NATIONAL GEOGRAPHIC
Dinosaurs

Created and produced by Firecrest Books Ltd., in association with
Tryo Edición Digital S.L., for the National Geographic Society

First U.S. Edition published by the National Geographic Society
1145 17th Street N.W.
Washington, D.C. 20036-4688
U.S.A.

Reprinted 2006, 2007 and 2008.

Library of Congress Cataloging-in-Publication Data:

Barrett, Paul M.
National Geographic dinosaurs / by Paul M. Barrett; illustrated by Raul Martín
p. cm.
ISBN 0-7922-8224-8
Dinosaurs—Juvenile literature. [1. Dinosaurs.]
I. Martín, Raul, ill. II. Title.
QE861.5.B37 2001
567.9—dc21   00-045263

Printed in China

NATIONAL GEOGRAPHIC
Dinosaurs

PAUL BARRETT
ILLUSTRATED BY RAUL MARTÍN
INTRODUCTION BY KEVIN PADIAN

NATIONAL GEOGRAPHIC

Washington, D.C.

Acknowledgments

Thanks are due to José Luis Sanz, Professor of Paleontology of the Universidad Autónoma de Madrid, for making available the text used for the CD-ROM *Historia Natural de los Dinosaurios* and for his authentication of the original artwork; and to Miguel Carrascal of Tryo Edición Digital and Rafael Casariego for helping to coordinate the project.

The publishers also wish to thank the following for permission to reproduce the pictures used in this book:

Natural History Museum, London:
pages 24, 25 (inset top right), 26, 27, 64 (top left), 65;
Paul Barrett: pages 50, 57 (inset top right),
61 (inset and bottom right), 66, 69, 74, 75, 102, 104, 108;
John Gurche: page 59 (illustration top right);
Paul C. Sereno: page 64 (illustrations top and center)
[originally published in the *Journal of Vertebrate Paleontology*];
O. Louis Mazzatenta: pages 152, 153, 162, 163;
The Kobal Collection: pages 186, 187 (top);
Walt Disney Pictures: page 187 (bottom) © Disney Enterprises, Inc.
José Luis Sanz and the Spanish organizations
and agencies who provided pictures for the CD-ROM

Color separation in Singapore by
Sang Choy International Pte Ltd
Printed in China by SC (Sang Choy) International Pte. Ltd.

Dr. Paul M. Barrett, *Editor and Chief Writer*

Emily Rayfield, Dr. Ian Jenkins, *Contributing Writers*

Dr. Kevin Padian, *Consultant*

Published by the National Geographic Society

John M. Fahey, Jr., *President and Chief Executive Officer*
Gilbert M. Grosvenor, *Chairman of the Board*
Nina D. Hoffman, *Executive Vice President, President of Books and School Publishing*
William R. Gray, *Vice President and Director*
Charles Kogod, *Assistant Director*
Barbara A. Payne, *Editorial Director and Managing Editor*
Marianne Koszorus, *Design Director*
Nancy Laties Feresten, *Publishing Director, Children's Books*
Jennifer Emmett, *Project Editor*
Bea Jackson, *Art Director, Children's Books*
Carl Mehler, *Director of Maps*
Suzanne Patrick Fonda, *Editor*
Jo Tunstall, *Assistant Editor*
Jocelyn Lindsay, Mary Collins, *Additional Text Research*
Judith Klein, *Copyediting*
R. Gary Colbert, *Production Director*
Vincent P. Ryan, *Manufacturing Manager*

Prepared for the National Geographic Society by
Firecrest Books Ltd.
from artwork originated by
Tryo Edición Digital SL for their CD-ROM
Historia Natural de los Dinosaurios

Peter Sackett, *Publishing Consultant*

Norman Barrett, *Editorial Director*

Phil Jacobs, *Designer*

Pat Jacobs, *Project Coordinator*

Contents

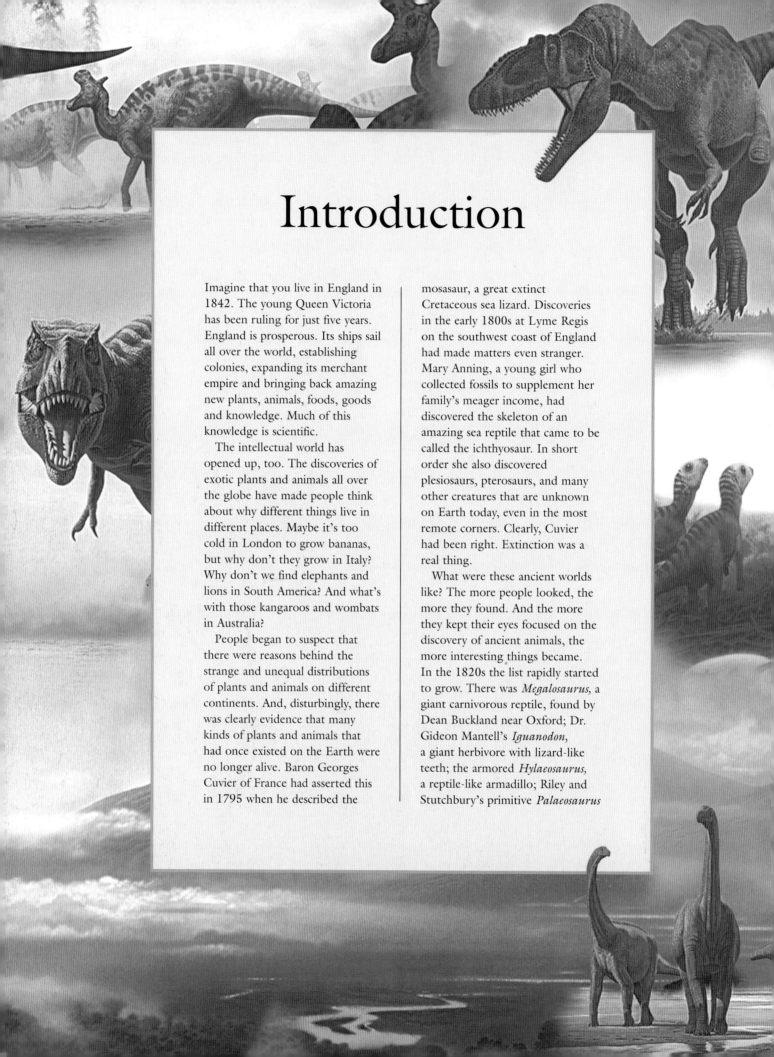

Introduction

Imagine that you live in England in 1842. The young Queen Victoria has been ruling for just five years. England is prosperous. Its ships sail all over the world, establishing colonies, expanding its merchant empire and bringing back amazing new plants, animals, foods, goods and knowledge. Much of this knowledge is scientific.

The intellectual world has opened up, too. The discoveries of exotic plants and animals all over the globe have made people think about why different things live in different places. Maybe it's too cold in London to grow bananas, but why don't they grow in Italy? Why don't we find elephants and lions in South America? And what's with those kangaroos and wombats in Australia?

People began to suspect that there were reasons behind the strange and unequal distributions of plants and animals on different continents. And, disturbingly, there was clearly evidence that many kinds of plants and animals that had once existed on the Earth were no longer alive. Baron Georges Cuvier of France had asserted this in 1795 when he described the

mosasaur, a great extinct Cretaceous sea lizard. Discoveries in the early 1800s at Lyme Regis on the southwest coast of England had made matters even stranger. Mary Anning, a young girl who collected fossils to supplement her family's meager income, had discovered the skeleton of an amazing sea reptile that came to be called the ichthyosaur. In short order she also discovered plesiosaurs, pterosaurs, and many other creatures that are unknown on Earth today, even in the most remote corners. Clearly, Cuvier had been right. Extinction was a real thing.

What were these ancient worlds like? The more people looked, the more they found. And the more they kept their eyes focused on the discovery of ancient animals, the more interesting things became. In the 1820s the list rapidly started to grow. There was *Megalosaurus*, a giant carnivorous reptile, found by Dean Buckland near Oxford; Dr. Gideon Mantell's *Iguanodon*, a giant herbivore with lizard-like teeth; the armored *Hylaeosaurus*, a reptile-like armadillo; Riley and Stutchbury's primitive *Palaeosaurus*

and *Thecodontosaurus;* and even what seemed to be a giant marine crocodile that was named *Cetiosaurus,* or "whale-lizard," although it didn't look exactly like a giant crocodile should.

All these animals were dinosaurs. But in the early 1800s no one knew they were dinosaurs. No one had seen them before. It fell to the great paleontologist Richard Owen to make sense of them in a new way. Owen knew that these were reptiles by the structure of their bones, yet they were not like any living reptiles. They had five hip vertebrae instead of two, and they were enormous. Most intriguingly, they held their limbs under their bodies, not sprawled to the side as in typical reptiles. In 1842 he gave them the name Dinosauria, which means "terrible lizards" or, perhaps more accurately, "fearfully great reptiles." The world has never been the same.

Fast-forward to the present. In the ensuing 150 years since Owen's christening, dinosaur fossils have been hunted and found on every continent, in forms and functions that would have delighted and terrified the Victorians, as they do us today. The National Geographic Society has been a leading supporter of dinosaur research for decades. It has brought paleontologists to the far reaches of the globe, including Mongolia, Africa, South America, India, Madagascar, Greenland, and Antarctica. It has helped discover some of the earliest dinosaurs in Argentina, Arizona, Texas, China, and Madagascar. It has helped shed light on the last days of the dinosaurs and their relatives in Uzbekistan, Morocco, Montana, New Zealand, and India. Most recently the Society has been a leading funder of the discoveries of the feathered dinosaurs of China. These amazing animals, over 125 million years old, are among the closest relatives of birds—the only group of dinosaurs that is still alive.

You're holding a catalog of some of the best known dinosaurs, as well as some of the most recently discovered ones. There's a great deal of information here about the origin, evolution, ecology, and behavior of these dinosaurs, organized for easy reference. Nearly anytime you open a newspaper, turn on the TV, or surf the dinosaur sites on the Web, new dinosaurs will be surfacing. This book is designed to help you understand the as-yet unknown ones, as well as the well-known ones. Happy discoveries!

Kevin Padian
Museum of Paleontology
University of California,
Berkeley

Dinosaurs
A natural history

Dinosaurs were some of the most spectacular creatures ever to have lived on our planet, and this book attempts to bring their extraordinary world to life. The popularity of television shows, books and movies that feature dinosaurs shows that there is a vast amount of interest in these animals among children and adults alike—indeed, it is possible that dinosaurs have never been more popular at any time since their original discovery in England over 150 years ago. Here, we have tried to capture the magic of the Age of Dinosaurs, as well as some of the excitement in what is currently a rapidly growing area of scientific knowledge.

The past 30 years or so have witnessed a revolution in the ways that scientists interpret dinosaur fossils. The scientific study of dinosaurs is not an end in itself but can provide many clues to the processes of evolution. It can also offer information on the way in which the earth has changed through time, on the way animals interact with their environments and on the causes of extinction. Far from being a "dead" subject, paleontology—the science of the reconstruction of ancient life—is now providing important information for biologists dealing with problems in today's world.

The profiles

The major part of this book presents profiles that give detailed information on the natural history of 53 different types of dinosaurs. These have been chosen from the 375 or so types of dinosaurs that have been discovered. The discovery of new types of dinosaurs continues apace, with about 6-10 new dinosaur genera being named each year. We cannot mention them all in this book, but these profiles provide a comprehensive cross-section of the different lifestyles, behaviors and structures of the whole range of dinosaurs. The features of these profiles are illustrated and explained on the opposite page—the size comparison scale, map showing the sites where the dinosaur has been discovered, and time chart putting the span of its existence into the perspective of the whole dinosaur era. The Fact File gives key information about the dinosaur in instantly accessible form—its place in the family tree, its physical dimensions, its "life dates" and where it lived. Each profile focuses on the genus rather than a species—*Tyrannosaurus* rather than *Tyrannosaurus rex.*

The dinosaur story

The complete dinosaur story is covered in the book at two levels—the first regarding their biology, behavior and habitat, the second from the point of view of our knowledge about them.

From studies of the rocks in which dinosaur remains are found, scientists can deduce their environment and date their existence with a fair degree of certainty. The other animals that lived in the time of the dinosaurs are also known from these studies. This book explains how evidence is obtained and put together, and why certain theories seem more likely than others. Some clues are even provided by living animals, such as birds and reptiles. Throughout the book, in both the text and the accompanying illustrations, we have striven to present the most accurate and up-to-date information currently available, while pointing out those ideas that are based more on guesswork than on hard fact. The close relationship of dinosaurs and birds is emphasized, highlighting the

Literal translation of the dinosaur's scientific name (usually based on Latin and Greek words).

Lengths (figures quoted include the tail), weights and ages of the various dinosaurs are all taken directly from the latest scientific literature.

The Classification entry traces the dinosaur's family tree but does not include two main branches of the Dinosauria— the Saurischia and Ornithischia.

The background color of the size chart and the human figure (see below) indicate the scale.

The color of this bar marks the group the dinosaur belongs to (see the family trees on pages 62-63 and 114-115).

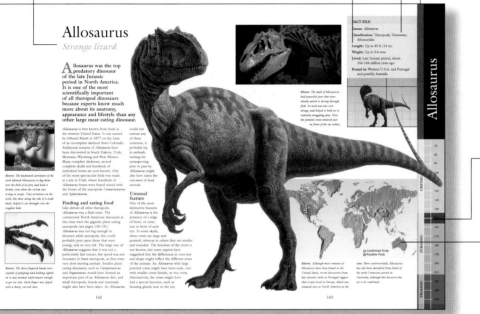

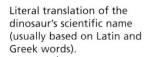

The years when the dinosaur lived are highlighted in the time bar.

Countries of the world where remains of the dinosaur have been found are highlighted in color. The definite discoveries are marked with solid circles ▣; the sites of probable finds are marked with open circles ▣.

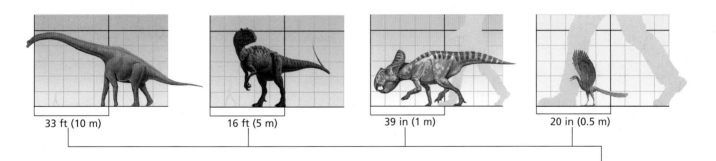

| 33 ft (10 m) | 16 ft (5 m) | 39 in (1 m) | 20 in (0.5 m) |

view among most scientists that birds are a group of dinosaurs.

The book covers the fascinating history of dinosaur discoveries and the early pioneers in dinosaur paleontology. A brief guide to dinosaur classification shows how the different types of dinosaurs are related to each other. And various theories proposed to account for the extinction of dinosaurs are discussed.

Our knowledge of dinosaurs is a tribute

to the dedicated teams of field workers, museum experts and scientists who, from age-old fossils of bones, teeth, footprints and even dung, piece together not only what dinosaurs looked like but how they moved, what they ate and how they hunted for prey or protected themselves from attack. The aim of this book is to bring alive the times, the places and the remarkable stories of these diverse and enchanting animals.

Four different scales of size charts are used, depending on the size of the dinosaur. The silhouette of an adult human (or part of one) is included to give an impression of the real size of these animals.

What is a dinosaur?

Dinosaurs are among the most successful land animals ever to have existed. They roamed the earth for more than 150 million years. They lived on every continent and evolved into a dazzling variety of forms. Gigantic plant-eaters—some larger than a house—shared their world with tiny chicken-size meat-eaters and with many other dinosaur species of all shapes and sizes. Their name means "terrible lizard." Dinosaurs dominated the earth until a combination of environmental disasters caused their extinction about 65 million years ago. But one group—the birds—survives.

Dinosaurs were reptiles—animals with a backbone and four legs and with a scaly, waterproof skin. Like most other reptiles, dinosaurs laid eggs with shells. Detailed studies of anatomy have shown that extinct dinosaurs are most closely related to the crocodiles and birds among living animals. The skeletons of birds and dinosaurs share a number of features not found in other animal groups, such as modifications to the legs that make them more efficient runners. Other shared features include lightly built limb bones, features of the skull and jaws, and a hinged ankle.

Built for speed

On the other hand, dinosaurs differ from their crocodilian cousins, and from all other reptiles, in a number of important ways. The most significant of these differences are found in the bones of the feet, legs and hips. Most kinds of reptiles hold their legs out from the sides of the body and move their legs through wide arcs as they walk. This style of walking is called "sprawling," and is not much different from how early vertebrates walked when they came out onto land.

Some lizards can run on their hind legs only, but their legs still stick out to the sides. And crocodiles, in addition to sprawling, can tuck their hind limbs under the body to do a "high walk" on land. In contrast, dinosaurs had legs that could only be held directly underneath the body, much like the legs of a mammal such as a dog or a horse. As a result, dinosaurs could not sprawl like other reptiles. The long, straight legs of dinosaurs could make very long strides, and footprints show that they put one foot in front of the other as they walked or ran.

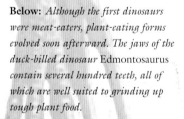

Below: *Although the first dinosaurs were meat-eaters, plant-eating forms evolved soon afterward. The jaws of the duck-billed dinosaur* Edmontosaurus *contain several hundred teeth, all of which are well suited to grinding up tough plant food.*

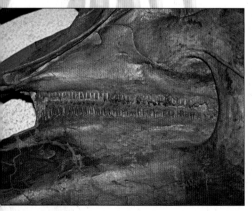

Right: *Small meat-eaters, such as this* Coelophysis, *were among the very first dinosaurs ever to walk the earth.*

The first dinosaurs appeared in what is now Argentina about 225 million years ago, during the late middle Triassic period. These animals were small meat-eaters that reached lengths of about 3 feet (1 m). By the end of the Triassic period, several new types of dinosaurs had appeared, including a number of small plant-eaters. Early dinosaurs were quite rare. But dinosaurs became more abundant as time passed. Many different types of dinosaurs evolved from these early forms.

Below: *Alligators and crocodiles are close relatives of dinosaurs and also have a long fossil record of their own. The earliest crocodile-like animals appeared about 210 million years ago.*

Left*: This is how the earth looked when the first dinosaurs appeared in what is now Argentina (highlighted in red).*

Below: *In this skeleton of the theropod dinosaur* Piatnitzkysaurus, *you can see that the legs are held directly under the body and would have easily supported the weight of the animal.*

Mesozoic era

Dinosaurs lived millions of years ago during a period of time that is known as the Mesozoic era. At this time, the earth was quite different from the planet we know today. The land, sea and sky were populated with many unfamiliar animals and plants, and even the shapes of the continents were different. Although all of these things seem strange to us, this world was also home to the ancestors of many of the living things that we see around us today.

Below: Insects, such as this fossil beetle, existed on earth well before the beginning of the Mesozoic era. Beetles are an ancient group of animals that first appeared about 270 million years ago, in what is known as the Permian period.

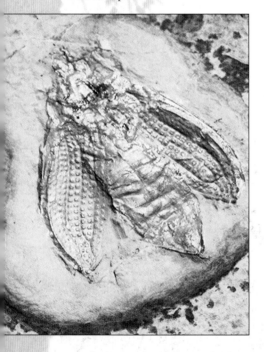

The Mesozoic era is divided into three periods: the Triassic, Jurassic and Cretaceous. The Triassic period is the earliest of these divisions. It lasted from about 245 to 213 million years ago. During the Triassic period, all of the continents were joined together in a huge single landmass that scientists call Pangaea. The earth was relatively warm and dry at this time and was covered with large deserts. The polar ice caps that now cover Antarctica and Greenland were absent during the entire Mesozoic era. Dinosaurs first evolved in this environment. Great monsoon seasons alternated with dry periods over much of the globe. Gradually, dinosaurs became more abundant, while a number of other animal groups, such as the ancestors of mammals, became scarcer. Meat-eaters, such as *Coelophysis,* and plant-eating prosauropods, such as *Plateosaurus,* were two kinds of dinosaurs that lived at this time. The late Triassic period can be regarded as the beginning of the Age of Dinosaurs.

Jurassic giants

Following the Triassic period, the Jurassic period began 213 million years ago and continued until the beginning of the Cretaceous period 144 million years ago. During this time, the world's weather became wetter, though it still remained warmer than today. The extra moisture helped plants to colonize the deserts and turn them into forests of huge trees and prairies of ferns and other low-growing plants. The continents started to break

apart from each other at the beginning of the Jurassic period. Great seas began to open up between North America and Europe and between Europe and Africa. These seas became today's Atlantic Ocean and Mediterranean Sea. During the Jurassic period, dinosaurs increased in number, and many more different types of dinosaurs appeared, including the gigantic long-necked sauropods, armored dinosaurs such as *Stegosaurus* and large meat-eaters such as *Allosaurus.*

The end of an era

The final division of the Mesozoic era is the Cretaceous period. Dinosaurs reached their greatest numbers at this time, in a world that was changing rapidly. By the end of the Cretaceous period, the continents were beginning to reach the positions they occupy today, although India was a large island isolated from all other land. Australia, Antarctica and South

Right: The first frogs appeared during the Triassic period. They looked somewhat like the frogs that are living today. This fossil frog is from the early Cretaceous period.

America were still joined to each other by narrow land bridges. The world's temperature peaked at the start of the Cretaceous period but cooled as time went on. This was the time of the great predator *Tyrannosaurus rex*, the three-horned *Triceratops* and the duck-billed hadrosaurs. But at the end of the Cretaceous period, 65 million years ago, all of these amazing animals disappeared, along with many other types of animals and plants. The reasons for this are still being debated by scientists, but the close of the Cretaceous period marks the end of the Age of Dinosaurs. No dinosaurs, except for the birds, survived into the following Cenozoic era, which is often called the Age of Mammals.

Below: The scales of this fish, called Lepidotes, *are very common fossils in rocks from the Jurassic and Cretaceous periods.* Lepidotes *was a large fish, as much as 20 inches (50 cm) or more long, and was a favorite food for some large crocodiles and dinosaurs.*

MESOZOIC PLANT LIFE

Fields full of grasses and flowers and forests filled with broad-leafed trees such as oak and beech are a common sight today in the countryside and parks of many lands. But these plants would have been unfamiliar to all but the last dinosaurs, because they did not appear until well into the Cretaceous period. Indeed, grasses did not evolve until after the last dinosaur had become extinct. For most of the Mesozoic era, plants such as ferns and cycads (pineapple-shaped plants with enormous fanlike leaves) made up most of the low-growing vegetation. They probably formed an important source of food for plant-eating dinosaurs. Forests of huge evergreen trees and tree ferns provided homes for many different types of animals.

Above: *Cycads were among the most common plants of the Mesozoic era. They are not particularly common today, being limited to living in hot, tropical habitats. During the Cretaceous period, when the earth was much warmer, cycads grew close to the North Pole.*

Other creatures

Dinosaurs shared their world with many other creatures that are now extinct. While dinosaurs roamed the land, enormous marine reptiles ruled the oceans. Flying reptiles swooped through the skies, catching insects and fish and occasionally tackling even larger prey. Alongside these animals, the small, early relatives of mammals and birds tried to make a living, while avoiding becoming a small meal for some larger animals.

Pterosaurs

Many of the animal groups alive today originated during the Mesozoic era. Mammals like the shrew-size *Morganucodon* appeared during the late Triassic period. But for most of the Mesozoic era, mammals were small, secretive animals about the size of rats or rabbits. They became the dominant animals only after the dinosaurs had disappeared. Frogs and crocodiles also evolved during the Triassic period, as did the turtles and tortoises. Lizards are first known in the Jurassic period, and the first bird, *Archaeopteryx*, flew though late Jurassic skies. Snakes slithered into existence during the Cretaceous period.

Marine monsters

Spectacular marine reptiles, including the ichthyosaurs, plesiosaurs, pliosaurs and mosasaurs, inhabited the Mesozoic seas. Of these animals, the ichthyosaurs were the most highly adapted to life in the sea. They looked extremely similar to dolphins, with long, pointed snouts full of sharp teeth, fins for steering, and a powerful crescent-shaped tail. Ichthyosaurs could not leave the sea to lay eggs, so they gave birth to live young while still in the water. Plesiosaurs had long, snakelike necks; short, squat bodies; and small heads equipped with sharp, pointed teeth. Their legs were modified into large paddles that they beat up and down to "fly" through the water. Pliosaurs were a group of plesiosaurs that had shorter necks and much larger heads. One type of pliosaur, *Liopleurodon*, had one of the largest meat-

eating skulls ever to have existed. The head of this creature was over 6 feet 6 inches (2 m) long! Mosasaurs were gigantic lizards closely related to living monitor lizards. They lived during the late Cretaceous period. All of these marine reptiles lived on a diet of fish, squid and shellfish. The largest pliosaurs often ate other marine reptiles. With the exception of turtles, all marine reptiles became extinct at the end of the Cretaceous period.

Flying reptiles

Flying reptiles, or pterosaurs (pictured top left), appeared in the late part of the Triassic period and survived until the end of the Cretaceous period. Pterosaurs came in a variety of sizes. Many were about the size of pigeons and crows, but others were as large as eagles and albatrosses. The largest flying animal ever was a pterosaur. *Quetzalcoatlus*, from the late Cretaceous period of North America, had a wingspan of about 36 feet (11 m)—larger than a small airplane! Pterosaur wings were each made from one very long finger that supported a thin, but very strong, flap of skin. This flap of skin attached to the side of the body. Many pterosaurs lived around rivers, lakes and shallow seas. Most pterosaurs ate insects, fish and other small animals.

Above: *This is the skull of a crocodile,* Bernissartia, *that was common during the early Cretaceous period. Its fossil remains have been found in southern England, Belgium, Germany, Spain and France.*

Above: *The fossil record of turtles is very good. Turtles and tortoises were more common in the past than they are today. The gradual cooling of the earth that has continued since the Cretaceous period has limited their distribution, as many reptiles cannot withstand low temperatures.*

Right: *A pair of mosasaurs feast upon* Nautilus. *Nautilus are part of the group of mollusks that also includes the ammonites.* Nautilus *are still alive today, and are often referred to as living fossils.*

Triassic

Dinosaurs first appeared during the late Triassic period. Herds of prosauropod dinosaurs, such as Plateosaurus, were common at this time.

During the Jurassic period, the gigantic sauropod dinosaurs, such as Diplodocus, dominated the earth. They shared the landscape with Allosaurus (right) and other large meat-eaters.

Cretaceous

Duck-billed dinosaurs, such as Parasaurolophus (front) and Edmontosaurus (rear), were common during the late Cretaceous period. Huge herds of these animals roamed through dense conifer forests.

Finds around the world

Dinosaur bones, eggs and footprints have been discovered all over the world in what are now deserts, quarries and forests. They have even been dredged from the bottom of the sea. Dinosaurs are known from every continent, including the now frozen wastes of Antarctica.

MAJOR DINOSAUR SITES

Listed are 12 of the world's most important areas where dinosaur remains have been unearthed, with examples of the dinosaurs found. See the map (right) for the locations.

1 Alberta, Canada: *Triceratops, Ankylosaurus, Troodon, Pachycephalosaurus*

2 Colorado, Montana, Wyoming and Utah, U.S.A.: *Diplodocus, Brachiosaurus, Camarasaurus, Stegosaurus, Camptosaurus, Maiasaura, Tyrannosaurus, Allosaurus*

3 Arizona and New Mexico, U.S.A.: *Coelophysis* and *Ceratosaurus*

4 Argentina: *Saltasaurus, Carnotaurus, Eoraptor, Patagosaurus, Herrerasaurus*

5 England: *Iguanodon, Hypsilophodon, Baryonyx, Hylaeosaurus*

6 Germany: *Plateosaurus, Compsognathus, Archaeopteryx*

7 Spain: *Pelecanimimus* and *Iberomesornis*

8 Niger: *Ouranosaurus*

9 Tanzania: *Brachiosaurus, Kentrosaurus*

10 Lesotho: *Lesothosaurus*

11 Mongolia: *Psittacosaurus, Velociraptor, Oviraptor, Protoceratops*

12 China: *Psittacosaurus, Sinosauropteryx* and a wide variety of other dinosaurs

North America

South America

Right: *The three maps of the world show the continents as they were in the main periods of the Age of Dinosaurs. By the late Triassic period, the continents had merged together into one large land mass called Pangaea.*

By the late Jurassic, Pangaea had begun to break up again, into Laurasia and Gondwanaland. The separation continued, and by the late Cretaceous the continents had drifted almost to the positions they occupy now.

Dinosaur remains are particularly common in North America, China, Argentina and western Europe. These areas are rich in the sedimentary rocks that contain dinosaur fossils. Until recently, scientists gained most of their knowledge of dinosaurs from finds in North America and Europe, in lands that have been explored, farmed, quarried and built on. But expeditions to many remote areas, often in search of oil or other valuable commodities, have opened up rich new sources of dinosaur fossils.

Below: *In addition to the major sites featured here, other important sources of dinosaur fossils are found in Brazil (A), France (B), Romania (C), Morocco (D), Madagascar (E), India (F) and Australia (G).*

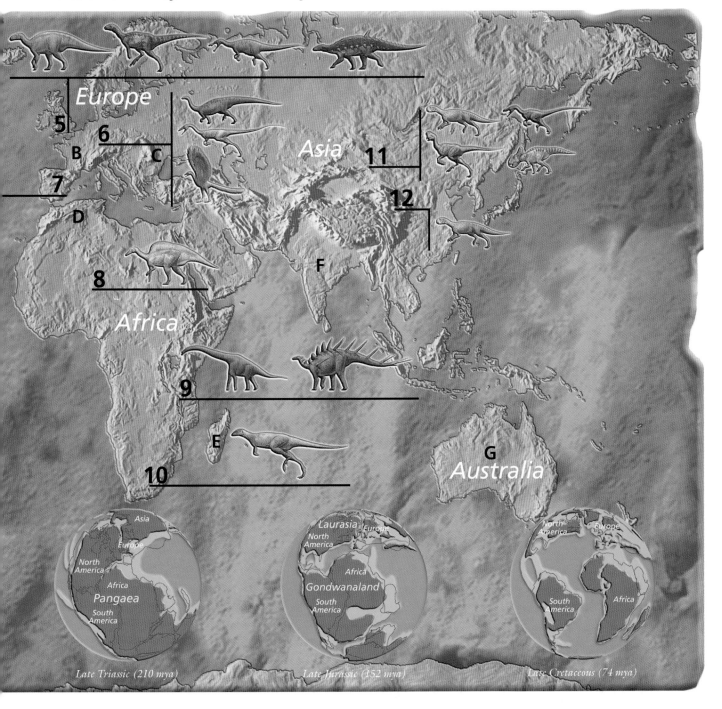

Europe

5

6

B

C

7

D

Asia

11

12

8

F

Africa

9

E

10

G

Australia

Pangaea

Asia

Europe

North America

Africa

South America

Late Triassic (210 mya)

Laurasia

North America

Europe

Africa

Gondwanaland

South America

Late Jurassic (152 mya)

North America

Europe

South America

Africa

Late Cretaceous (74 mya)

From dragons to dinosaurs

People have always been fascinated by the remains of extinct creatures, although for many years the origin and real identity of these fossil bones and teeth remained mysterious. Many early scholars believed that the remains of dinosaurs, and other prehistoric animals such as mammoths, were the bones of giant men and mythological monsters. Others thought that these fossils represented the remnants of animals that had died during the Great Flood described in the Bible. It is only in the last 200 years that scientists have recognized fossils as the remains of long-extinct animals (or plants), many of which were very different from any creature alive today.

Above: *English naturalist Robert Plot published a drawing in 1677 of a bone fragment found in Oxfordshire. He did not know it, but this was the first known illustration of a dinosaur.*

Above: *The British geologist William Buckland, of Oxford University, was the first person to give a dinosaur a proper scientific name when he described* Megalosaurus *in 1824.*

The earliest written records that describe dinosaur remains come from China. Fossil bones are mentioned in a number of manuscripts, some of which date back over 1,700 years. It was thought that these huge bones, found buried in the ground, must be the remains of great dragons. The Chinese believed that these "dragon bones" had magical properties, and the bones were sometimes ground up to be used as an ingredient in traditional medicines.

Fabulous animals

It seems likely that stories about a mythological animal called the griffin, a creature with the body of a lion and the head, wings and claws of an eagle, began as a result of early encounters with the remains of dinosaurs. When tribesmen from Central Asia first made contact with the ancient Greeks about 2,500 years ago, they brought with them stories of terrifying creatures in the desert that guarded chests of gold. This myth probably arose from the discovery of *Protoceratops* skeletons, which are extremely common in some parts of Mongolia's desert, the Gobi. The large beak of *Protoceratops* could easily be mistaken for that of an eagle, and the outlandish appearance of these animals probably instilled fear into all those who saw them.

European discoveries

The Englishman Robert Plot was the first person to illustrate a dinosaur bone, when he published a drawing in 1677, in a book on the natural history of Oxfordshire. The bone was originally thought to belong to an elephant, which could have been brought to Britain by the Romans. Later, it was identified as part of a giant man. Unfortunately, this bone is now lost, but Plot's descriptions and illustrations show that it was actually a part of a thighbone from a large meat-eating dinosaur.

Discovery of *Megalosaurus*

William Buckland, the eccentric Reader in Geology at Oxford University, was the first person to describe and name a dinosaur. The bones of a gigantic fossil reptile had been unearthed from the limestone quarries of Stonesfield, near Oxford, about 1815 and were given to Buckland to study. Buckland named this dinosaur *Megalosaurus* (enormous lizard) in 1824, and concluded that it was a gigantic meat-eating lizard.

The doctor and the dinosaur

Gideon Mantell, a doctor in Lewes, on the south coast of England, was an enthusiastic fossil collector. He used to go on many collecting trips to the numerous small quarries that dotted the surrounding countryside. On one of these trips, Mantell and his wife discovered the fossilized teeth of an unfamiliar animal. In 1825, he named these teeth *Iguanodon* and suggested that this creature was an enormous plant-eating lizard. This idea was revolutionary at the time, as plant-eating reptiles are very rare today. *Iguanodon* was the second dinosaur to be named and described scientifically.

Naming names

Although we now know that *Megalosaurus* and *Iguanodon* are dinosaurs, the name "dinosaur" had not yet been invented when Buckland and Mantell were publishing their work. Indeed, *Megalosaurus* and *Iguanodon* were thought of as huge lizards, whereas we now consider the dinosaurs to form a special group of animals on their own. The recognition of the "Dinosauria" came a few years later, when a brilliant scientist named Richard Owen looked again at their fossil skeletons and found that they differed from those of other reptiles in a number of ways.

Terrible lizard

Richard Owen coined the name "dinosaur" in 1842 in a milestone scientific paper on the fossil reptiles of Great Britain. The name dinosaur, meaning "terrible lizard," refers to the great size of these extinct beasts. The three original members of the Dinosauria were *Megalosaurus*, *Iguanodon* and *Hylaeosaurus*. Owen demonstrated that the structure of the skeleton in these three animals was very different from that seen in any other reptile, living or extinct. At one stroke, Owen changed our view of life in the Mesozoic era forever.

DINING IN A DINOSAUR

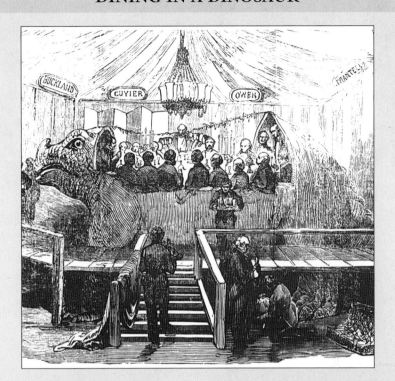

Plaster models of *Iguanodon*, *Megalosaurus* and *Hylaeosaurus* were made under the guidance of Richard Owen for the Great Exhibition of London, held in 1850-51. Before the exhibition opened, Owen hosted a meal for distinguished scientists inside the uncompleted model of the *Iguanodon*. After the exhibition, the models were moved to Crystal Palace Park (below), in south London, where they can still be seen to this day.

The "Bone Wars"

From the mid-1800s, more finds in Europe and abundant discoveries of more complete skeletons in North America enabled scientists to make dramatic breakthroughs in the study of dinosaurs. The science of dinosaurs advanced in leaps and bounds. More discoveries throughout the 1900s, on other continents, showed us how these creatures had dominated the earth for millions of years.

Above: *Gideon Mantell, a British fossil collector, was an early pioneer of dinosaur research. He showed the big teeth he found to the French anatomist Georges Cuvier, who believed they belonged to a new kind of animal, a plant-eating reptile. Mantell named it* Iguanodon.

New dinosaur fossils continued to be found in southern England, France and Germany during the rest of the 1800s. This led to the description and recognition of several "new" types of dinosaur, including the prosauropod *Thecodontosaurus* (socket-toothed lizard), the sauropod *Cetiosaurus* (whale lizard) and the small ornithopod *Hypsilophodon*. Although scientists collected a large number of individual bones, few complete skeletons were found. This led to mistakes in the scientists' early reconstructions of these mysterious animals. For example, Gideon Mantell believed that a strange cone-shaped bone he had discovered was the horn of *Iguanodon*. However, the spectacular discovery of dozens of almost complete *Iguanodon* skeletons in a coal mine at Bernissart, Belgium, in 1878 showed that the "horns" were actually large spikes, which had been attached to the ends of the thumbs.

American discoveries

The discoveries in Europe were soon followed by a number of spectacular discoveries in North America. Prospectors looking for gold, coal and other valuable minerals, and engineers building bridges and railways, began to unearth huge treasure troves of dinosaur material in the western interior of the United States. These finds soon attracted the attention of scientists, and many expeditions went out into the badlands of Colorado, Wyoming and Montana in search of fossils. In Europe, finding a complete dinosaur skeleton was a rare event, but in the United States skeletons were found in abundance. These new discoveries showed that dinosaurs were even more spectacular than the European scientists had dared to imagine.

The "Bone Wars"

Edward Drinker Cope and Othniel Charles Marsh were rival scientists, both heavily involved in the naming and description of many of the fossil skeletons discovered in the American West during the late 1800s. The two men started their careers as friends but soon became bitter enemies as each tried to upstage the other by describing more and more new types of dinosaurs. Both scientists paid crews of workmen to go and collect dinosaur fossils, and the workmen would often become involved in fights over prize specimens. The scientific disputes between Cope and

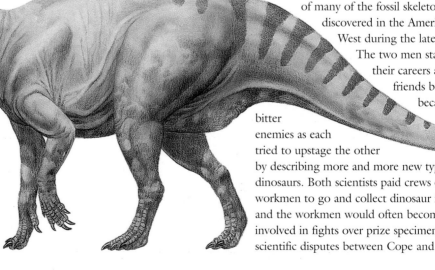

Right: Leptoceratops *(narrow horned face) was one of the many dinosaurs discovered and named by Barnum Brown, an American dinosaur hunter of the early 1900s. Despite its name,* Leptoceratops *did not have horns—it was a member of the protoceratopsid family. Brown's other discoveries included* Ankylosaurus, Corythosaurus, Pachycephalosaurus *and* Tyrannosaurus.

Marsh, and the sometimes violent clashes between their work crews, became known as the "Bone Wars." The keen competition between these two scientists led to the discovery of many new types of dinosaurs, including *Diplodocus, Allosaurus* and *Camarasaurus.*

The 20th century

Up until about 1900, almost all dinosaur remains had been found in Europe and North America, with only a handful of species being described from any of the other continents. As methods of travel and communication improved during the early part of the 1900s, scientists started to explore more remote regions of the earth in search of dinosaurs. It soon became clear, as their fossilized remains began to turn up in Africa, South America and Asia, that dinosaurs once had a worldwide distribution. The most impressive discoveries were made in East Africa, China, Mongolia and Argentina, areas that continue to yield many new fossils. Scientists are still exploring new areas today, and recent finds have shown that dinosaurs even lived in what is now Antarctica.

The dinosaur "comeback"

For much of the 1800s and 1900s, dinosaurs were regarded as sluggish, slow-moving animals that were an evolutionary "dead-end." But discoveries of small, agile, large-brained dinosaurs such as *Deinonychus* during the 1960s began to change scientists' ideas of these creatures. Scientists now regard dinosaurs as dynamic animals with complex behavior—a view that also fits in with the theory that some dinosaurs were the direct ancestors of birds.

Above: *British scientist Richard Owen studied the early discoveries of fossil skeletons and coined the term "Dinosauria" to describe a new group of animals. He had models made of these creatures, reconstructing them as huge mammal-like quadrupeds.*

IMPORTANT DATES IN DINOSAUR DISCOVERY

600 BC	Central Asian traders bring stories of griffins—based on the fossil skeletons of *Protoceratops*—to the ancient Greeks.
AD 300	Chinese scholars record the presence of "dragon bones."
1677	Robert Plot illustrates a thighbone, possibly of *Megalosaurus.*
1824	William Buckland names *Megalosaurus*—the first dinosaur to be scientifically described.
1825	Gideon Mantell names *Iguanodon.*
1842	Richard Owen coins the name "Dinosauria."
1850-1	Models of *Iguanodon, Megalosaurus* and *Hylaeosaurus* are displayed at the Great Exhibition in London.
1856	The first dinosaur remains from the United States are described.
1867	Thomas Henry Huxley is the first scientist to suggest that birds are the direct descendants of dinosaurs.
1877-95	"The Bone Wars"—fierce scientific rivalry between Othniel C. Marsh and Edward D. Cope sparks the discovery of hundreds of new dinosaur specimens in the American West.
1878	Miners discover dozens of *Iguanodon* skeletons at Bernissart, Belgium.
1920s	A series of expeditions to Mongolia's desert, the Gobi, by the American Museum of Natural History results in the first discovery of dinosaur eggs and of many new types of dinosaur.
1930s	The Chinese scientist C.C. Young begins a series of expeditions to excavate dinosaurs in China.
1969	John Ostrom, of Yale University, publishes a description of *Deinonychus*, beginning a revolution in the way that dinosaurs were perceived by scientists and the public.
1970 onward	More and more evidence suggests that dinosaurs are indeed the ancestors of birds. Continued study of dinosaur specimens shows that dinosaurs were active, complex animals.

Digging and dressing

T he impressive mounted skeletons of dinosaurs on display in the world's museums are the results of many years of painstaking work. The processes of discovery, excavation, cleaning and study require large teams of dedicated scientists and craftsmen. The scientists who study dinosaurs and other fossils are called paleontologists. They require many different skills for their work, including those of the anatomist, the geologist, the quarryman and the artist. These skills enable them to make accurate reconstructions of the appearance, behavior and lifestyle of dinosaurs.

Several factors need to be considered when hunting for dinosaur fossils. First, dinosaurs are found mainly in rocks that were deposited during the Mesozoic era. Rocks that are older or younger than this will yield other types of fossils, but no dinosaurs. Second, dinosaur fossils are found mainly in rocks such as mudstones, limestones and sandstones. These types of rocks, known as sedimentary rocks, are formed from layers of mud, clay or sand that represent typical land environments. Rocks that were formed by volcanic activity, or that have been greatly altered by heat and pressure, seldom contain dinosaur fossils. Finally, dinosaur remains are most abundant in rocks that formed on land or close to land. They are very rare in rocks that were once at the bottom of the sea. All of these factors limit the places where dinosaur remains can be found, and it is

sometimes necessary to travel to remote regions of the world in order to find suitable rocks. Even when all of these conditions are met, it may still be difficult to find a dinosaur. Scientists sometimes have to rely on luck, noticing, perhaps, a small piece of bone sticking out of a cliff or a hill—a find that might lead them to the discovery of a buried skeleton.

Digging for bones

Once a dinosaur fossil has been located, scientists need to remove it from the surrounding rock. To start with, they use brushes and shovels to clear the loose rock and earth away from the fossil. The way in which the bones are removed depends upon the hardness of the rock and the condition of the bones. If the bones are very fragile, as they often are, great care needs to be taken

Below: *Some dinosaur fossils are found in very hard rocks. In these cases it is necessary to use jackhammers, mechanical diggers and even explosives in order to remove the overlying rocks. Great care needs to be taken when using these methods, as they can easily damage the fossils, and they often pose dangers for the scientists themselves.*

Right: *Scientists take great care when excavating fossil bones, as the bones are usually quite fragile. It may take many weeks or even months to excavate a large skeleton.*

Far right: *Scientists are preparing a fossil for transport by wrapping it in a plaster jacket. These jackets are very tough and give the fossils protection and support as they are eventually opened and prepared.*

to prevent damage. If the fossils are found in soft clays and mudstones, the bones can be removed by scraping the mud away with trowels or hosing it off with jets of water. For harder rocks it may be necessary to use large hammers and drills to remove a block of rock containing the fossil from a cliff face. In extreme situations it may be necessary to use pneumatic drills and even explosives in order to remove the encasing rock from the bones. The scientists make drawings to record the positions of the bones as they lay in the rock, because this information is useful when trying to work out how the dinosaur's skeleton should be put back together.

DRESSED FOR TRANSPORT

As the fossils are removed from the cliff face, they are wrapped in strips of paper and cloth soaked in plaster. As the plaster dries and sets, the fossils become encased in a hard plaster cast, just like the casts that doctors put onto people's broken arms and legs. Scientists call these plaster casts "jackets." The jackets help to protect the fossils while they are being transported back to the laboratory for study. Because many dinosaur fossils are found in remote areas, without trains, trucks or good roads, their journey to the laboratory requires good protection. When working in these regions, scientists have to be particularly careful that they do not injure themselves or become sick, as medical treatment may be difficult to obtain.

Preparing the exhibit

W hen the fossil bones of a dinosaur reach the laboratory, saws and scissors are used to remove the plaster jackets. Work can now begin on freeing the bones from the remaining rock. This can be an extremely delicate operation, and it may take teams of scientists, technicians and volunteers several years to completely remove all the rock and debris from a single dinosaur skeleton. This process is known as "preparation." How the fossils are cleaned depends on the hardness and chemical composition of the rock.

Below: *When the fossils arrive in the laboratory, they are usually still encased in a thick covering of rock. This photograph shows a block of limestone containing the skeleton of the small theropod* Pelecanimimus. *Only the tip of the snout can be seen.*

Below: *This is the same block of limestone after preparation. Much more of the snout can now be seen, and some of the teeth.*

Scientists often plaster large chunks of rock, because the rock encasing the fossils gives them added protection during transport. Sometimes the rock also contains important information on the biology of the dinosaur, such as the remains of fossilized gut contents or impressions of the skin. Once the jackets are opened, large chunks of rock that do not contain bones or any other useful material can be sawn off from the boulders with large diamond-tipped saws. When removing rock close to the fossilized bones, however, scientists need to be much more careful—they cannot use such powerful equipment. For this fine work, needles and small dentist's tools are used. These implements are made from very strong metals, such as steel and tungsten, and are used to pick the rock from the fossil bones a grain at a time. Sometimes it is possible to use electric "air pens" to blast the rock away from the fossil's surface. Air pens use compressed air to fire tiny pellets of very hard material, similar to small grains of sand, at the rock.

Acid baths

Certain types of rock, such as limestone, will dissolve if they come into contact with acid. In some cases, scientists immerse blocks of rock containing fossil bones into tanks filled with weak solutions of acid. Acetic acid, the chemical that gives vinegar its strong smell and flavor, is commonly used for

this purpose. The acid slowly eats away at the rock, exposing the bone within. Great care must be taken so that the acid does not start to dissolve the bone. In order to avoid this, the block is occasionally removed from the acid so the exposed bones can be painted with a preservative chemical that protects them from the acid.

The next steps

Once the fragments have been completely removed from the surrounding rock, they must be pieced back together. This is rather like attempting a very large three-dimensional jigsaw puzzle! The pieces have to be carefully cleaned and hardened with preservatives. Then the bone fragments are reassembled with permanent glue. Missing pieces can be filled in with strong plastics to prevent further breakage.

Building an exhibit

Scientists aim to make the exhibits in museums depict dinosaurs as exciting, dynamic animals. Usually, the original bones are not placed on public exhibit. Instead, molds and casts are made.

Each bone is molded in a modeling material such as plasticine. Then the bone is removed and fiberglass and other substances are used to fill the mold, so that they create an exact replica of the original bone. These replicas, or casts, are mounted to other bones using metal frames. The assembled skeleton can then be posed in a lifelike way.

WHERE TO SEE DINOSAURS

Australia
Queensland Museum, South Brisbane
Victoria Museum, Melbourne

Canada
Royal Ontario Museum, Toronto
Tyrrell Museum of Paleontology, Drumheller,
   Alberta

China
Zigong Dinosaur Museum, Sichuan

France
Musée d'Histoire Naturelle, Paris
Musée des Dinosaures, Espéraza

Germany
Humboldt Museum für Naturkunde, Berlin
Staatliches Museum für Naturkunde,
   Stuttgart

Japan
National Science Museum, Tokyo
Gunma Museum of Natural History,
Tomioka

Poland
Institute of Paleobiology, Warsaw

Russia
Paleontological Institute, Moscow

South Africa
South African Museum, Cape Town

Spain
Museo Nacional de Ciencias Naturales,
   Madrid

United Kingdom
The Natural History Museum, London
University Museum of Natural History,
   Oxford
Sedgwick Museum of Earth Sciences,
   University of Cambridge
Bristol City Museum and Art Gallery
Isle of Wight Museum of Geology
Leicester City Museum

United States
American Museum of Natural History,
   New York
National Museum of Natural History,
   Washington, D.C.
Carnegie Museum of Natural History,
   Pittsburgh
Peabody Museum, Yale University
Field Museum of Natural History, Chicago
Utah University Museum of Natural History,
   Salt Lake City
University of California Museum of
   Paleontology, Berkeley
Jensen Dinosaur National Monument,
   Jensen, Utah
Museum of the Rockies, Bozeman, Montana

Above: *Baths of dilute acetic acid are used to remove certain types of rock from fossil bones.*

Below: *The mounted reconstructions we see in museums are the result of many years of hard work. The spectacular results are well worth all of the effort.*

33

Dinosaur biology and behavior

Like detectives attempting to solve a crime, paleontologists try to reconstruct the appearance and behaviors of dinosaurs by using all of the available evidence. Most of the time, all that remains of a dinosaur are bones and teeth. But consideration of other fossils, such as footprints and skin impressions, provides a valuable source of additional information. However, there are many aspects of dinosaur biology that will always be a mystery, as so many different parts of these animals, and many of their behaviors, are never preserved as fossils.

Paleontologists working on dinosaurs and other extinct creatures need to have a thorough knowledge of the biology and natural history of living animals. By seeing how the muscles, organs and bones of living animals are put together, scientists can attempt to reconstruct the skeleton and soft parts of a dinosaur from their fossilized remains. Birds, crocodiles and lizards, the closest living relatives of dinosaurs, provide important clues to dinosaur biology.

Warm- or cold-blooded?

Today's warm-blooded animals—birds and mammals—have a higher metabolic rate than living cold-blooded animals such as fishes, amphibians and reptiles. This means that their body's chemical processes occur at faster rates and higher temperatures, so that they yield more sustained energy for the animal. However, this higher energy level requires a much greater intake of food.

But that is not the only difference. Warm-blooded animals make most of their own energy by burning food. In contrast, cold-blooded animals get only part of their energy this way. They use heat from the environment, such as sunlight, to warm up enough to be more active, so they depend on the climate much more than warm-blooded animals do. As a result, their body temperatures tend to go up and down with the climate, whereas warm-blooded animals have a more constant temperature. Another difference is that many cold-blooded reptiles such as lizards and snakes can move very quickly—but only for a short time, after which they seem to run out of gas. Their lifestyles—and metabolisms—are based more on short, rapid bursts than on sustained periods of activity, such as we see in birds and mammals.

Were dinosaurs more like today's reptiles or like birds and mammals? The question is not easy. Some scientists think they were more reptilian because, after all, dinosaurs were reptiles. But birds, which are warm-blooded, are descended from dinosaurs, so somewhere along the line warm-bloodedness evolved, as it did when mammals evolved from their cold-blooded ancestors.

How can we tell if dinosaurs were warm- or cold-blooded? Large dinosaurs almost

Right: *Scientists reconstruct the muscles and organs of dinosaurs from fossils and from their knowledge of living reptiles and birds. But features such as color cannot be determined on the basis of fossil evidence.*

Right: *This cassowary has a large horny crest on its skull that is brightly colored. Some dinosaurs have similar crests, but did they use them for display and species recognition, as the cassowary does? Dinosaur behavior is not always easy to interpret.*

certainly kept fairly constant body temperatures, if only because it would take so long to warm or cool such large body masses. What about smaller dinosaurs—and babies? Studies show that dinosaurs grew very quickly—much as large birds and mammals grow today. A typical duck-billed dinosaur may have become 23 feet (7 m) long in just seven years! To grow so fast for such a long time would seem to require a sustained high metabolic rate, because we know no animals today that can grow so fast and yet are cold-blooded. Mesozoic dinosaurs may not have been exactly like large birds and mammals of today, but they were apparently more like them than like crocodiles and lizards in these respects.

FEATHERS, SKIN AND COLORS

Fossilized skin impressions show that many dinosaurs had scaly skin, similar to that of living reptiles. But a few exceptionally well preserved fossils show that some dinosaurs had coatings of fluffy down, or even of feathers.

The most spectacular of these fossils are those of small theropod dinosaurs from the early Cretaceous period of China. *Sinosauropteryx* has the remains of small downlike structures running along the length of the back, whereas *Protarchaeopteryx* (before the ancient wing) has a small fan of feathers attached to the end of the tail. The presence of feathers in these dinosaurs is not too surprising, however, as other features of their skeletons show that they were closely related to birds.

But although feathers and skin impressions are sometimes preserved as fossils, the original color of the skin never survives the fossilization process. In their reconstructions of dinosaurs, scientists use the colors of living lizards, crocodiles, birds and large mammals.

Skin impressions, such as this one from a Corythosaurus *fossil, display a complicated pattern of small bony plates. Unfortunately, the original color of the skin is not preserved.*

Eggs and nests

Dinosaur eggs and nests were first recognized from discoveries by the American Museum of Natural History in Mongolia's desert, the Gobi, led by Roy Chapman Andrews in the 1920s. They provided scientists with their first ideas about how dinosaurs might have raised and cared for their young. A number of recent discoveries in the western United States and in Mongolia, including embryos and baby dinosaurs, have greatly improved our knowledge of dinosaur birth. Careful study of these precious fossils has shown that dinosaur nesting behavior was very similar to that of living birds.

Below: *Scientists from the American Museum of Natural History recently discovered an* Oviraptor *egg that contained the beautifully preserved remains of an embryonic skeleton. This is an artist's reconstruction of how the embryo might have looked just before it was due to hatch out of the egg.*

Dinosaur eggs come in a wide variety of shapes and sizes. Some eggs are circular and about the size of a tennis ball, whereas others are up to 21 inches (53 cm) in length and have an elliptical shape. This might seem very big, but even these eggs are not as large as those laid by the biggest birds, such as the extinct elephant birds of Madagascar.

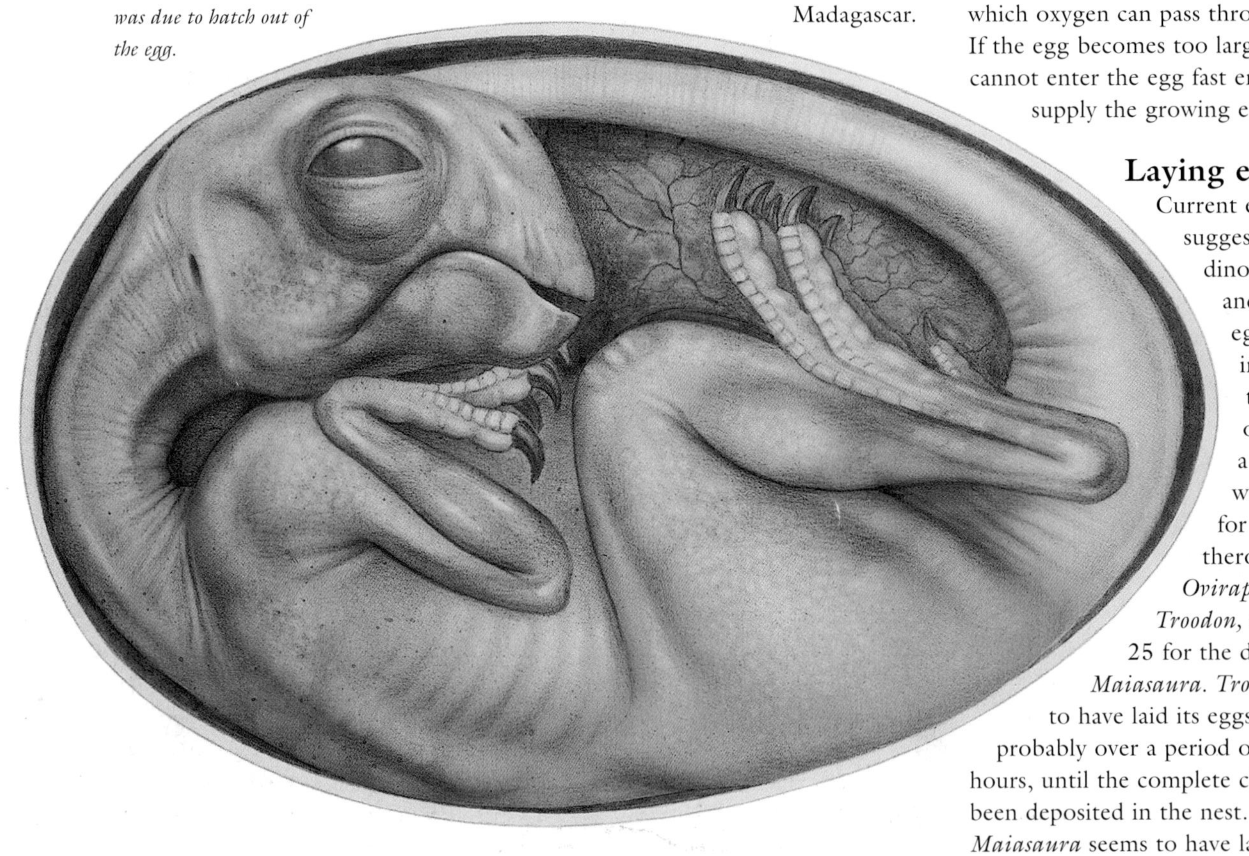

Dinosaurs generally laid many more eggs in their nests than living birds do, even though the eggs were larger. In addition, there are limits to egg size. The eggshells of dinosaurs, birds and reptiles are perforated with many tiny holes, called pores, which allow the life-giving gas oxygen to enter the egg. The maximum size of all eggs is controlled by the rate at which oxygen can pass through the egg. If the egg becomes too large, oxygen cannot enter the egg fast enough to supply the growing embryo.

Laying eggs

Current evidence suggests that all dinosaurs laid eggs and that the eggs were laid in nests. The total number of eggs laid in a single nest was about 22 for the small theropods *Oviraptor* and *Troodon,* and up to 25 for the duck-billed *Maiasaura. Troodon* appears to have laid its eggs in pairs, probably over a period of several hours, until the complete clutch had been deposited in the nest. In contrast, *Maiasaura* seems to have laid its eggs in a spiral pattern, starting at one side of the nest and working around it until all of the eggs were in place.

Nests and nest sites

The nests of *Troodon* and *Maiasaura* were quite different. Those belonging to *Troodon* were simple bowl-like structures formed by digging a shallow hollow in the soil. A *Maiasaura* nest was much more impressive. It consisted of a tall mound of earth up to 6 feet (2 m) across. The eggs were laid in a shallow hollow on top of the mound, which might have been lined with plant material that helped to cushion the eggs and keep them warm—*Maiasaura* was much too large to sit on its eggs! Some living birds, such as the scrub-fowl, as well as crocodiles still make similar nests today. Detailed study of *Maiasaura* nests shows that they are made up of several layers of mud and other material piled on top of each other. This suggests that they were reused year after year.

Egg Mountain

Most of our information on *Maiasaura* nests comes from a spectacular locality in Montana called Egg Mountain. This area contains evidence of many dozens of nests. Analysis of the rock types on Egg Mountain shows that this area was an island in a shallow lake during the late Cretaceous period. It appears that herds of *Maiasaura* used this island as a communal nest site. The nests are situated very close to each other, but are separated by just enough space for an adult *Maiasaura* to move around in without trampling on its eggs. These nesting colonies must have been very noisy, smelly and crowded places, much like penguin colonies of modern times. However, by living together so closely, the *Maiasaura* herd were able to protect their young much more easily. The shallow waters that surrounded the island might also have offered some protection from predators.

Above: *This fossil egg contains the remains of a* Troodon *embryo. If you look carefully, you will see two tiny limb bones (above the white markings).*

Left: *This is a nest of the small theropod dinosaur* Troodon. *It was discovered in rocks of late Cretaceous age in Montana. The eggs are preserved in an upright position, suggesting that they became embedded in the soil as they were laid.*

Left: *Dinosaur eggs are not particularly common, but they are abundant in certain parts of China, the United States, Argentina and Spain. It is often difficult to decide which dinosaur laid a particular egg—only those eggs that contain fossil embryos can be identified with confidence. Note the wrinkled surface texture of the eggs. This feature helps to keep the pores free of dirt, allowing gases such as oxygen to enter and leave the egg.*

Caring for the babies

I n a handful of cases, scientists have been lucky enough to discover the remains of embryos within dinosaur eggs. So far, embryos are known for the theropods *Troodon, Oviraptor* and *Therizinosaurus,* the ornithopod *Maiasaura* and an unnamed sauropod from South America. A number of skeletons from very young baby dinosaurs have also been discovered. These fossils provide important information on the ways in which dinosaurs grew and developed, and also tell us something about the ways that parents cared for their young.

Below: Mussaurus *(mouse lizard) was a prosauropod dinosaur that lived during the late Triassic period in what is now Argentina. All the known remains of* Mussaurus *are from baby animals. Their skeletons are so small that they can easily fit into the palm of your hand! The one here is pictured with a centimeter ruler. The size of the adults is unknown at present, but they probably reached a body length of about 10 feet (3 m).*

Parental care

Examination of the tiny bones from *Maiasaura* babies has shown that the leg bones were not fully formed at the time when the animals hatched. It appears that the legs were quite weak and that the young hatchlings were incapable of running or walking properly. As a result, the babies were probably confined to the nest during the first few weeks of their lives. This idea is confirmed by the presence of many fragments of trampled, broken eggshell in the nests. If the babies had left the nests soon after hatching, the eggshells would not have been broken up

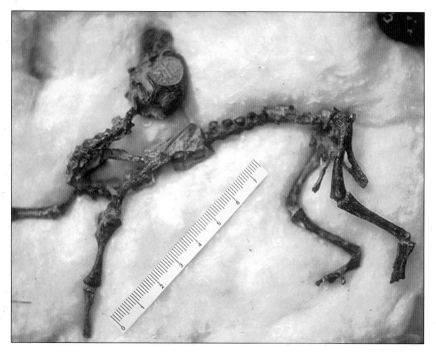

in this way. While the babies were restricted to their nests, their parents would supply them with food, water and protection. Newly hatched *Maiasaura* were about 12 inches (30 cm) in length. But they grew very quickly, and reached a length of about 5 feet (1.5 m) in only a few weeks. At this point, the babies were big enough and strong enough to leave the nest and join the rest of the herd.

Fending for themselves

In contrast to the high levels of parental care seen in *Maiasaura, Troodon* babies were left to fend for themselves as soon as they had hatched. *Troodon* nests often contain the remains of hatched eggs. These eggs lack the top part of the shell (which was removed by the baby as it hatched out), but otherwise show little evidence of trampling. This suggests that the babies did not remain in the nest for long after hatching. The limb bones of *Troodon* babies were well formed and strong, so the youngsters could scamper away from the nest and begin searching for their own food almost immediately. These tiny predators probably ate insects and other small animals but were themselves vulnerable to attack by larger meat-eating animals such as other theropods and large monitor lizards.

A brooding dinosaur

Skeletons of the small plant-eating dinosaur *Protoceratops* are extremely abundant in Mongolia, in the Gobi. For this reason, when dinosaur eggs and nests were discovered in this area during the 1920s it was assumed that they must have belonged to this animal. During the same series of expeditions, the skeleton of a bizarre theropod was found close to one of these nests, and it was suggested that this animal had died while attempting to steal eggs from the nest. It was given the name *Oviraptor* (egg thief) as a result. Recent fieldwork in the Gobi has led to the discovery of many more dinosaur nests, some of which are preserved underneath the fossilized skeleton of an *Oviraptor*. The *Oviraptor* skeletons appeared to be sitting on top of the eggs, and it was suggested that the nests might belong to *Oviraptor* rather than to *Protoceratops*. This idea was proved to be true when an egg containing an *Oviraptor* embryo was discovered in one of the nests. It seems that *Oviraptor* was actually a caring parent that brooded its eggs just like a bird, rather than the devious egg thief that it was once thought to be. This is a good example of how new discoveries can overturn long-held views on dinosaur biology and evolution.

Below: *This is a reconstruction of a nest of the duck-billed dinosaur* Maiasaura. *It contains the skeletons of several newly hatched animals. Fossil leaves, seeds and fruits found within the nests show that the parents brought food to the baby animals.*

Baby dinosaurs

A mother Maiasaura brings a mouthful of succulent plants to the nest to feed her brood of fast-growing babies. The babies could not leave the nest until they were several months old.

Hunting and fighting
The predators and the prey

Dinosaurs interacted with each other, and with the other animals that shared their environment, in an astonishing number of ways. Meat-eating dinosaurs such as *Tyrannosaurus* and *Allosaurus* needed the equipment to hunt down and subdue prey animals. They had the teeth and claws to penetrate the superb defenses of plant-eaters such as *Triceratops* and *Iguanodon* if they could catch them. Within the same species, individuals would probably have fought each other in contests for mates, food, territory or dominance within a group. To cope with all of these demands, dinosaurs possessed a wide variety of weapons for both attack and defense.

The principal weapons of predatory dinosaurs, from the enormous *Tyrannosaurus* to the diminutive *Compsognathus*, were mouths lined with rows of bladelike teeth, and hands and feet tipped by razor-sharp claws.

the edges of these teeth, allowing them to slice through meat with ease. In *Tyrannosaurus*, the teeth were up to 12 inches (30 cm) long and were strong enough to crush and puncture solid bone. Other theropods, such as *Baryonyx*, had teeth similar to those of living crocodiles that were ideal for impaling slippery prey such as fish.

Above: *The skull of* Albertosaurus *(Alberta lizard) shows several of the predatory features seen in all theropod dinosaurs. The jaws hold many large, curved and finely serrated teeth. There are large spaces to house powerful jaw muscles, and the skull is robustly built to withstand the forces generated by holding on to struggling prey.*

Teeth

The teeth of most theropod dinosaurs were pointed and strongly curved so that they could easily pierce flesh and get a firm grip on a struggling prey animal. Tiny serrations, like those on a steak knife, lined

Claws

All theropods possessed curved, hooklike claws on their hands and feet. Each claw ended in a sharp point that was ideally suited for digging into the flesh of unfortunate prey animals. During life, a sheath of a hard, hornlike substance called keratin—the same material that makes up our hair and fingernails—would have covered the bony claws. As the sheath was worn down by use, it would develop a sharp edge, making it a very efficient weapon for cutting and slashing. But the sheath was also a living tissue and could be partially replaced by new growth as it was worn away. The curved shape of the claws, similar to that seen in living birds of prey such as eagles and hawks, would have been useful in pinning prey to the ground when feeding. Some of these claws were enormous. For example, the claws on the hands of *Baryonyx* would have been over 12 inches (30 cm) long! In other cases, the claws were small, but deadly.

Like switchblade knives

Several small theropods, such as *Deinonychus* and *Troodon,* had specially enlarged claws on their feet that could be used like switchblade knives. A reversed joint in the second toe forced the claw to be folded back during running and walking. However, when attacking, the claw could be flicked forward at high speed. This action could have been performed in combination with a jump or a kick and would have caused a great deal of damage to any animal unlucky enough to be within range.

Pack hunting

Teeth of *Deinonychus* are sometimes found alongside skeletons of *Tenontosaurus,* a large plant-eating dinosaur. Careful study of the shape and size of the teeth by scientists has shown that they often belonged to several different individuals. In addition, *Deinonychus* skeletons are often found together, indicating that these small but vicious hunters lived in groups. These two observations suggest that *Deinonychus* hunted in packs, using teamwork to attack and kill much larger animals than themselves. The brain of *Deinonychus* is very large for a dinosaur of its small body size, and this might have allowed it to coordinate its hunting behavior and strategy with other members of the pack.

Below: *This reconstruction shows the small theropod* Saurornitholestes *(robbing bird-lizard) attacking the much larger duck-billed dinosaur* Lambeosaurus. *Small theropods would normally be limited to preying upon small animals such as lizards and mammals, but pack-hunting animals, like* Saurornitholestes, *could work together to bring down much larger prey.*

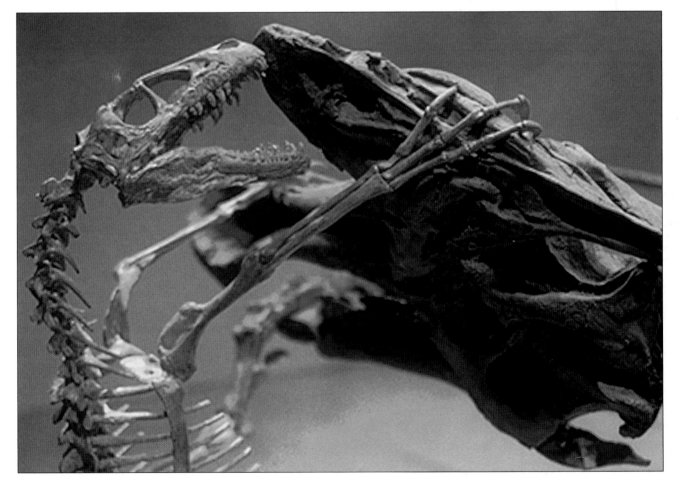

Scavenging

A hungry tyrannosaurus disturbs a scavenging pair of Quetzalcoatlus as it moves in on the carcass that the giant pterosaurs had been eating.

Arms and armor
Self-protection

Many plant-eating dinosaurs possessed impressive defensive weapons that provided them with some security in a world populated by large predatory dinosaurs. These weapons ranged from thumb spikes to tail clubs, horns and heavy hoofs. Some dinosaurs were able to rely on sheer size as a defense—adult sauropods were so large that they probably weren't threatened by even the largest meat-eaters. Others, like the ankylosaurs and the sauropod *Saltasaurus,* relied on coats of armor that could resist the sharp teeth and claws of all but the most determined predators.

Below: *A stegosaur's tail was protected by plates and spines. The two sets of paired tail spines can be seen in this picture. They would have been covered in a horny sheath.*

Below: *The skull of* Ankylosaurus *was completely encased in a covering of thick bony plates. Similar plates covered much of the rest of the body, providing an almost impenetrable covering of armor.* Euoplocephalus *(well-armored skull) a close relative of* Ankylosaurus *even had armor-plated eyelids!*

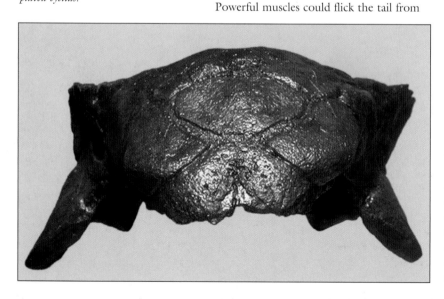

Stegosaurs possessed pairs of large spikes, up to 2 feet (60 cm) long, situated at the end of a powerful tail. A sideways swipe with this formidable weapon might have severely injured a marauding theropod. Some ankylosaurs might have used massive tail clubs made out of solid bone in a similar way. A few sauropods, including the Chinese *Omeisaurus* (Omei lizard), also had bony tail clubs. The thickset, heavy tails of large ornithopods, such as *Iguanodon* and *Parasaurolophus,* and sauropods might have provided them with some protection. A well-aimed blow from one of these tails could throw an attacker off balance or knock it off its feet. Other sauropods, such as *Diplodocus* and *Apatosaurus,* had long, whiplike tails. Powerful muscles could flick the tail from side to side, and the end of the tail could strike a predator at blistering speed.

Horns and frills
The horns of some ceratopsian dinosaurs might have been formidable weapons. The arrangement and number of the horns varied from species to species. For example, *Triceratops* had a short horn on the tip of its nose and a long brow horn over each of the eyes, whereas *Monoclonius* (one-horned) had a single large horn on its nose. The horns would have been covered with a sharp sheath made of keratin. In *Triceratops,* a large bony frill over the neck would have provided some protection from predators.

Other defenses
Many plant-eaters lacked such impressive defenses and had to rely on other means in order to evade or escape their attackers. Some of these animals had heightened senses, such as keen eyesight, that enabled them to detect the approach of predators from a great distance, giving them ample time to escape. Many small ornithopods, such as *Hypsilophodon,* with long hind limbs could run at great speed in order to avoid capture. Some dinosaurs, such as the hadrosaur *Maiasaura* and the horned dinosaur *Chasmosaurus,* lived in great herds that offered some protection from attackers. Finally, it is possible that many dinosaurs used skin patterns to camouflage themselves and merge into the background to hide from predators.

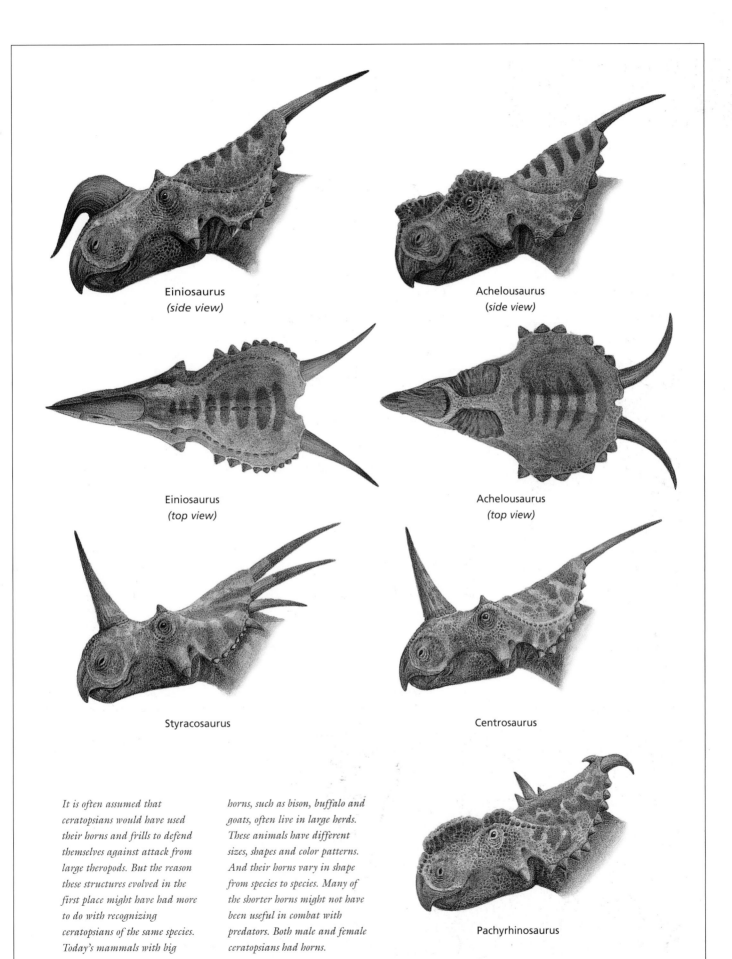

Einiosaurus
(side view)

Achelousaurus
(side view)

Einiosaurus
(top view)

Achelousaurus
(top view)

Styracosaurus

Centrosaurus

Pachyrhinosaurus

It is often assumed that ceratopsians would have used their horns and frills to defend themselves against attack from large theropods. But the reason these structures evolved in the first place might have had more to do with recognizing ceratopsians of the same species. Today's mammals with big horns, such as bison, buffalo and goats, often live in large herds. These animals have different sizes, shapes and color patterns. And their horns vary in shape from species to species. Many of the shorter horns might not have been useful in combat with predators. Both male and female ceratopsians had horns.

Tyrannosaurus tries to attack the armored dinosaur Edmontonia. Although much smaller Edmontonia is well protected by bony plates and spines embedded within its skin.

What dinosaurs ate
The evidence

Knowing what an animal eats is extremely important. Diet controls almost all aspects of an animal's life, including its behavior and the place where it lives. Animals may be divided into herbivores (plant-eaters), carnivores (meat-eaters) and omnivores (those that eat both).

Direct evidence of dinosaur eating habits is hard to come by. Scientists look for different clues. In rare cases, the remains of the dinosaur's last meal have been found inside the skeleton. We know that the theropod *Coelophysis* sometimes practiced cannibalism, because scientists have discovered adult skeletons containing small bones of baby *Coelophysis*. Another small theropod, *Compsognathus*, has been found with the remains of a small lizard in its ribcage, close to the original position of the stomach. There is also an example of an *Edmontosaurus*, a duck-billed dinosaur, with stomach contents that included fragments of bark, pine needles and conifer cones.

Coprolites
Examination of fossilized feces (animal waste), called coprolites, can also provide direct evidence of diet. Coprolites contain bits and pieces of the animals or plants that the dinosaur was eating. Unfortunately, there are only a few cases in which a coprolite has been found inside a dinosaur skeleton—the direct link that would enable scientists to confidently assign a coprolite to a specific type of dinosaur. In 1991, an expedition from the American Museum of Natural History to Mongolia's desert, the Gobi, made such a find. The coprolite, discovered inside a dromaeosaurid theropod similar to *Velociraptor*, contained the remains of a small lizardlike animal.

Many coprolites have been found that cannot be directly associated with any particular types of dinosaur. Some large coprolites from the Upper Cretaceous period of North America contain several fragments of plant material. Scientists speculate that these may have been produced by hadrosaurs, the duck-billed dinosaurs that were so abundant at that time. Other coprolites found in the same

Below: Coprolites have been found in many different parts of the world and come in all shapes and sizes. Some coprolites are less than half an inch in length, whereas others reach lengths of over 12 inches (30 cm).

WHO ATE WHAT

Experts divide dinosaurs into plant- or meat-eaters on the basis of many different features. Here's how the dinosaurs in this book are grouped.

Herbivores

Ankylosaurus	*Maiasaura*
Apatosaurus	*Ouranosaurus*
Aragosaurus	*Pachycephalosaurus*
Brachiosaurus	*Pachyrhinosaurus*
Camarasaurus	*Parasaurolophus*
Camptosaurus	*Patagosaurus*
Chasmosaurus	*Plateosaurus*
Corythosaurus	*Protoceratops*
Diplodocus	*Psittacosaurus*
Hylaeosaurus	*Saltasaurus*
Hypsilophodon	*Scelidosaurus*
Iguanodon	*Stegosaurus*
Kentrosaurus	*Styracosaurus*
Lambeosaurus	*Tenontosaurus*
Lesothosaurus	*Triceratops*

Carnivores

Allosaurus	*Deinonychus*
Archaeopteryx	*Dilophosaurus*
Baptornis	*Eoraptor*
Baryonyx	*Herrerasaurus*
Carcharodontosaurus	*Iberomesornis*
Carnotaurus	*Sinosautopteryx*
Ceratosaurus	*Troodon*
Coelophysis	*Tyrannosaurus*
Compsognathus	*Velociraptor*

Omnivores

Caudipteryx	*Struthiomimus*
Oviraptor	*Therizinosaurus*
Pelecanimimus	

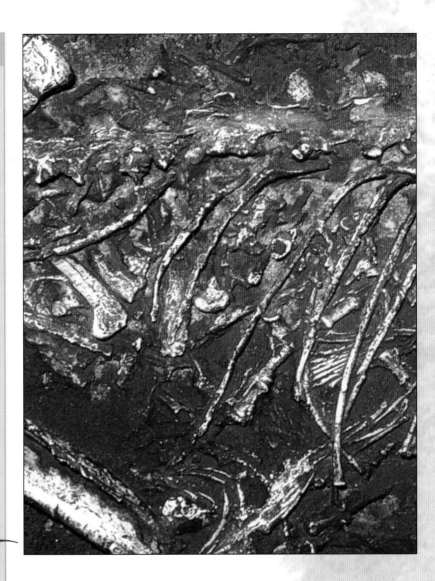

region contain fragments of bone, demonstrating that meat-eating dinosaurs made them. One recent find, an enormous coprolite over 16 inches (40 cm) long and containing smashed pieces of bone, is thought to have belonged to *Tyrannosaurus.*

Indirect methods

Scientists rely mostly on indirect ways to learn about dinosaur diet. The most common method is to look at the shape of the teeth and the way in which the jaws of the dinosaur were able to chew food. Study of living animals has shown that particular dietary behavior, such as eating plants, is closely linked to specific tooth shapes. Scientists can use this information to draw conclusions about what dinosaurs ate. The ways in which scientists use this information are discussed on the following pages.

Above: *The ribcage of this adult* Coelophysis *is filled with many tiny bones that represent the remains of its last meal. Scientists have discovered that these small bones belonged to baby* Coelophysis, *suggesting that this vicious predator was a cannibal.*

The dinosaur diet
Analyzing the clues

In most cases, scientists have to deduce the diet of dinosaurs by looking at the clues left behind in the structure of their teeth, skulls and skeletons. The shape of the teeth is particularly informative, as studies on living animals have shown that tooth shape is closely related to the type of food that an animal eats. Other types of evidence are also useful. These include claw shape, the general form of the body, and the way in which the jaws worked.

Clues to carnivory

Living carnivorous reptiles, such as monitor lizards, have flat bladelike teeth. The tips of the teeth are curved back so that they can hook into the flesh of their prey. Both the front and the back edges of the teeth are lined with tiny serrations, rather like those on a steak knife. These serrations enable the tooth to saw its way through flesh. Such teeth are particularly useful for feeding on large land-living animals with tough hides. Other

Above: *The teeth of the iguana are leaf shaped. The tooth edges are covered with a few large serrations, ideal for puncturing plant material.*

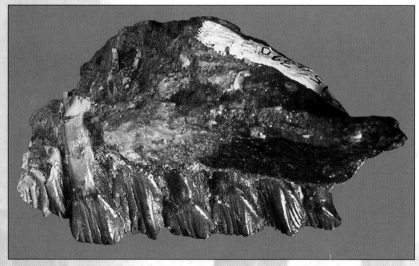

Above: *The teeth of* Atlascopcosaurus, *a small plant-eating dinosaur from Australia, are extremely similar to those of the iguana. These teeth have been heavily worn.*

carnivores, such as crocodiles, have simple spikelike teeth, lacking serrations. These are ideal for grasping slippery, soft-bodied prey such as fish.

Dinosaurs such as *Tyrannosaurus* and *Allosaurus* have teeth very similar to those of monitor lizards—although the dinosaur's teeth are much larger. *Baryonyx* has teeth just like a crocodile's. These

similarities tell us that these dinosaurs were very likely carnivores, and even tell us a little about the types of animals that they probably fed on.

Living carnivores, such as birds of prey, crocodiles and some mammals, have large, sharp, highly curved claws that they use for holding on to, and dismembering, prey. Those dinosaurs with large curved claws are also likely to have been carnivores. Some theropod dinosaurs had claws up to 12 inches (30 cm) long.

Hints at herbivory

The teeth of living herbivorous lizards, such as iguanas, are quite different from those of carnivores. They are wide and are often described as leaf shaped. They have very rough serrations along the sides, much larger than those seen on carnivore teeth, giving them a zigzag appearance. These serrations are ideal for puncturing and cutting plant material. Very similar teeth are seen in some dinosaurs, such as *Lesothosaurus* and *Scelidosaurus,* suggesting that these animals were herbivores. Other dinosaurs, such as the hadrosaurs, have flat teeth that lack these large serrations. These teeth are very similar to those of animals such as sheep and cows that spend a lot of time chewing tough vegetation.

Herbivores also need very large guts, to help process their meals of hard-to-digest plant food. As a result, they tend to have very large stomach regions, too. The shape of a dinosaur's ribcage can give clues to the size of its gut and, therefore, its diet.

Above: *This lower jaw of a monitor lizard shows the kind of flat, bladelike teeth that are found in the jaws of many different types of carnivorous reptile. The sides of the teeth bear many very fine, sharp serrations.*

Below: *Although they are much larger, the teeth of* Tyrannosaurus *are almost identical in shape to those of monitor lizards. In combination with the powerful jaw muscles, they enabled* Tyrannosaurus *to puncture through solid bone.*

STOMACH STONES

Occasionally, dinosaur skeletons are discovered with small piles of highly polished stones in the area where the stomach once was. These stones are called gastroliths, meaning "stomach stones." Some living herbivores are known to swallow stones that then become trapped in the stomach. The stones are rubbed against each other by movements of the stomach muscles and help to grind food up into smaller pieces. The gastroliths in herbivorous dinosaurs probably acted in the same way.

How big were they?

All shapes and sizes

Dinosaurs are generally thought of as gigantic animals that were much larger than any of the animals that are alive today. In reality, however, dinosaurs came in a wide range of sizes. Although many dinosaurs were huge, some were surprisingly small.

The animals depicted here provide a dramatic comparison of the sizes of the different types of dinosaurs, from the gigantic sauropods to the smallest carnivores and birds.

Some dinosaurs, such as the herbivores *Lesothosaurus* and *Hypsilophodon* and the carnivores *Troodon* and

Compsognathus, reached adult body sizes of only 3-6 feet (1-2 m) and weighed no more than the average family dog. Baby dinosaurs were also very small. Some, such as *Mussaurus*, were only a few inches

Iberomesornis   Compsognathus   Deinonychus   Triceratops   Tyrannosaurus

long when they hatched. But baby dinosaurs grew quickly and could reach much larger body sizes by the time they were fully grown.

Dinosaurs included the largest land animals of all time. Some sauropod dinosaurs, such as *Seismosaurus*, were the longest animals ever to live on earth. But although many dinosaurs were far longer and heavier than living elephants and rhinoceroses, even the heaviest dinosaurs weighed much less than the largest animal of all time. The blue whale can reach a length of over 100 feet (30 m) and weigh almost 200 tons—twice as much as the largest dinosaur. Blue whales can become so large because the weight of their massive bodies is supported by the water in which they live. Dinosaurs, on the other hand, had to support their body weight on land, which is much harder to do.

FACT FILE

Longest: *Seismosaurus,* a sauropod from North America, up to 160 feet (50 m)

Heaviest: *Argentinosaurus,* an Argentinian sauropod, up to 100 tons

Tallest: *Brachiosaurus* fed on leaves from the tops of trees perhaps 40 feet (12 m) high

Smallest: *Compsognathus* reached a maximum 3 feet (1 m) and weighed about the same as a chicken; many birds from the Jurassic and Cretaceous periods were even smaller, and some, such as *Iberomesornis,* were no larger than a sparrow

Largest meat-eater: *Giganotosaurus,* an Argentinian theropod, up to 48 feet (14.5 m) in length

Largest head: *Pentaceratops,* a horned dinosaur from North America, had a skull more than 10 feet (3 m) long

Brachiosaurus

Footprints in rock
Making tracks

Scientists use two main methods to determine the ways in which dinosaurs moved—they make detailed studies of the skeleton and they examine fossilized footprints. The skeleton can show the possible range of limb movements and the size and positions of the muscles that were responsible for moving the limbs. It also indicates the strength of the individual limb bones and the position of the animal's center of balance. Footprints can yield information on many other aspects of dinosaur behavior, such as herding, in addition to evidence of walking speeds and styles.

Below: *This trackway was made by an ornithopod dinosaur walking on its hind limbs. Ornithopod footprints can be recognized from the impressions of three large toes, each of which ends in a blunt, rounded hoof. Ornithopod footprints are very common in the early Cretaceous rocks of Spain and southern England.*

Below: *Theropod footprints look much like those of ornithopods, and the trackways of these two very different kinds of dinosaurs are sometimes confused. Theropod footprints can be recognized by the sharp point at the ends of the toes made by the claws.*

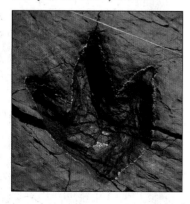

Unfortunately it is not possible to decide exactly which species of dinosaur made a particular footprint. This is because the shape of the feet is usually very similar within a broad group of dinosaurs. For instance, almost all theropods had three-toed feet that ended in sharp, pointed claws. However, the trackways of these broader dinosaur groups can be distinguished from each other. The large circular footprints of sauropods, for example, can easily be distinguished from the three-toed footprints of theropods and ornithopods. This allows some general statements to be made about the identity of the dinosaurs responsible for making the tracks.

Running and walking

Experiments on running and walking in living mammals, birds and reptiles have shown that it is possible to calculate an animal's speed from a few simple measurements of its footprints. The two most important measurements are the stride length—the distance between consecutive prints from the same foot—and the length of the footprint itself. These can be entered into some simple equations to estimate the animal's speed. Some calculations suggest that certain large theropods, such as *Allosaurus*, could attain speeds of about 25 mph (40 km/h). Lightly built theropods such as *Struthiomimus* and small ornithopods such as *Hypsilophodon* might have been

able to run at almost twice that speed. The enormous sauropods and the heavily built ankylosaurs, stegosaurs and ceratopsians were slower moving. They probably reached maximum speeds of 10-20 mph (15-30 km/h).

Swimming

One remarkable trackway appears to record a swimming sauropod. When the track was first discovered, it was noticed that, although many handprints were preserved, there were few footprints. It looked a little like the sauropod had been walking on its hands! It was suggested, however, that this trackway could have been formed if the sauropod had been in a river, using its front legs to pull itself along while its back legs floated clear of the riverbed. The footprints would have formed when the sauropod occasionally gave an extra push against the bottom of the river.

Right: *These spectacular trackways were made by a pair of big sauropod dinosaurs. Note the large circular footprints and the smaller crescent-shaped handprints that lie in front of them. When these trackways were made, the mud that makes up these rocks was next to a large lake. It might appear that the dinosaurs were climbing up a rock face, but the rocks have been tilted vertically by the action of geological forces over many millions of years.*

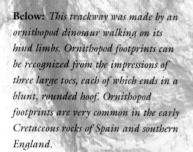

When they walked on soft, muddy surfaces, sauropods left large circular impressions of their broad feet, similar to the tracks of living elephants. Broad feet spread the weight of the animal over a large area, preventing it sinking too far into spongy ground. In well-preserved sauropod footprints, an impression of a large claw, which was present on the first toe of these animals, is often visible.

Above: *Note the claw on this* Apatosaurus *foot.*

Two legs or four?

Walking and running

Animals may be classified according to the way in which they walk and run. Bipedal animals, or bipeds, are those that walk on their hind limbs only. These include human beings and birds. Quadrupedal animals, or quadrupeds, such as most mammals and reptiles, walk on all fours. But these categories are not strictly defined. Some animals can switch between these two different methods of locomotion. Scientists are able to work out how dinosaurs carried themselves by studying the proportions of their skeletons and examining the handprints and footprints preserved in trackways.

Below: *These footprints were made by a large bipedal ornithopod. The short distance between each of the footprints suggests that the animal was walking very slowly at the time.*

Below: *This skeleton of* Camptosaurus *is mounted in a quadrupedal pose. It is likely that this animal might have run on its hind limbs, too, but perhaps only when startled by a predator.*

Right: Plateosaurus *could rear up onto its hind limbs in order to feed higher up in the trees. Note the short arms. But they were powerfully built, enabling* Plateosaurus *to rest or walk on all fours.*

Quadrupeds have arms and legs that are about the same length. In this way, the weight of the body is equally supported at the front and back. In contrast, bipeds tend to have very long hind legs, but arms that are very short and incapable of bearing a large part of the animal's weight. The bodies of bipeds tend to be very short also, so that most of the body weight is positioned just above the hips. In quadrupeds, the body can be longer, as more of the weight is supported by the arms.

Bipedal dinosaurs

Theropod dinosaurs have extremely long hind limbs and short, compact bodies. The arms are usually quite short in relation to the hind legs and usually not strong enough to support the weight of the body. These features are also seen in some small ornithopods and pachycephalosaurs, and suggest that all these animals were bipedal.

Quadrupedal dinosaurs

Sauropods, ankylosaurs and ceratopsians had very stout arms, capable of bearing heavy loads, and large, barrel-shaped bodies, suggesting that they were quadrupedal. Evidence from trackways confirms these predictions. Handprints are seldom found in the trackways of theropods or small ornithopods, but sauropod, ankylosaur and ceratopsian trackways always show the impressions of the hands and feet.

On two or four legs

Large ornithopods, such as *Iguanodon*, and prosauropods, such as *Plateosaurus*, were able to switch between bipedal and quadrupedal walking and running as the situation demanded. Their bodies show a mixture of features including long hind legs and short but strong arms with broad hands—capable of providing support for the body when they were placed on the ground. Trackways made by both of these types of dinosaur confirm that the hands were occasionally used while walking.

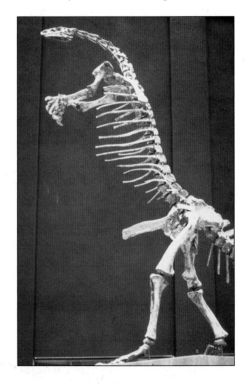

In air and water
Flying and swimming

Many scientists used to believe that some dinosaurs spent much of their time living in water, but detailed studies of dinosaur skeletons have shown that all of the most familiar dinosaurs were land animals. This does not mean that dinosaurs could not swim at all, however. Some geological evidence suggests that a few dinosaur species crossed rivers and lakes. Among members of the birds branch (Aves) of the dinosaur family tree, *Archaeopteryx* was equipped to fly and *Baptornis* to swim.

The skeletons of many dinosaurs do not show any special features, such as large paddle-shaped hands and feet, that are suggestive of an aquatic lifestyle. However, many living animals such as dogs and horses also lack such features but are known to be strong swimmers. There is some evidence that the horned dinosaur *Centrosaurus* lived in herds, as the bones of many different individuals have been found together in the same quarries. Studies of the rocks in which these bones are found indicate that all the skeletons were deposited at the same time in a large river. It is possible that the *Centrosaurus* herd was trying to swim across the river and that some of the animals died in the attempt.

Learning to fly
Although *Archaeopteryx* is the earliest known bird, it is thought that living birds are the direct descendants of small, fast-running theropod dinosaurs. Scientists have developed two major theories to explain the evolution of flight in birds from their non-flying ancestors. The first suggests that the ancestors of birds lived in the tops of trees and had to leap from branch to branch. The other theory proposes that ground-living dinosaurs sped along the ground and jumped into the air in order to catch prey. Scientists are not sure which of these theories is correct. But in either case, any features of the animals that helped them to jump longer distances would be advantageous and would be passed on to their descendants. One such feature might have been the development of small feathers on the arms. This would be the first stage in developing a wing useful in gliding. Over time, many additional small changes to the structure of the arms, tail and other parts of the body would eventually lead to the evolution of true flapping flight.

Above: *Archaeopteryx, the earliest-known bird, had well-developed feathers. But there is much debate over its flying abilities. Current evidence suggests that* Archaeopteryx *could fly, but that it was not a particularly strong or agile flier.*

Below: *It is possible that herds of* Centrosaurus *often crossed large rivers, as wildebeest—a type of African antelope—do today, on long journeys in search of food.*

59

The dinosaurs
Origins

The first known dinosaur fossils appear in rocks that were deposited during the late Triassic period, about 225 million years ago. At this time, we find the remains of the earliest prosauropods, ornithischians and theropods. These three dinosaur groups all have a large number of features in common, particularly in the structure of their legs and hips. This suggests they are descended from the same common ancestor. As these different dinosaur groups appeared at the beginning of the late Triassic period, their common ancestor must have lived at an even earlier time.

Right: Lagosuchus *was not a dinosaur, but is thought to have shared a common ancestor with the dinosaurs. No evidence of this common ancestor has yet been found. The term Dinosauromorpha is used for the group that includes the dinosaurs (Dinosauria) and* Lagosuchus *and its close relatives* Marasuchus *and* Lagerpeton.

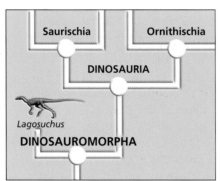

During the middle Triassic period, a small reptile called *Lagosuchus* (rabbit crocodile) lived in what is now Argentina. *Lagosuchus* was lightly built and had long, slim hind legs that were well suited to running. Like the earliest dinosaurs, it walked on its hind legs only. In fact, *Lagosuchus* and its close relatives *Marasuchus* (mara crocodile) and *Lagerpeton* (rabbit reptile) were among the earliest-known bipedal animals. The development of bipedal walking was a major event in evolution, as all but one of the animals known to have lived before the middle Triassic period had walked on all fours. This exception was *Eudibamus* (original two legs), a little animal the remains of which have been found in Germany. Walking on the hind legs only allows the front legs to be used for other purposes, such as catching prey, and running is much more efficient.

Common ancestor
The structure of the legs and hips in *Lagosuchus* is very similar to that seen in

Above: Lagosuchus *fossils have been found only in Argentina. As the earliest dinosaur fossils are also found in this region, it has been suggested that dinosaurs evolved from* Lagosuchus-*like animals in this area of the world during the middle or late Triassic period.*

the earliest dinosaurs, differing from them only in a few minor details. The long tail of *Lagosuchus* helped to counterbalance the weight of the slim, graceful neck, and the body was short and compact, as in many early theropods and ornithischians. These shared features suggest that an animal very similar to *Lagosuchus* was the common ancestor to all of the different dinosaur groups.

Classification and relationships

Scientists divide dinosaurs into a number of groups, reflecting the ways in which the different species were related to one another. These divisions are based upon characteristics unique to particular groups of dinosaurs. For example, stegosaurs are recognized as a distinctive group of dinosaurs because they all possessed large bony plates and spines that extended in rows along the back and tail. The identification of such features in dinosaur skeletons enables scientists to deduce the relationships between the various kinds of dinosaurs.

Scientists can work out how the dinosaurs evolved, building up a kind of "family tree" of dinosaurs. This is called a cladogram.

Experts divide dinosaurs into two major groups. These can be distinguished from each other by the shapes of the hipbones. Those dinosaurs with hips similar to those of living reptiles, such as crocodiles and lizards, are called saurischians (meaning lizard-hipped), whereas those with hips more similar to those of living birds are called ornithischians (bird-hipped). Confusingly, bird-hipped dinosaurs are only distantly related to birds, whereas the direct ancestors of birds are to be found among the lizard-hipped dinosaurs.

Ornithischians (bird-hipped)

The best-known groups of ornithischian dinosaurs are the Ornithopoda, Ankylosauria, Stegosauria, Ceratopsia and Pachycephalosauria. All ornithischians were plant-eaters. Ornithopods, such as *Iguanodon* and *Hypsilophodon*, were usually bipedal, although they sometimes walked on all fours. They had heads with long snout regions. The tanklike ankylosaurs, such as *Ankylosaurus*, can be recognized from their covering of armor plates, whereas the stegosaurs, such as *Kentrosaurus*, possessed large bony plates and spines. Ceratopsians, such as *Triceratops*, usually possessed impressive horns and frills on their skull. The pachycephalosaurs, such as *Pachycephalosaurus*, had high-domed skulls, with thick layers of solid bone.

Saurischians (lizard-hipped)

Saurischian dinosaurs are split into two groups—the Theropoda and Sauropodomorpha. Theropods were bipedal, meat-eating dinosaurs that possessed sharp serrated teeth and grasping hands with powerful claws. This group includes *Allosaurus, Tyrannosaurus* and *Oviraptor*. The Sauropodomorpha is subdivided into the Prosauropoda and Sauropoda. Both of these groups were plant-eaters that had long necks, small heads and large barrel-shaped bodies. They differed in a number of features, such as the number of bones in the neck (sauropods have much longer necks than prosauropods). *Plateosaurus* is an example of a prosauropod, whereas the sauropods include *Diplodocus* and *Brachiosaurus*.

Below: *The hips of all dinosaurs are composed of three bones—the ilium, the pubis and the ischium. The ilium is the large bone that makes up the top part of the hip. It connects the hips to the backbone. The ischium and pubis both point downward and are used for the attachment of powerful leg muscles.*

In saurischian dinosaurs, such as this Allosaurus (larger picture), the arrangement of these bones is very similar to that seen in other reptiles. The ischium points backward, and the pubis points forward, giving the hip a three-pronged appearance.

In ornithischian dinosaurs, such as Scelidosaurus (small picture), the arrangement of the hipbones is similar to that seen in birds. Instead of pointing forward, as in saurischians, the pubis has rotated backward so that it lies alongside the ischium.

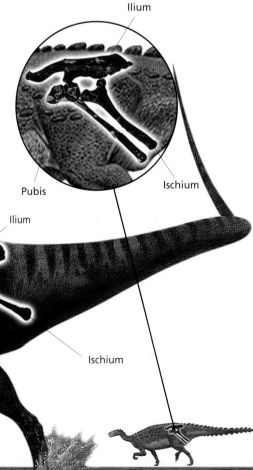

Ilium

Pubis

Ischium

Ilium

Ischium

Pubis

Bird-hipped dinosaurs
Ornithischia

The relationships of the different ornithischian (bird-hipped) dinosaurs to each other are shown in this family tree. There were many different types of ornithischians, ranging from *Lesothosaurus*, a very early form from the early Jurassic period, to the impressive hadrosaurs and ceratopsians of the late Cretaceous.

Ornithischians first appeared during the late Triassic period but were very rare at this time. In fact, ornithischians were rare until the late Jurassic, at which time they began to increase in numbers and importance. By the end of the Cretaceous, ornithischians were the most abundant dinosaurs. All ornithischians were plant-eaters, and some were able to chew their food in ways similar to that seen in living mammals. Ornithischians are subdivided into three main subgroups: Thyreophora (stegosaurs, ankylosaurs and their relatives), Marginocephalia (pachycephalosaurs, ceratopsians and relatives) and Ornithopoda.

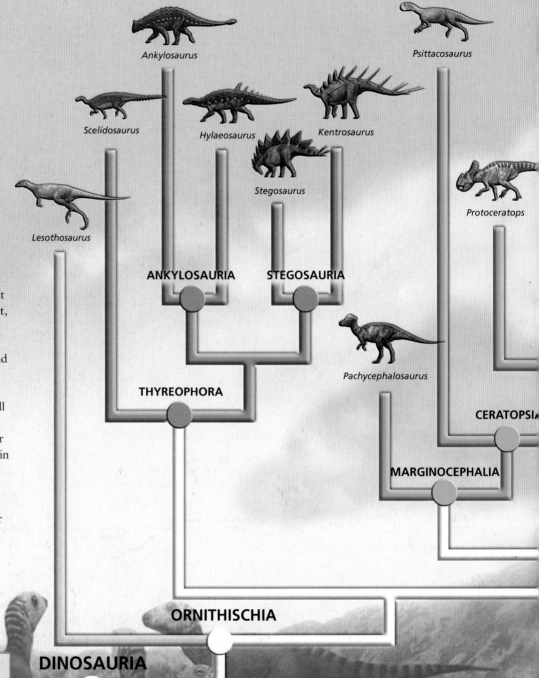

Ankylosaurus

Scelidosaurus

Hylaeosaurus

Kentrosaurus

Psittacosaurus

Stegosaurus

Protoceratops

Lesothosaurus

ANKYLOSAURIA

STEGOSAURIA

Pachycephalosaurus

THYREOPHORA

CERATOPSIA

MARGINOCEPHALIA

ORNITHISCHIA

DINOSAURIA

MAJOR SUBGROUPS

Thyreophora

Marginocephalia

Ornithopoda

Not in major subgroup

Chasmosaurus

Pachyrhinosaurus

Camptosaurus

Parasaurolophus

Corythosaurus

Styracosaurus

Tenontosaurus

Maiasaura

Triceratops

Hypsilophodon

Lambeosaurus

Ouranosaurus

HADROSAURIDAE

Iguanodon

NEOCERATOPSIA

IGUANODONTIA

ORNITHOPODA

63

Lesothosaurus
Lesotho lizard

Lesothosaurus was a small, lightweight dinosaur whose only defense was to be able to outrun its attackers. Its legs were long and graceful, and its bones were hollow, making them light but strong. In some ways, its life must have been similar to that of living gazelles, which spend much of their time trying to feed while keeping a sharp lookout for predators.

Lesothosaurus was one of the earliest, and also one of the most primitive, of all ornithischian dinosaurs. Its skeleton offers many important clues as to the origin of this group of plant-eaters from their meat-eating ancestors. *Lesothosaurus* was

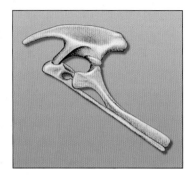

Above: *All ornithischian dinosaurs, including* Lesothosaurus, *had a birdlike arrangement of hipbones. The pubis and ischium both point backward, rather than pointing in opposite directions as in saurischian dinosaurs.*

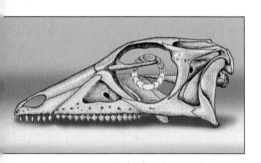

Above: *This is a reconstruction of the skull of* Lesothosaurus. *Note the very large eye socket, which might indicate that* Lesothosaurus *had good vision. The skull is very lightly built, with many openings.*

Above: *The toe bones of* Lesothosaurus *were long and thin, as is also the case in many other fast-running animals.*

carried on the front of the upper jaw. Ornithischians also possess a bone that crosses the top of the eye socket called the "palpebral" bone. This bone helps to support the eye and the eyelid. Similar bones are also found in living crocodiles.

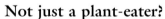

an agile biped with a short neck, a short, deep body and a very long, slim tail. It had the characteristic birdlike arrangement of hipbones. The reason for the evolution of the "bird-hipped" arrangement is not clear, but it might have been related to changes in the ways that the leg muscles were attached to the hipbones. Alternatively, the pubic bone might have rotated backward to allow more room for a larger gut—a feature that is needed in plant-eating animals, as plants are much more difficult to digest than meat.

Shared features

All ornithischian dinosaurs, including *Lesothosaurus*, share a large number of anatomical features in addition to the possession of birdlike hipbones. A special bone called the "predentary" is found at the front of the lower jaw and links the left and right sides of the lower jaw together. The predentary bone was covered by a horny sheath, making a beak that fitted against a similar structure

Not just a plant-eater?

The jaws of *Lesothosaurus* were lined with teeth that look very similar to those of the living iguana, a plant-eating lizard. The edges of the teeth became worn as they sliced past each other, leaving sharp cutting edges that were well suited for chopping plant food into small pieces. But the teeth at the very front of the mouth were sharply pointed, and it may be that this little herbivore ate small animals from time to time. This would not be a particularly surprising behavior, as many living herbivores, such as small antelopes, occasionally need a little meat in their diet.

FACT FILE

Genus: *Lesothosaurus*

Classification: Ornithischia

Length: Up to 40 in (1 m)

Weight: 20 lb (10 kg)

Lived: Early Jurassic period, about 213-200 million years ago

Found in: Lesotho and South Africa

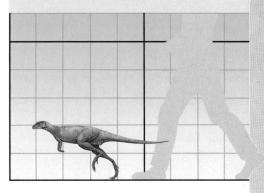

Left: *This photograph shows a skull of* Lesothosaurus *that has been partially removed from the encasing rock. The upper and lower jaws, with their rows of small pointed teeth, can be seen in the lower right of the picture.*

Above: *Lesotho is a small country situated entirely in the mountainous eastern part of South Africa. Remains* of Lesothosaurus *are known from Lesotho and from neighboring parts of South Africa.*

CRETACEOUS
70
80
90
100
110
120
130
140

JURASSIC
150
160
170
180
190
200

TRIASSIC
210
220
230
240

FACT FILE

Genus: *Scelidosaurus*

Classification: Thyreophora

Length: Up to 13 ft (4 m)

Weight: Up to 550 lb (250 kg)

Lived: Early Jurassic period, about 206-200 million years ago

Found in: England and the United States

Scelidosaurus
Limb lizard

An armored dinosaur, *Scelidosaurus* is one of the earliest members of the group that also contains the plated stegosaurs and the tanklike ankylosaurs. It is also one of the earliest of all ornithischian dinosaurs. As a result, *Scelidosaurus* provides scientists with a great deal of information about the origin and evolution of this major group as a whole. *Scelidosaurus* is known from two beautifully preserved skeletons, two skulls and a few isolated bones and armor plates.

Right: *Many detailed features may be seen in this skull of a young* Scelidosaurus.

Below: *Remains of* Scelidosaurus *have been found in Dorset, southern England. Scutes (armor plates), recently uncovered in Arizona, possibly came from* Scelidosaurus *or a very close relative.*

Scelidosaurus was a low-slung, plant-eating dinosaur that had many rows of oval, ridged bony studs extending along its back and tail. This armor was an early version of the more extensive armor plating found in ankylosaurs. It would have helped to protect *Scelidosaurus* from the attacks of large theropods such as *Magnosaurus* (great lizard). Fossilized skin impressions show that small hexagonal scales covered the spaces between the armor plates.

Walking on all fours

Scelidosaurus walked on all fours, but its hind legs were much longer than its forelimbs. This feature suggests that it might occasionally have been able to run on its hind legs alone. Or it might have been able to rear up on its hind legs in order to reach higher up into the bushes to feed. The stoutness of its body and the structure of its legs and feet suggest

☐ Confirmed finds
◙ Possible finds

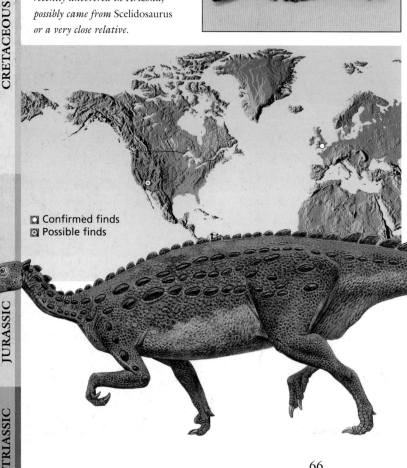

that *Scelidosaurus* was not a particularly fast runner.

The head of *Scelidosaurus* was quite small, with a horny beak situated at the front of the jaws. Its teeth were small and leaf shaped, and had a few large serrations extending along each edge. These were used for cutting through plant material.

70
80
90
100
110
120
130
140
150
160
170
180
190
200
210
220
230
240

CRETACEOUS

JURASSIC

TRIASSIC

Hylaeosaurus
Forest lizard

This dinosaur owes its name to a forest in Sussex, in southern England. Its remains were first found in 1832 by local quarrymen and studied by the famous fossil collector Gideon Mantell. *Hylaeosaurus* is known from a single partial skeleton and from numerous isolated bones and armor plates. It was the first armored dinosaur to be discovered and was the third animal to be recognized as a dinosaur—after *Megalosaurus* and another Mantell discovery, *Iguanodon*.

FACT FILE

Genus: *Hylaeosaurus*

Classification: Thyreophora; Ankylosauria; Nodosauridae

Length: Up to 16 ft (5 m)

Weight: 1.5 tons

Lived: Early Cretaceous period, about 140-131 million years ago

Found in: England

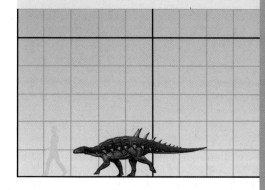

Hylaeosaurus is an ankylosaur. The Ankylosauria are subdivided into two groups called the Nodosauridae and the Ankylosauridae. These two groups differ in a number of ways. Members of the Ankylosauridae have a tail club and a skull with an elaborate covering of armor plates. Nodosaurs lack a tail club and have much less armor on their skull. *Hylaeosaurus* is a nodosaur. It possessed a large number of bony plates that lined its back and tail. The plates came in a variety of shapes and sizes. Some were flat and had oval or circular outlines, whereas others were modified into large spines over the shoulders. These features would have deterred all but the most determined meat-eaters from attacking *Hylaeosaurus*.

Subtropical habitat

Like all other ankylosaurs, *Hylaeosaurus* was a slow-moving plant-eater that walked on all fours. It would

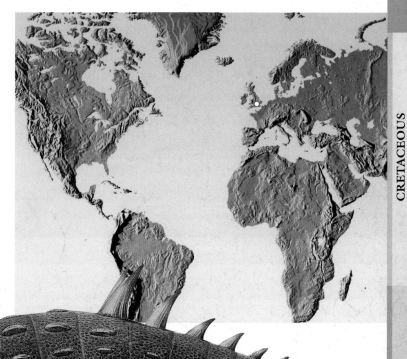

have fed on low-growing plants, cropping huge mouthfuls of vegetation with its wide horny beak. It lived in a subtropical environment covered by rivers, lakes and forests.

Above: *The remains of* Hylaeosaurus *have been found only in southern England. Close relatives of* Hylaeosaurus *lived in England, the United States, Spain and Romania.*

CRETACEOUS	70
	80
	90
	100
	110
	120
	130
	140
	150
JURASSIC	160
	170
	180
	190
	200
	210
TRIASSIC	220
	230
	240

Ankylosaurus
Fused lizard

A large dinosaur from the late Cretaceous period in North America, *Ankylosaurus* was covered from head to tail in sheets of thick bony armor. Large triangular horns projected from the back of its skull. And all along its body, the armor plates were embedded in the skin, with sharp spines sticking up along back and tail. Its tail was thickened at the end into a heavy, bony club. As it shared its habitat with fearsome predators such as *Tyrannosaurus* and *Albertosaurus*, it probably needed all this heavy armor.

Below: *The tip of the skull ends in a large, toothless beak. Behind the beak is a row of small, leaf-shaped teeth. It used to be thought that the teeth of ankylosaurs were of little use in breaking down plant food. But recent studies have shown that they were surprisingly good at chewing.*

Below: *The skull is very broad and strongly constructed, and completely enclosed within bony plates. In some ankylosaurs there is even a bony eyelid! The large, triangular horns can be seen projecting from the rear of the skull.*

Scientists think the tail club was formed from bony nodules that were originally embedded in the skin. As these nodules grew, they fused together and to the bones of the tail. In front of the tail club, the individual tail bones were tightly interlocked, making the end of the tail very stiff and strong. Club movement was controlled by the action of muscles near the base of the tail, muscles that normally pulled the hind limbs backward during walking. These muscles could swing the tail from side to side.

Defense

The thick bony plates would have been a good defense against even the most determined theropod. But its underside was unarmored, so, when attacked, *Ankylosaurus* probably crouched down to protect this vulnerable region. It might have been in danger if a predator could flip it over. But as *Ankylosaurus* weighed several tons, this would have been difficult to do.

Attack!

Theropods preying upon *Ankylosaurus* were tall, heavy two-legged animals. As a result, they were slightly less stable than a short four-legged dinosaur. Because of the weight of their bodies, a simple fall could cause them to break some of their bones—especially their slender leg bones. A well-timed blow from the

Ankylosaurus tail club could have knocked a predator over or broken one of its legs, resulting in serious injury or even death.

Crossing into North America

Ankylosaurus is one of only two members of the family Ankylosauridae known from North America. All other ankylosaurids lived in eastern Asia. It appears that the group first evolved in Asia, at some time in the earliest Cretaceous period, when eastern Asia and North America were connected by a land bridge. The ancestors of *Ankylosaurus* probably crossed into North America from Asia using this route.

FACT FILE

Genus: *Ankylosaurus*

Classification: Thyreophora;
Ankylosauria; Ankylosauridae

Length: 33-36 ft (10-11 m)

Weight: 4 tons

Lived: Late Cretaceous period, about
68-65 million years ago

Found in: Montana and Wyoming,
western U.S.A., and Alberta, Canada

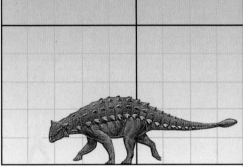

Left: *This skeleton of* Euoplocephalus,
a close relative of Ankylosaurus, *shows
how the separate armor plates could be
arranged in large defensive shields of
bone that covered the back, neck and
sides of the body.*

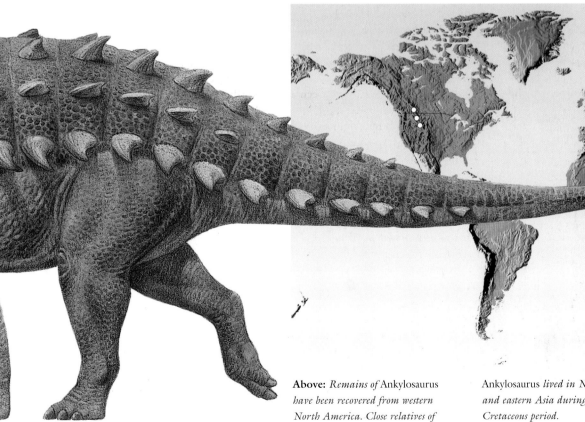

Above: *Remains of* Ankylosaurus
*have been recovered from western
North America. Close relatives of*
Ankylosaurus *lived in North America
and eastern Asia during the late
Cretaceous period.*

CRETACEOUS

70
80
90
100
110
120
130
140
150
160
170
180
190
200
210
220
230
240

JURASSIC

TRIASSIC

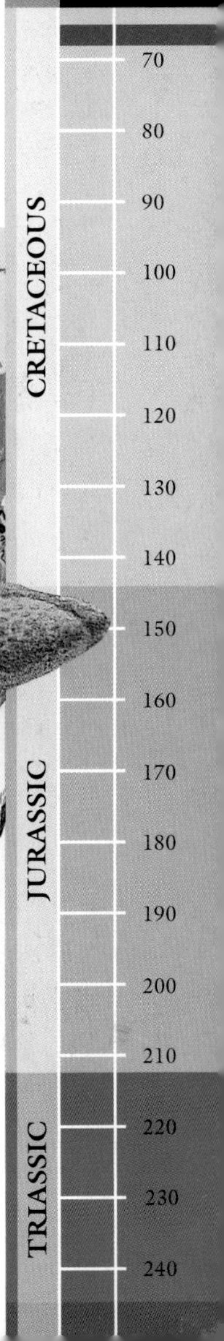

Kentrosaurus
Pointed reptile

Kentrosaurus is the smaller, spikier cousin of the famous *Stegosaurus*. Both stegosaurs lived in the late Jurassic period. *Stegosaurus* could be found in North America, whereas *Kentrosaurus* roamed the landscape of what is now Tanzania, in eastern Africa. A plant-eating animal, *Kentrosaurus* walked on all fours. It had long bony spines projecting from its back that might have deterred predators, with the extra protection of spines sticking out from its shoulders. It might have used its spiky tail to lash out against attackers.

Below: *Owing to the difference in size between the forelimbs and hind limbs, the head of* Kentrosaurus *was held close to the ground. Its neck was also quite short. These features suggest that* Kentrosaurus *fed on low-growing plants, such as ferns and cycads. It cropped and chopped up plants with its horny beak and with simple leaf-shaped teeth, before passing them to the stomach for digestion.*

The bony plates along the back of its neck and on the front part of its back probably helped *Kentrosaurus* regulate body temperature, in the same way as similar plates might have for *Stegosaurus* (see pages 72-73). The outwardly pointing shoulder spines helped deter attacks from the sides. Most other stegosaurs possessed spines on this area of the body. Spines also protected the lower back and the tail, which could be swung from side to side. As it was also studded with sharp spines along its length, and ended in a pair of extralarge spines, predators could not afford to get too close to the tail without taking a huge risk. But the neck, belly and legs of *Kentrosaurus* were still exposed and largely unprotected.

Body armor
The large paired plates and spines are characteristic of the stegosaurs, extending all of the way along the backbone from the base of the neck to the tip of the tail. The plates were not joined to the backbone, but were embedded in the tough skin. In *Kentrosaurus,* this series of bony projections begins just behind the head, with a sequence of flat, triangular plates. The series of plates continues along the back, increasing in size but retaining the same shape. At the hips, the plates start to become more pointed and more spinelike. The spines are longer and sharper along the tail.

Bulky body and huge stomach
Stegosaurs had very bulky bodies and huge stomachs for digesting their meals of tough, dry plants. Their forelimbs were much shorter than their hind limbs, but the large size of its gut meant that *Kentrosaurus* had to walk on all fours. If it tried to walk on its hind legs only, the weight of its body would have pulled it back down to the ground again.

It is possible that *Kentrosaurus* could have reared up on its hind legs in order to reach up into bushes and nip off parts of plants. But it would not have been able to stand in this position for very long.

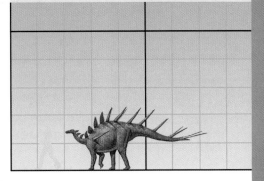

FACT FILE

Genus: *Kentrosaurus*

Classification: Thyreophora; Stegosauria; Stegosauridae

Length: 16 ft (5m)

Weight: 1 ton

Lived: Late Jurassic period, about 156-150 million years ago

Found in: Tanzania, East Africa

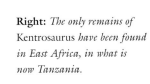

Left: *Sharp spines might have warned away any predator planning to attack* Kentrosaurus *from the rear.*

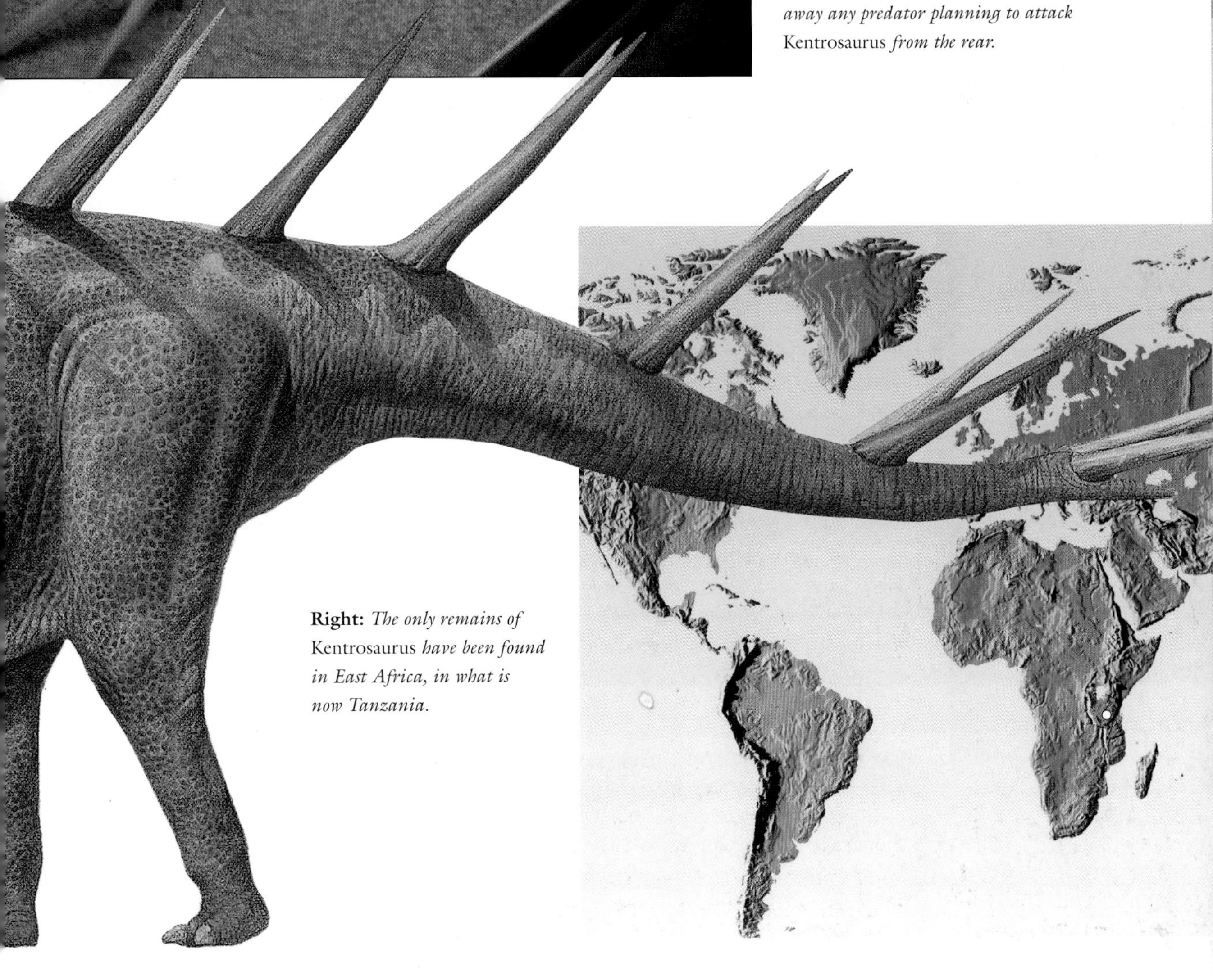

Right: *The only remains of* Kentrosaurus *have been found in East Africa, in what is now Tanzania.*

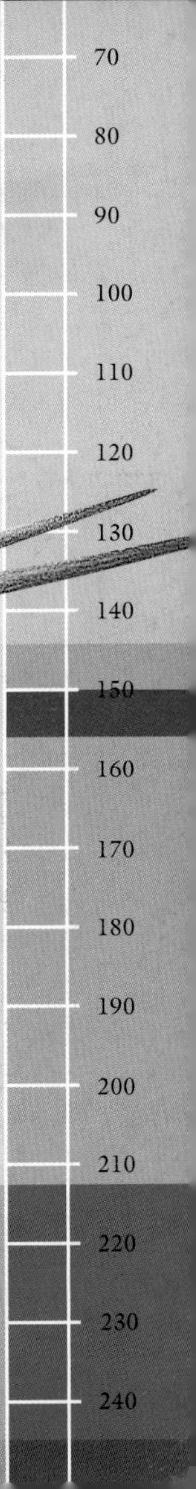

Stegosaurus
Roofed reptile

This is the most familiar member of the Stegosauria, a group of dinosaurs that were characterized by a series of bony plates and spines extending along their backs. Although this group existed from the middle Jurassic period through to the late Cretaceous period, *Stegosaurus* is found only in the late Jurassic rocks of western North America. It is a large, slow-moving plant-eating dinosaur that lived among, and probably fell prey to, other famous North American dinosaurs of that time, such as *Allosaurus* and *Ceratosaurus*.

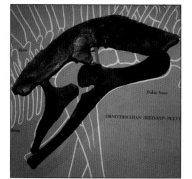

Above: *The massive hipbones of* Stegosaurus *provided anchorage for the huge muscles of the tail and hind limbs.*

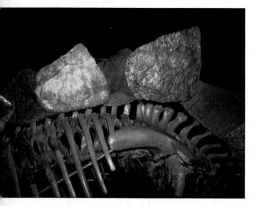

Above: *There has been some debate as to whether the two rows of plates sat in pairs that were exactly opposite each other, or whether the plates alternated in position along the back. Recent discoveries suggest they alternated.*

Though parts of *Stegosaurus* are covered in numerous small bony protrusions, including bony nodules over the throat region, the large plates and tail spines are by far its most impressive features. The plates vary in size along the backbone. They are tallest and broadest just above the hip region. In a large *Stegosaurus*, these plates can be nearly 3 feet (1 m) tall. The two pairs of tail spines can be up to 2 feet (0.6 m) or more in length.

Defensive measures
Although large, the plates were relatively thin and blunt and would have offered little protection against an attack by one of the large meat-eating theropods. The heavy structure of its legs, its strange curved back and the sheer size of *Stegosaurus* all suggest that it was not an animal capable of a quick getaway when under attack. As a result, its only defense against fierce Jurassic predators might have been to swing its powerful tail from side to side so that the spikes could be aimed at the delicate legs and belly regions of marauding carnivores.

Stegosaur plates
The plates of stegosaurs might have been used for warning off predators or for recognition between members of a species. But one interesting suggestion is that they functioned as a device for controlling body temperature. Tiny grooves along the plate surfaces indicate the possible presence of numerous blood vessels. These could have served to absorb or discharge body heat. If this were the case, *Stegosaurus* could probably have controlled the amount of blood passed into the plates to avoid heating up or cooling down at the wrong times.

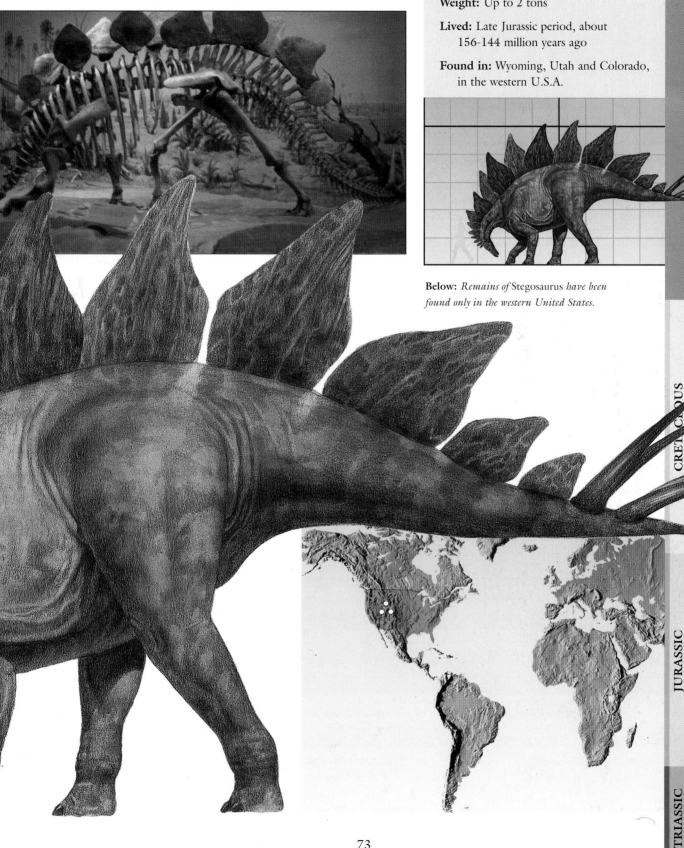

Below: *Apart from the plates, other features of* Stegosaurus *to note are the short, sprawling forelimbs and the much longer hind limbs. This suggests it had* an enormous gut. Because its tiny teeth and beak were not capable of grinding plant matter, it had to ferment food for some time to release nutrients.

FACT FILE

Genus: *Stegosaurus*

Classification: Thyreophora; Stegosauria; Stegosauridae

Length: Up to 30 ft (9 m)

Weight: Up to 2 tons

Lived: Late Jurassic period, about 156-144 million years ago

Found in: Wyoming, Utah and Colorado, in the western U.S.A.

Below: *Remains of* Stegosaurus *have been found only in the western United States.*

CRETACEOUS

70
80
90
100
110
120
130
140
150
160

JURASSIC

170
180
190
200
210

TRIASSIC

220
230
240

Pachycephalosaurus
Thick-headed lizard

Pachycephalosaurus was a plant-eating dinosaur that roamed western North America in the late Cretaceous period. It is notable for the huge dome on top of its head that was up to 10 inches (25 cm) thick. The function of this dome is uncertain, and has been the subject of considerable argument among experts ever since the first remains of the dinosaur were discovered in 1940.

The dome might have acted like a dinosaur "crash helmet" to shield the head during attack. But, unlike armored dinosaurs such as ankylosaurs, the rest of the body is not protected. So protecting only the head would be of little use against the jaws of *Tyrannosaurus* or other meat-eating dinosaurs.

Another theory is that the dome might have enabled *Pachycephalosaurus* to recognize one another. Each species of *Pachycephalosaurus* had a differently shaped dome.

The dome as a weapon

Yet another possibility is that the chief use of the dome was as a weapon against predators and in fights with other *Pachycephalosaurus*. If two males rammed into each other at high speed, shockwaves caused by a head-butt could be carried through the skull, down the specially strengthened backbone and through the hind limbs to the ground.

However, some experts argue that *Pachycephalosaurus* would not have butted their heads together, because the bone forming the dome does not itself appear to be very strong. Instead, they suggest, two males might have pushed domes together as a test of strength. Alternatively, one male might have butted into the side of another male's body. Not all *Pachycephalosaurus* domes were built in the same way. Some were flat and thin, some tall and ridged—a poor design for head-butting!

Living together?

Direct combat is not the only kind of confrontation. Some pachycephalosaurs had spikes projecting down and back behind the head. When the head was lowered, the spikes might have presented a large, formidable display to a rival— much as moose antlers do.

Existing alongside *Pachycephalosaurus* were the stout, heavily armored ankylosaurs and the trumpet-headed *Parasaurolophus*. All of these plant-eating dinosaurs probably fell prey to the giant meat-eaters of the time such as *Albertosaurus* and *Tyrannosaurus rex*.

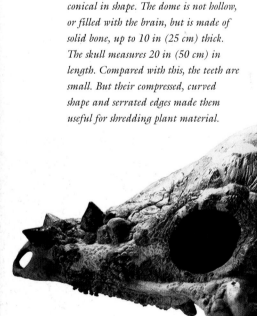

Below: *The skull of* Pachycephalosaurus *is notable not only for the dome, which rises above and behind the eye socket, but also for all its other protusions. There is a series of rounded, bony projections under the dome at the back, and bony knobs along the snout that are more conical in shape. The dome is not hollow, or filled with the brain, but is made of solid bone, up to 10 in (25 cm) thick. The skull measures 20 in (50 cm) in length. Compared with this, the teeth are small. But their compressed, curved shape and serrated edges made them useful for shredding plant material.*

FACT FILE

Genus: *Pachycephalosaurus*

Classification: Marginocephalia;
Pachycephalosauria;
Pachycephalosauridae

Length: Up to 26 ft (8 m)

Weight: 1–2 tons

Lived: Late Cretaceous period, about
68–65 million years ago

Found in: Western U.S.A. and Canada

Left: *The skulls of* Pachycephalosaurus *and its close relatives show a variety of shapes and thicknesses that may reflect varied functions.*

Above: *In 1940, the first* Pachycephalosaurus *fossil was found in Montana, in the western United States. Since then, remains have been discovered in Wyoming and South Dakota and in Alberta, Canada.*

CRETACEOUS	70
	80
	90
	100
	110
	120
	130
	140
	150
JURASSIC	160
	170
	180
	190
	200
	210
TRIASSIC	220
	230
	240

Psittacosaurus
Parrot lizard

Although it lacks the impressive horns and neck frills found in *Triceratops, Styracosaurus* and the other horned dinosaurs, many features of *Psittacosaurus* show that it was an early member of this group. All of these dinosaurs, known as ceratopsians, had a sharply curved beak at the front of the jaws, similar to that of a parrot. The beak was covered with a sharp sheath of horn and would have been ideal for slicing through the stems and leaves of plants.

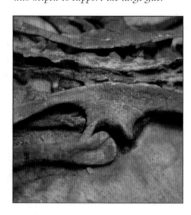

Below: *The hip region of* Psittacosaurus *provided an area for the attachment of powerful leg muscles and also helped to support the large gut.*

Below: *This is a close-up of the stomach region in* Psittacosaurus. *You can see a large number of small polished stones within the ribcage. These are the gastroliths, which are responsible for grinding food in the stomach.*

The upper part of the beak is formed from a special bone, called the rostral, which is unique to this group of animals. Other features that link *Psittacosaurus* to the horned dinosaurs include the beginnings of a neck frill, formed from a small ledge of bone that juts out from the back of the skull, and strange, pointed cheekbones. The function of these cheekbones is not known for certain, but they are found in all horned dinosaurs. They might have been useful in pushing contests, in which rivals would lock their heads together and then try to shove each other backward in trials of strength. These contests might have been important in fighting for mates or territory.

An elegant herbivore

Unlike the later horned dinosaurs, *Psittacosaurus* was a small, lightly built animal that walked on its hind legs only. The hands had long, slender fingers that ended in small, sharp claws and were used for collecting food. The hind legs were long and graceful, suggesting that it could run quite quickly. *Psittacosaurus* chewed its food in an unusual way. Instead of simply moving the jaws up and down, like a pair of scissors, as did most other dinosaurs, the lower jaws could slide back and forth against the upper teeth to produce an efficient grinding motion. Later ceratopsians inherited this jaw action.

Grinding stones

Several skeletons of *Psittacosaurus* contain a mass of small, highly polished stones in the area of the belly. It appears that *Psittacosaurus* would deliberately swallow small stones that then became embedded in the walls of the gut. Movements of the gut muscles then caused the stones to grind up food within the gut, making digestion easier. Scientists call these stomach stones gastroliths (see also page 53). *Psittacosaurus* is the only ornithischian dinosaur known to have definitely used gastroliths, although there is some evidence that *Stegosaurus* might also have used them. Gastroliths are also found in the stomachs of some prosauropods, sauropods and theropods. Scientists know that the stomach stones were used in this way because many modern birds, such as chickens and ostriches, also have gastroliths.

FACT FILE

Genus: *Psittacosaurus*

Classification: Marginocephalia; Ceratopsia; Psittacosauridae

Length: Up to 6 ft 6 in (2 m)

Weight: Up to 55 lb (25 kg)

Lived: Early Cretaceous period, about 125-97 million years ago

Found in: Mongolia, northern and western China, Thailand and central Russia

Left: Psittacosaurus *is known from a large number of skeletons. Some of these skeletons, like the one shown here, are beautifully preserved and provide scientists with a great deal of detailed information.*

Above: Psittacosaurus *fossils have been recovered from all over eastern and central Asia, and are particularly common in Mongolia and northern China.*

CRETACEOUS

70
80
90
100
110
120
130
140
150

JURASSIC

160
170
180
190
200
210

TRIASSIC

220
230
240

Protoceratops
First horned face

The remains of *Protoceratops* were discovered in Mongolia's desert, the Gobi, by an expedition from the American Museum of Natural History in New York during the 1920s. It is one of the earliest known members of the group that contains the horned dinosaurs, such as *Triceratops*. The name *Protoceratops* is rather misleading, as it has no real horns on its skull—merely low bumps of bone on the top of its nose and on its cheeks. But the bony neck frill and parrotlike beak show that it belonged to the same group as the other horned dinosaurs.

Above: *The curious triangular shape of the* Protoceratops *head comes from the bony projections that stick out from the cheeks. These might have helped individuals to recognize each other, or they might have had a defensive function.*

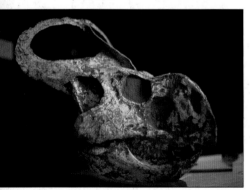

Above: *Seen from the side,* Protoceratops's *beak shows its huge, curving lower jaw. Its jaws look like a great pair of gardener's shears—no coincidence, because* Protoceratops *used its jaws in just the same way.*

Protoceratops is more primitive than the other—much bigger—horned dinosaurs. Its body was barrel shaped and probably looked a little like that of a large pig. However, unlike a pig, the body was strongly arched at the hips. Because of this, the long, deep tail might have drooped downward from the rear of its body. The hind limbs were strong and straight, with large feet. One reconstruction suggested that the front limbs were sprawled out to the sides, rather like a modern reptile, giving *Protoceratops* a crouched appearance. But most evidence now indicates that the front limbs were held under the body just like the hind limbs. This arrangement would have supported the head well above ground level.

Scientists have discovered the skeletons of baby, juvenile and adult *Protoceratops*, enabling them to work out the details of their growth. As young *Protoceratops* grew, their faces became deeper and shorter, their mouths wider, and their bony neck frills wider and taller.

Living like pigs
The wide ribcage housed a big stomach that was used to digest large amounts of plant food. Because of its slight resemblance to pigs, some scientists have suggested that *Protoceratops* might have lived a little like them by rooting and grubbing around in the soil for roots, tubers and other nutritious plants. It might

have behaved like this, but its impressive set of grinding teeth and its parrotlike beak indicate that it could probably chop up much tougher foodstuffs than pigs do.

Defending the young
The powerful, stocky build and strong beak of *Protoceratops* made it a formidable defender of its eggs and young. One remarkable fossil shows the preserved remains of a *Protoceratops* and a *Velociraptor* (a theropod dinosaur) entangled together. It appears that these two dinosaurs died in combat as they were overcome by slumping sand dunes. Many eggs

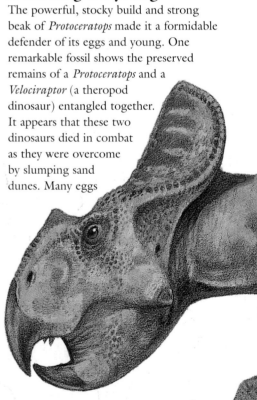

and nests first thought to belong to *Protoceratops* have been unearthed in Mongolia, but most of these nests are now known to have belonged to the theropod *Oviraptor*.

FACT FILE

Genus: *Protoceratops*

Classification: Marginocephalia;
Ceratopsia; Protoceratopsidae

Length: 8 ft (2.4 m)

Weight: 390 lb (177 kg)

Lived: Late Cretaceous period, about
80-73 million years ago

Found in: Mongolia and China

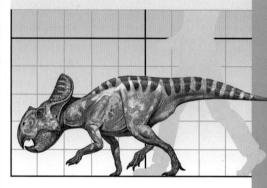

Left: Protoceratops's *teeth were locked together in
long rows and in several vertical columns. As the
teeth along the cutting edge of the jaws were worn
down, they were shed and replaced from below by
new teeth. In this way* Protoceratops *kept a
sharpened battery of rough grinding teeth in good
condition for chewing on plants.*

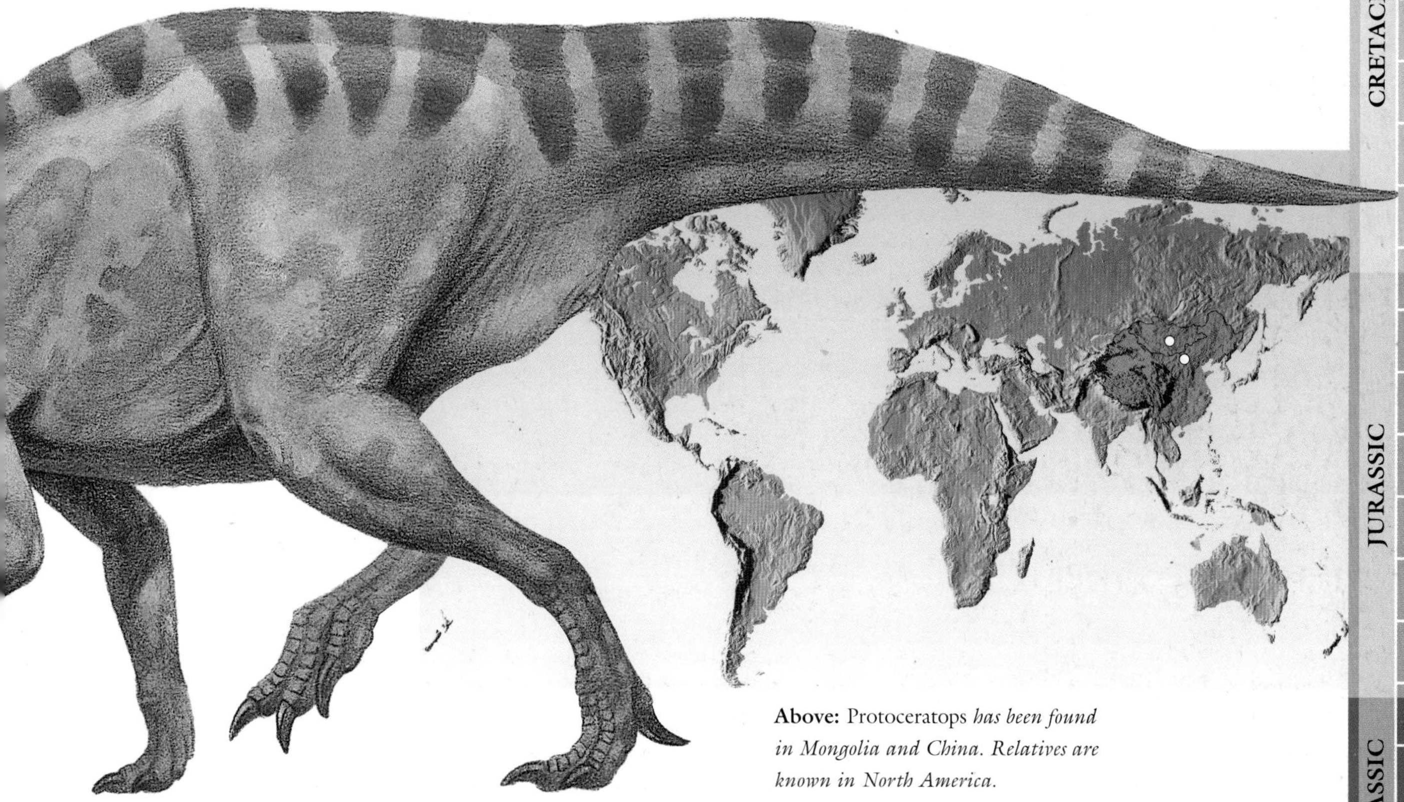

Above: Protoceratops *has been found
in Mongolia and China. Relatives are
known in North America.*

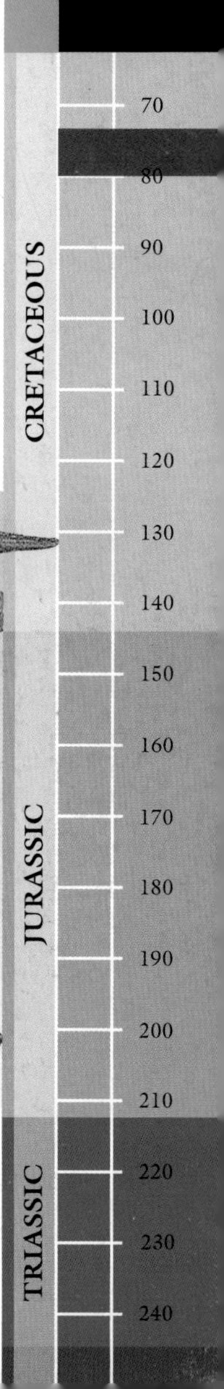

CRETACEOUS

JURASSIC

TRIASSIC

- 70
- 80
- 90
- 100
- 110
- 120
- 130
- 140
- 150
- 160
- 170
- 180
- 190
- 200
- 210
- 220
- 230
- 240

Chasmosaurus
Chasm lizard

A medium to large horned dinosaur, *Chasmosaurus* had one of the longest skulls of any known land-living animal. The skull reached over 6 and a half feet (2 m) in length and made up about a quarter of the entire length of the animal's body. There is a great deal of variation in the arrangement of the horns and in the orientation of the frill in the different species of the plant-eating *Chasmosaurus*. Finds of bone-beds with many *Chasmosaurus* individuals together suggest they lived in herds (see next pages).

Below: *This* Chasmosaurus *skull has a small nose horn and moderately developed brow horns. Note the very large holes that puncture the frill. Nearly all the large ceratopsians except* Triceratops *had these large openings in the frill.* Chasmosaurus *gets its name from these large holes, a chasm being a deep hole or fissure.*

All species of *Chasmosaurus* had a small nose horn and two brow horns, but the sizes of the brow horns differed considerably. Some species had very small brow horns that were no more than pointed bumps of bone above the eyes. Others had much longer brow horns, though none of these horns was as impressive as those of other horned dinosaurs, such as *Triceratops*. In all species of *Chasmosaurus*, the frill was a broad shieldlike structure that lacked the impressive spikes seen in animals such as *Styracosaurus* and *Pachyrhinosaurus*. But one or two small spines might sometimes have been present at the corners of the frill. The advanced horned dinosaurs, called ceratopsids, can be divided into two groups. Chasmosaurs, such as *Chasmosaurus*, had very long frills, whereas centrosaurs, such as *Pachyrhinosaurus*, had much shorter frills. Although all ceratopsians are often referred to collectively as "horned dinosaurs", only the ceratopsids possessed large horns.

Supporting that head

All scientists agree that the hind legs of horned dinosaurs were held straight beneath the body, like pillars. But there has been some debate about the way in which the front legs were held. Some scientists think that the legs were held out sideways, in a similar fashion to that seen in lizards and crocodiles. However, if this were the case, it is difficult to see how *Chasmosaurus* and its relatives could have

supported the massive weight of their huge, horned heads. It seems more likely that the front limbs were also held straight beneath the body, as this would have made carrying the head much easier. Some evidence from trackways supports this view. If the front legs were held out to the sides, the trackways of horned dinosaurs would be very wide. However, the trackways are actually very narrow, showing that the limbs must have been held directly underneath the body.

A North American group

The fossil remains of ceratopsians are known only from Central Asia and North America. The most primitive ceratopsians, such as *Psittacosaurus*, lived in China and Mongolia during the early Cretaceous period, suggesting that the group first evolved in Asia. *(continued on page 82)*

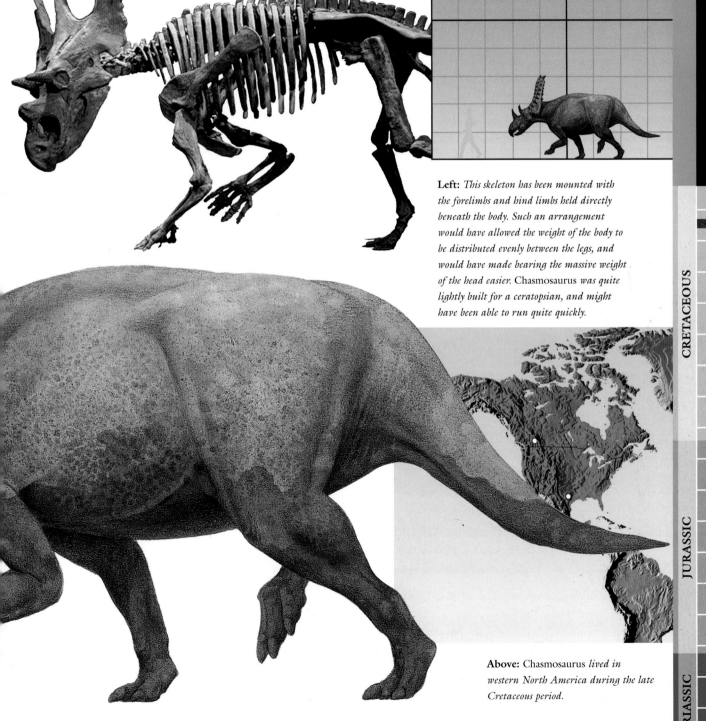

FACT FILE

Genus: *Chasmosaurus*

Classification: Marginocephalia; Ceratopsia; Ceratopsidae

Length: Up to 26 ft (8 m)

Weight: 1.5-2 tons

Lived: Late Cretaceous period, about 76-73 million years ago.

Found in: Texas and Alberta (Canada)

Left: *This skeleton has been mounted with the forelimbs and hind limbs held directly beneath the body. Such an arrangement would have allowed the weight of the body to be distributed evenly between the legs, and would have made bearing the massive weight of the head easier.* Chasmosaurus *was quite lightly built for a ceratopsian, and might have been able to run quite quickly.*

Above: Chasmosaurus *lived in western North America during the late Cretaceous period.*

CRETACEOUS

70
80
90
100
110
120
130
140
150
160
170
180
190
200
210
220
230
240

JURASSIC

TRIASSIC

81

A land bridge existed between eastern Asia and North America during the late Cretaceous period, allowing some ceratopsians to migrate into North America from Asia at this time. These animals gave rise to the advanced ceratopsids, such as *Chasmosaurus* and *Triceratops*. No such ceratopsids have been discovered in Asia to date, suggesting that this particular group of ceratopsians was limited to North America.

Migrating herds?

Chasmosaurus has been found in large bone-beds in Alberta, Canada. Some bone-beds contain the remains from tens, or even hundreds, of individuals of *Chasmosaurus*. Bone-beds are formed extremely rapidly by a single catastrophic event, such as the flooding of a river or the eruption of a volcano. Study of the *Chasmosaurus* bone-beds has shown that they were formed during a flood, suggesting that an entire herd of these animals perished as they tried to swim across a river. Similar events are known to occur today. As herds of wildebeest migrate across the African plains, they often have to cross large rivers. If the river is in flood, many wildebeests drown and are washed downriver, where their bodies accumulate in large piles. The *Chasmosaurus* bone-beds may be telling us that this horned dinosaur also migrated over large distances, but this idea is difficult to prove.

Chasmosaurus

A group of charging Chasmosaurus must have been a fearsome sight even to the largest of predators. Chasmosaurus was bigger than the largest rhinoceroses living today.

Pachyrhinosaurus
Thick-nosed lizard

FACT FILE

Genus: *Pachyrhinosaurus*

Classification: Marginocephalia; Ceratopsia; Ceratopsidae

Length: 23 ft (7 m)

Weight: 4 tons

Lived: During the late Cretaceous period, about 73-65 million years ago

Found in: Alaska and Canada

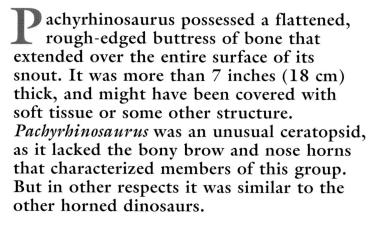

P achyrhinosaurus possessed a flattened, rough-edged buttress of bone that extended over the entire surface of its snout. It was more than 7 inches (18 cm) thick, and might have been covered with soft tissue or some other structure. *Pachyrhinosaurus* was an unusual ceratopsid, as it lacked the bony brow and nose horns that characterized members of this group. But in other respects it was similar to the other horned dinosaurs.

Below: Pachyrhinosaurus *remains have been discovered in the cold badlands and tundra of North America, although in the late Cretaceous period these regions had a warm climate.*

Some scientists have suggested that the nose buttress might have supported a horn made of keratin, the same substance that makes up the horns of rhinoceroses. But keratin is not usually fossilized, so this idea is difficult to investigate.

Frill, spines and spikes

The frill of *Pachyrhinosaurus* was adorned with characteristic spines and spikes. Two large, curved spines extended backward from the rear of the frill, and a short spine pointed forward from the center of the frill, just above and between the eyes. These structures probably helped *Pachyrhinosaurus* to recognize others of its own kind. The frill was perforated by two large holes, as in nearly all other horned dinosaurs. It used to be thought that the edges of these holes were areas of attachment for large jaw muscles, but the muscles didn't attach there. The holes lightened a skull that, at about 6 feet (2 m) in length, would have been extremely heavy. Presumably, skin was stretched across the frill's opening.

Styracosaurus
Spike lizard

FACT FILE

Genus: *Styracosaurus*

Classification: Marginocephalia; Ceratopsia; Ceratopsidae

Length: 18 ft (5.5 m)

Weight: 3 tons

Lived: Late Cretaceous period, about 80-73 million years ago

Found in: Alberta, Canada, and Montana

Like the other advanced horned dinosaurs, *Styracosaurus* was a large-bodied, plant-eating animal that walked on all fours. It differed from the other types, such as *Triceratops* and *Chasmosaurus*, in the structure of the bony frill and the arrangement of the horns. The back of the frill gave rise to six long backward-pointing spines. Smaller spines lined the edges of the frill. There was a large single nose horn, but no brow horns—only small horns above the eyes.

The fringe of spikes might have given some protection to the back of the neck, an area vulnerable to predators. But the frill of *Styracosaurus* was lightly constructed and, once again, perforated by large openings. It is more likely that the frill and spines were used for visual display, to attract mates, perhaps, or to defend territory.

Left: *This mounted skeleton of* Styracosaurus *clearly shows the elaborate structure of the skull.*

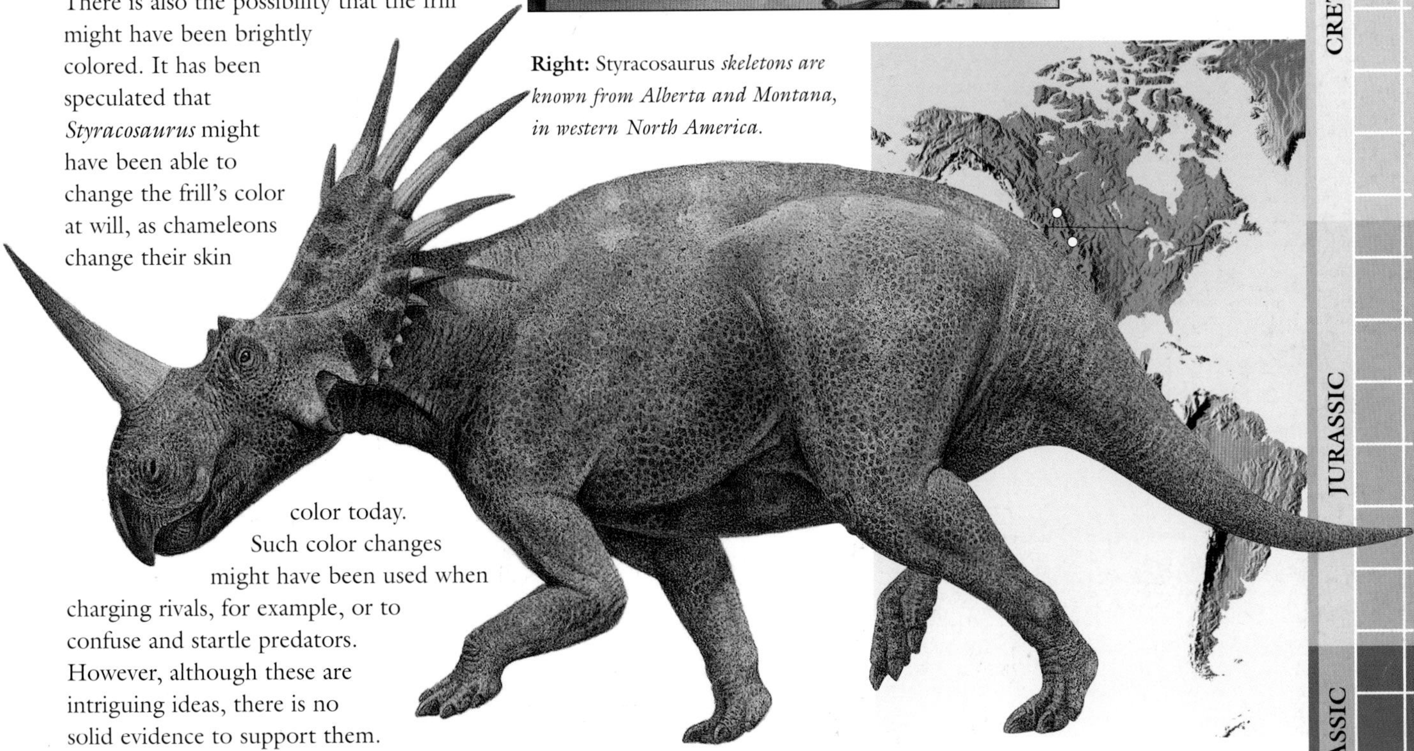

Colored frill?

There is also the possibility that the frill might have been brightly colored. It has been speculated that *Styracosaurus* might have been able to change the frill's color at will, as chameleons change their skin color today. Such color changes might have been used when charging rivals, for example, or to confuse and startle predators. However, although these are intriguing ideas, there is no solid evidence to support them.

Right: Styracosaurus *skeletons are known from Alberta and Montana, in western North America.*

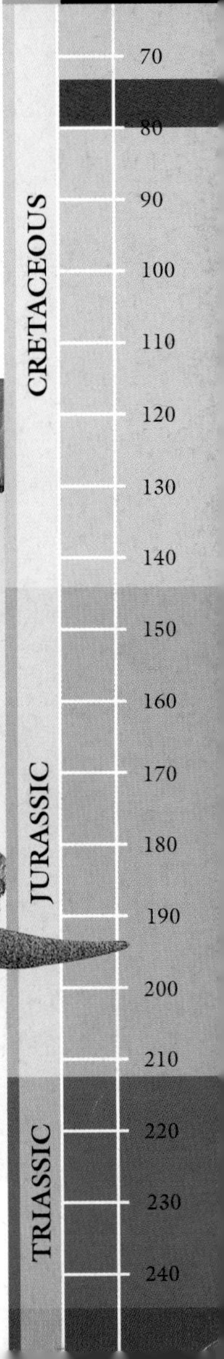

CRETACEOUS

JURASSIC

TRIASSIC

70
80
90
100
110
120
130
140
150
160
170
180
190
200
210
220
230
240

Triceratops
Three-horned face

This was the largest, and in some ways the most unusual, of the magnificent horned dinosaurs of the late Cretaceous period. No complete skeletons of *Triceratops* have ever been unearthed. But the discovery of numerous skulls, horns and teeth indicate that it was one of the most common dinosaurs of this time.

The skull of *Triceratops* had three prominent horns—one short horn on the nose and two long horns above the eyes. Its impressive bony neck frill could reach up to 6 feet 6 inches (2 m) in width, extended outward from the back of the skull, covering the neck. The snout formed a curved, parrot-like beak that was tipped with horn. This imposing head was as much as 5 feet (1.5 m) across—one of the largest skulls known in any land animal.

Function of the frill

Long ago it was proposed that the frill protected the neck of *Triceratops* against the attacks of big meat-eating dinosaurs such as *Tyrannosaurus rex*. This might have been true some of the time, but a number of frills have been found with *Tyrannosaurus* bite marks puncturing them. Another idea is that the frill might have been used for display during contests for mates, territory, or social position within the group. It is likely, as with other ceratopsians, the frill allowed members of the same species to recognize each other. Another intriguing idea is that the frill was used to regulate body temperature.

Rhinolike lifestyle?

Triceratops had a stout, barrel-shaped body and powerful limbs that were much more strongly built than those of living elephants. The limbs were probably this strong to withstand the weight of the animal as it ran. But its large size probably meant *Triceratops* could not run very fast. In addition, the front limbs needed to be very strong to help support the weight of that enormous head. *Triceratops* looks a little like the dinosaur equivalent of a rhinoceros. It might have behaved in quite a similar way, spending most of its time eating plants and occasionally defending itself with its horns when threatened.

Powerful jaws

The jaws of *Triceratops* were lined with dozens of closely packed teeth that formed "dental batteries" similar to those of the duck-billed dinosaurs. The jaws had a powerful scissorlike action, and the rows of teeth formed elongated cutting blades that were ideal for shredding tough plants into short pieces.

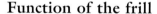

Below: *The beak and teeth of* Triceratops *were suited to slicing and crushing plant food. It probably ate cycads, ferns and palm leaves. The impressive horns would have been used in defense and would have been capable of inflicting nasty wounds on an attacker.*

FACT FILE

Genus: *Triceratops*

Classification: Marginocephalia; Ceratopsia; Ceratopsidae

Length: 30 ft (9 m)

Weight: Up to 6 tons

Lived: Late Cretaceous period, about 68-65 million years ago

Found in: U.S.A. (Wyoming, Montana, South Dakota, Colorado) and Canada (Alberta, Saskatchewan)

Left: *Its huge body housed an enormous stomach that would have been suitable for digesting the tough, high-fiber plants that made up the* Triceratops *diet.*

Above: *Remains of* Triceratops *have been found in western North America.*

CRETACEOUS

JURASSIC

TRIASSIC

70
80
90
100
110
120
130
140
150
160
170
180
190
200
210
220
230
240

Hypsilophodon
High-ridged tooth

Hypsilophodon was one of the smallest dinosaurs, reaching only 6 and a half feet (2 m) in length when fully grown. It was a slender plant-eater whose head was no bigger than a child's hand. Its jaws were lined with a set of ridged, leaf-shaped teeth that were used for slicing through leaves and other parts of plants. In addition to a set of good cutting teeth, *Hypsilophodon* also had a turtlelike beak, made of horn, at the front of its snout. This was useful in nipping the shoots and leaves off juicy plants.

Below: *The turtlelike beak and leaf-shaped teeth of* Hypsilophodon *enabled it to make short work of its plant food.* Hypsilophodon *had large eye sockets. Each socket contained a ring of tiny bones. These bones are seen in many dinosaurs and in birds. They probably help the eyes to focus properly.*

Most reptiles lack cheeks, but *Hypsilophodon*— like most other ornithischians— might have had fleshy cheeks that helped to keep food in its mouth while chewing. Large holes at the back of the skull provided plenty of room for the attachment of powerful muscles that worked the jaws.

Avoiding predators
The leg bones of *Hypsilophodon* were long, slender and lightweight. Its long hind legs had big thigh muscles, which helped it to run and dodge speedily. These muscles might have made its legs look a bit like smaller versions of the legs of some of the big flightless birds alive today, such as ostriches of Africa and emus of Australia.

Hypsilophodon stood with its body slung quite close to the ground and was well balanced at the hips, a good build for twisting and turning to escape its enemies. Another aid to sharp maneuvering was its long, powerful tail muscles, which drew the hind legs back in running.

Speedy runner
All of these features suggest that *Hypsilophodon* was a speedy little runner. It might have had a way of life a little like some of the very small antelope in Africa today, such as gazelles, which eat delicate shoots and leaves and escape from their attackers by running very fast.

Dinosaur tree-climber?
When scientists first examined the foot bones of *Hypsilophodon* they thought that they were similar to those of perching birds with opposable toes. As a result, early reconstructions of *Hypsilophodon* often show it perched up in the branches of a tree. Scientists have rejected this idea, as later studies of the foot bones showed that the toes could not have been used to clamp the feet onto branches—so climbing would have been impossible.

88

FACT FILE

Genus: *Hypsilophodon*

Classification: Ornithopoda;
  Euornithopoda; Hypsilophodontidae

Length: Up to 6 ft 6 in (2 m)

Weight: Up to 55 lb (25 kg)

Lived: Early Cretaceous period, about
  125-119 million years ago

Found in: England, Spain and possibly
  the U.S.A.

Left: Hypsilophodon's *long, slim hind legs gave
it a fast getaway from enemies such as the big
meat-eater* Altispinax (*tall spines*).

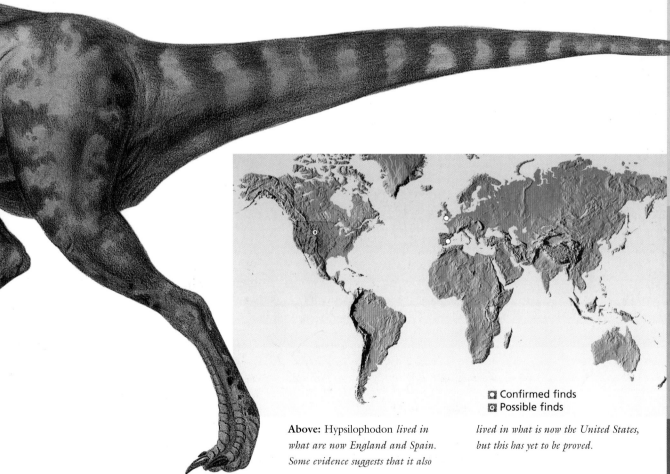

Above: Hypsilophodon *lived in
what are now England and Spain.
Some evidence suggests that it also*

*lived in what is now the United States,
but this has yet to be proved.*

□ Confirmed finds
◉ Possible finds

CRETACEOUS

70
80
90
100
110
120
130
140

JURASSIC

150
160
170
180
190
200
210

TRIASSIC

220
230
240

Hypsilophodon

Hypsilophodon was a small, fast-running dinosaur. It lived in the forests of what would later be England and Spain during the early Cretaceous period and ate plants.

Camptosaurus
Bent lizard

Camptosaurus was well equipped to feed on the tough plants that grew during the late Jurassic and early Cretaceous periods. Its lower jaw was filled with many rows of rough-edged teeth that were good at grinding and shredding plant material.

The teeth had edges with many small spiky points along them that could easily puncture plant leaves and stems. Because the plants were so tough, the tops of the teeth would become worn down until they were almost flat. At the end of its long, low head, *Camptosaurus* had a broad, horny beak for cropping plant material.

Back support

Tendons are the tough stringlike structures that connect muscles to bones. There were lots of big, long tendons along the back of *Camptosaurus*. In most animals, the tendons are made of a soft but strong material called collagen. The tendons of a young *Camptosaurus* started off as soft, strong collagen fibers, but as the animal grew, these tendons gradually turned into bone. Eventually, the tendons of an adult *Camptosaurus* would look like a network of very long, thin bones.

Above: *Lots of rough teeth in its jaws enabled* Camptosaurus *to grind up tough plants.*

Reaching up and bending down

Camptosaurus was a rather bulky animal because it had a large stomach in which to digest its huge meals of leaves, shoots and twigs. It had long, strong hind legs but rather small arms. As a result, it could probably walk only on its two hind legs. But although the arms were not strong enough to use when walking, the wrist bones were shaped so that they could help bear the weight of the animal when necessary. This allowed *Camptosaurus* to feed on plants that grew close to the ground. It could bend down quite easily and use its arms as props for short periods of time. *Camptosaurus* could also rear up on its hind legs in order to reach higher into the trees to get at juicy new shoots on the tips of the branches. Its long, heavy tail provided muscle support and counterbalance for the body.

Above: *A network of bony tendons helped to keep the back stiff and straight.*

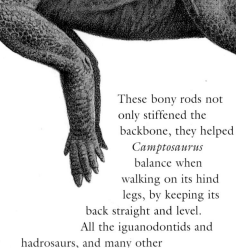

These bony rods not only stiffened the backbone, they helped *Camptosaurus* balance when walking on its hind legs, by keeping its back straight and level. All the iguanodontids and hadrosaurs, and many other ornithischians, had such tendons.

FACT FILE

Genus: *Camptosaurus*

Classification: Ornithopoda; Euornithopoda; Iguanodontia; Camptosauridae

Length: Up to 20 ft (6 m)

Weight: Up to 4 tons

Lived: Late Jurassic and early Cretaceous periods, about 156-138 million years ago

Found in: U.S.A. and England

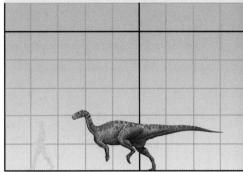

Left: Camptosaurus *is intermediate in many ways between hypsilophodontids and iguanodontids.*

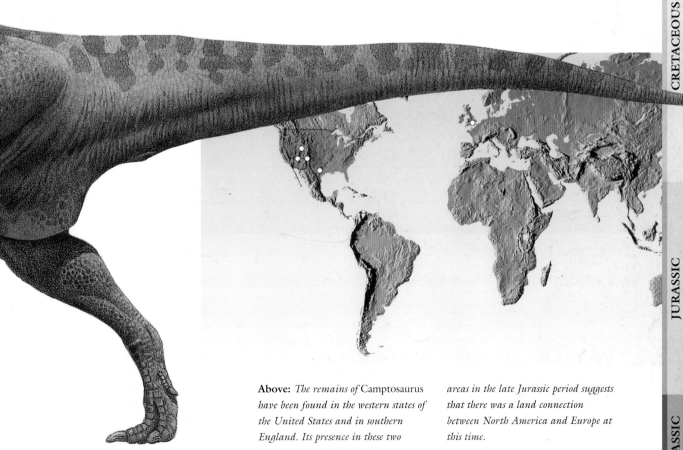

Above: *The remains of* Camptosaurus *have been found in the western states of the United States and in southern England. Its presence in these two* areas in the late Jurassic period suggests *that there was a land connection between North America and Europe at this time.*

CRETACEOUS

70

80

90

100

110

130

140

160

JURASSIC

170

180

190

200

210

TRIASSIC

220

230

240

93

Camptosaurus

The plant-eating dinosaur Camptosaurus tries to escape from an attacking Allosaurus. Camptosaurus had few defenses and was not a fast runner.

Ouranosaurus

Valiant lizard

FACT FILE

Genus: *Ouranosaurus*

Classification: Ornithopoda;
  Euornithopoda; Iguanodontia

Length: 23 ft (7 m)

Weight: Up to 2 tons

Lived: Early Cretaceous period, about
  102-97 million years ago

Found in: Niger

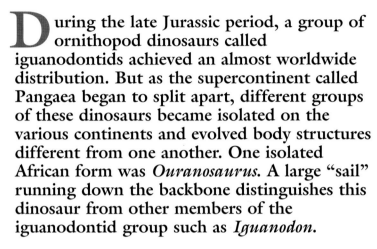

During the late Jurassic period, a group of ornithopod dinosaurs called iguanodontids achieved an almost worldwide distribution. But as the supercontinent called Pangaea began to split apart, different groups of these dinosaurs became isolated on the various continents and evolved body structures different from one another. One isolated African form was *Ouranosaurus*. A large "sail" running down the backbone distinguishes this dinosaur from other members of the iguanodontid group such as *Iguanodon*.

Below: Ouranosaurus
*was discovered in 1966
in the part of the Sahara
that lies within Niger,
western Africa.*

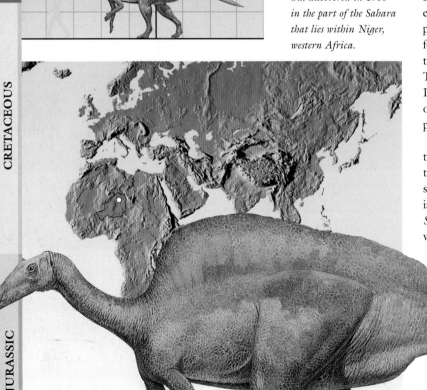

Ouranosaurus walked on its hind limbs. But the forelimbs were also quite long and ended in hooflike claws. So it could probably have walked and rested on all fours when necessary. The elongated skull tapered toward a broad, flattened snout. This was covered by a ducklike beak. Large teeth and a powerful arrangement of jaw muscles aided in the chewing of plant matter.

Bony projections extended upward from the backbone. Some reconstructions show these spines connected with skin, as if this structure acted as a "heat exchanger." This is similar to the theory about the plates of *Stegosaurus* (page 72). It suggests that when *Ouranosaurus* was cool, it could raise its body temperature by pumping the skin full of blood. As the blood flowed through the skin, it would absorb heat. Warm blood returning to the body would increase its temperature. The animal could cool itself in a similar way, losing heat to the outside. Some other dinosaurs, such as the theropod *Spinosaurus* (spiny lizard) and the sauropod *Rebbachisaurus* (Rebbach lizard), evolved similar sail-back heat exchangers.

Tenontosaurus

Sinew lizard

FACT FILE

Genus: *Tenontosaurus*

Classification: Ornithopoda;
  Hypsilophodontidae (?)

Length: Up to 21 ft (6.5 m)

Weight: Up to 1 ton

Lived: Early Cretaceous period, about
  119-113 million years ago

Found in: U.S.A.

In relation to its overall length, *Tenontosaurus* probably had the longest tail of any known dinosaur. The tail was almost four times as long as the main part of the body, and reached a length of over 13 feet (4 m). It was also very thick, well muscled and extremely strong. It was strengthened by many tendons extending alongside the bones of the back and tail. These turned into bony rods as the animal grew older.

This cowlike plant-eater had a short, deep body and long hind legs, and could walk on two or four legs. Long, powerful arms ended in broad five-fingered hands that could be used to support the weight of the body. Teeth of the theropod *Deinonychus* are often found close to the skeletons of *Tenontosaurus*. In many cases, there are too many shed tooth crowns to have come from fewer than a pack of animals. This has suggested to scientists that these vicious predators must have hunted in groups.

Left: *The structure of its long, bony tail may be seen clearly in this reconstructed skeleton of* Tenontosaurus.

Below: Tenontosaurus *fossils are found in the western and southern states of the United States.*

Relatively uncertain

Because of its large body size and the long snout region of the skull, *Tenontosaurus* was originally considered to have been an *Iguanodon*-like dinosaur. But some features have indicated that it was actually more like a giant *Hypsilophodon*. The relationship of *Tenontosaurus* to the other ornithopods is still uncertain.

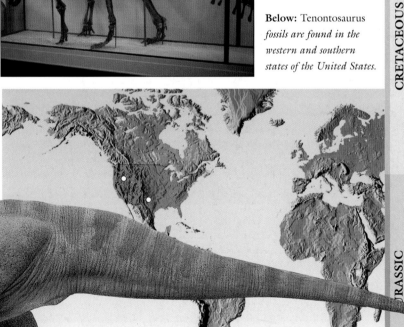

Iguanodon
Iguana tooth

Iguanodon was one of the first dinosaurs to be discovered—its remains were found in England in the 1820s. Scientists first reconstructed the animal as a large, lumbering creature, walking on all fours, with a spike on the end of its nose. But as more skeletons were unearthed, it became clear that *Iguanodon* was more lightly built than previously thought.

Below: Iguanodon *means "iguana tooth." When the first* Iguanodon *tooth was discovered, it looked a lot like the tooth of a giant iguana, a modern plant-eating lizard. Note the size of the tooth (shown against a centimeter scale) and the plant-shredding serrations along the front and back edges.*

Below: *Jaw muscles leave scars on the skull, showing where they attached to the skull bones. Using this evidence, scientists can reconstruct the jaw muscles of extinct animals. By adding a covering of skin and eyes, we can gain some idea of what the animal might have looked like when alive. Note the large, horny beak at the front of the jaws.*

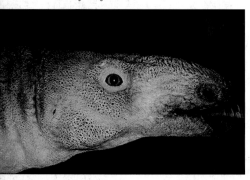

However, it still took some time for scientists to agree about how *Iguanodon* had moved. The next reconstructions featured it standing bolt upright on its hind limbs. The long tail was thought to have acted as a prop to help support the weight of the animal, so this reconstruction made *Iguanodon* look rather like a giant kangaroo. For a large part of the 1900s, this image remained. Only in the 1980s was it noticed that to keep *Iguanodon* in an upright pose, the tail would have to be broken halfway along its length!

On all fours—or just two

We now know that the tail was held out straight behind the body to provide a type of counterbalance. The backbone is held more horizontally, too. This means that, when it wanted to, *Iguanodon* could walk on its front and its back legs. The structure of the hand supports this idea. The middle three fingers are strongly built and are capped by hoofs. The chest bones are also heavy and strengthened. But *Iguanodon* was equally comfortable walking on its back legs alone.

Nose spike?

The so-called "nose spike" actually attaches to the end of the thumb. The thumb sticks out from the rest of the hand, and the spike might have made an effective weapon against some predators.

Grinding skills

Iguanodon was a plant-eater, and its jaws and teeth were well adapted for this type of food. There is a broad beak at the front of the jaws for cropping vegetation and many parallel rows of teeth farther back. These teeth formed a broad cutting and grinding surface. When the jaws closed, the upper and lower teeth fitted together, and hinges between bones in the skull allowed the upper jaws to slide sideways as the teeth of the lower jaws slid underneath them.

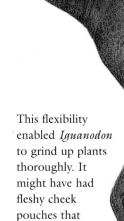

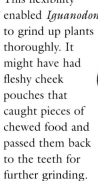

This flexibility enabled *Iguanodon* to grind up plants thoroughly. It might have had fleshy cheek pouches that caught pieces of chewed food and passed them back to the teeth for further grinding.

FACT FILE

Genus: *Iguanodon*

Classification: Ornithopoda; Euornithopoda; Iguanodontia; Iguanodontidae

Length: Up to 33 ft (10 m)

Weight: 4-5 tons

Lived: Early Cretaceous period, about 140-97 million years ago

Found in: Europe, the U.S.A. and Mongolia

Left: *This is the three-toed foot of* Iguanodon. *The bones are strong and thick to support the weight of the animal. Each toe ends in a blunt claw. The tips of the toes are held flat to the ground, whereas the longer bones of the foot are held more upright. This suggests that* Iguanodon *probably walked on its toes, and footprints confirm this idea.*

Above: Iguanodon *was widely distributed during the early Cretaceous period. It ranged from what is now the central United States, through Europe, where it was especially common in England, Germany, Spain and Belgium, and into eastern Asia (Mongolia).*

CRETACEOUS

70
80
90
100
110
120
130
140
160
170
180
190
200
210
220
230
240

JURASSIC

TRIASSIC

Iguanodon

Iguanodon was the commonest plant-eating dinosaur during the early Cretaceous period. Here, a herd of Iguanodon walk through the marshy forests that covered southern England at this time.

Maiasaura

Good mother lizard

One of the hadrosaurs, or duck-billed dinosaurs, *Maiasaura* possessed the flattened, toothless beak at the front of the snout that characterized this group. It lived and nested along the shores of an ancient sea that stretched across the center of North America during the Cretaceous period. The discovery of large numbers of *Maiasaura* fossils, many of which represent animals at different stages of life, and of their fossilized nesting grounds has enabled scientists to study the family behavior and growth rates of these dinosaurs.

Maiasaura was first discovered in 1978, when 15 babies and a fossilized nest were uncovered in Montana. These animals were about 3 ft (1 m) in length and had been approximately four weeks old when they died. Despite their age, the hipbones and the backbone were not fused together tightly, and the ends of the limbs had not turned completely to bone. This means that they were not able to walk properly. But their teeth were well worn, which suggests they had been feeding on plant matter for some time. Food must have been brought to the nest by the parents, and the babies cared for in the nest for some period of time.

Fast growth

Since these early discoveries, many more *Maiasaura* fossils have been found, and scientists have identified distinct growth stages in the life of a developing *Maiasaura*. When newly hatched, the young were just under 20 inches (50 cm) long. They remained in the nest for one to two months, and at this stage were growing very fast. They continued to grow rapidly until they were between one and two years old and over 10 feet (3 m) long. After the age of two, growth appeared to slow down, and *Maiasaura* reached adulthood at about seven to eight years. At this point, they may have been up to 23 feet (7 m) long. This growth rate is faster than any living reptile and similar to that of living, warm-blooded birds and mammals. This evidence strongly suggests that *Maiasaura*, like other large dinosaurs, were warm-blooded.

Fossil bone-beds

Some *Maiasaura* fossils are found in "bone-beds," fossil deposits composed of the remains of hundreds of individuals. Some of these cover areas many miles wide. The animals in these bone-beds might have died suddenly and been covered by ashes from a nearby volcanic eruption.

The large number of skeletons in these bone-beds provides strong support for the idea that *Maiasaura* nested in colonies.

Below: *The fossil nests of* Maiasaura *have yielded a great deal of information about dinosaur family life. Large bowl-like structures, they were more than 3 ft (1 m) across.*

FACT FILE

Genus: *Maiasaura*

Classification: Ornithopoda;
Iguanodontia; Hadrosauridae

Length: 23-30 ft (7-9 m)

Weight: 2-3 tons

Lived: Late Cretaceous period, about
80-73 million years ago

Found in: Montana, western
United States

Below: Maiasaura *used its "duckbill" to crop leaves and twigs and carry food back to its babies in the nest. The skeleton below is about 28 inches (70 cm) long. It was assembled from* hundreds of fragmentary bones that were scattered in nests. This animal, a few months old, still remained in and near the nest and was fed by the parents.

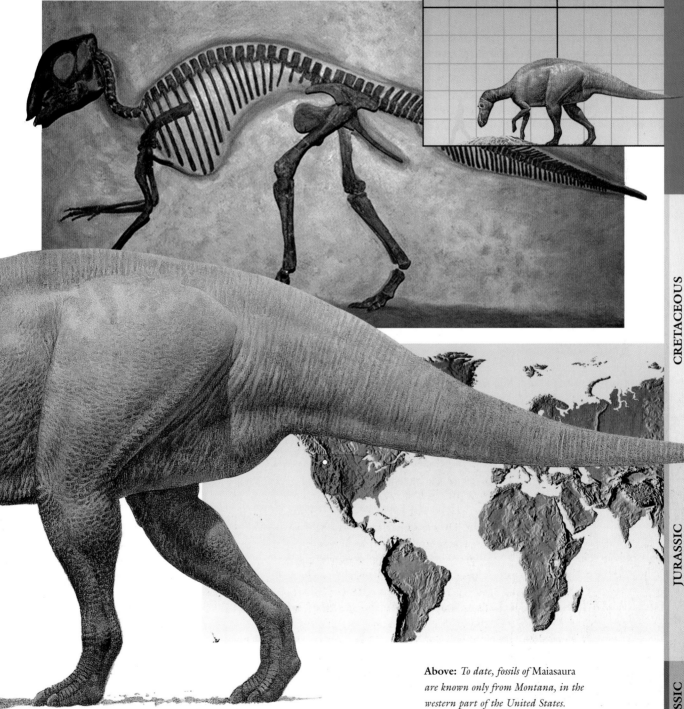

Above: *To date, fossils of Maiasaura are known only from Montana, in the western part of the United States.*

CRETACEOUS

JURASSIC

TRIASSIC

70
80
90
100
110
120
130
140
150
160
170
180
190
200
210
220
230
240

Corythosaurus
Corinthian helmet lizard

The most obvious feature of *Corythosaurus* is the large bony crest on top of its head. Other duck-billed dinosaurs, such as *Parasaurolophus*, also had crests, but the distinctive helmet-shaped crest of *Corythosaurus* must have made it particularly easy for it to recognize others of its own kind.

A plant-eater, *Corythosaurus* had a broad, turtlelike beak at the front of its snout, which it used to slice and chop through vegetation. Fossilized stomach contents from *Edmontosaurus,* a duck-billed dinosaur related to *Corythosaurus,* suggest that these kinds of dinosaurs ate the leaves of trees similar to living pine and fir trees. These tough leaves were powerfully ground up by rows of rough teeth lining the jaws.

Below: *The skull of* Corythosaurus *shows its distinctive helmet-shaped crest.*

Spotting the difference

Subtle differences in the shape and size of their crests might have enabled *Corythosaurus* to spot the difference between their species and other species from some distance away. The crest could also have helped *Corythosaurus* in another way. Hollow tubes connected to the nose ran through the inside of the crest. By blowing air though these tubes, *Corythosaurus* might have made a high trumpeting sound quite unlike that of any other dinosaur. This sound might have been useful for attracting mates, for signaling to other members of the herd, or for keeping in touch with young if they wandered away from the mother. *Corythosaurus* might also have used this call as an emergency alarm to warn others in the herd of the arrival of a predator.

Below: *Like many other "duck-billed" dinosaurs,* Corythosaurus *had tendons running alongside its backbone that turned into little bony rods as the animal grew. These rods helped to strengthen the spine and stopped it from bending. Several patches of fossilized skin can also been seen on this skeleton.*

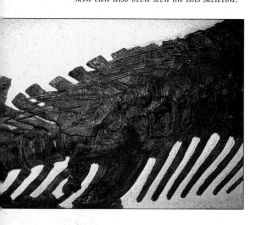

Preserved skin

Some skeletons of *Corythosaurus* have been preserved with the fossilized traces of the skin. This is a very rare event, as skin usually rots away before the body of an animal becomes fossilized. In *Corythosaurus,* the skin contained many small bony plates of different shapes and sizes. Some of the plates are circular, and some are oval. Other plates are pyramid-shaped or are many-sided. The largest of these plates are about 2 inches (5 cm) long and 1 inch (2-3 cm) wide. Although the skin would have been quite tough, these plates would probably not have been a particularly good defense against the teeth and jaws of big meat-eaters such as tyrannosaurs. But they might have given some protection against other, smaller predators such as packs of *Dromaeosaurus.*

FACT FILE

Genus: *Corythosaurus*

Classification: Ornithopoda; Euornithopoda; Iguanodontia; Hadrosauridae

Length: Up to 33 ft (10 m)

Weight: Up to 3 tons

Lived: Late Cretaceous period, about 80-73 million years ago

Found in: U.S.A. and Canada

Left: *The shoulders of* Corythosaurus *are bent downward, giving a "humpbacked" appearance similar to that seen in North American bison of today. Large pads of fat might have surrounded the shoulders, forming a reserve of energy for times when food was not available.*

Right: *Remains of* Corythosaurus *have been discovered in the badlands of Alberta, Canada, and in Montana, U.S.A.*

CRETACEOUS

— 70
— 80
— 90
— 100
— 110
— 130
— 140

JURASSIC

— 150
— 160
— 170
— 180
— 190
— 200
— 210

TRIASSIC

— 220
— 230
— 240

Corythosaurus tries to evade an attacking tyrannosaur by running out into a lake. Large meat-eating dinosaurs often preyed upon duck-bill ■ dinosaurs during the late ■retaceous period.

Corythosaurus

Lambeosaurus
Lambe's lizard

The most distinctive feature of *Lambeosaurus* is the hatchet-shaped crest on its head. This is tall and flat and points forward at the front. It looks like a bizarre version of the helmetlike crest of its close cousin *Corythosaurus*. Unlike *Corythosaurus*, it has a smaller prong of bone jutting out from the back. Such features, as well as possible differences in color patterns and the noises they made, would have helped these two plant-eating dinosaurs to tell each other apart when gathered in large herds next to or in lakes and water holes.

Lambeosaurus held its tail off the ground at all times and used it as a balance when walking. It seems to have been able to choose whether it walked on its two hind legs or on all limbs. Like other hadrosaurs and iguanodontids, it had hooflike front toes, so it was well adapted for both modes of life.

Changing with age
Over the years, many different *Lambeosaurus* fossils have been discovered. In the early 1900s, scientists noticed that the shape of the crest varied among different animals, leading them to infer that there were several different types of *Lambeosaurus*. But recent studies of these fossils have revealed that many of these differences resulted from the way in which *Lambeosaurus* grew. Babies, young adults and mature individuals have now been identified from the fossils. Youngsters have shorter, rounder beaks than adults, and short, low crests that often lack the backward-pointing bony prong. In older animals, the beaks became longer and narrower, whereas the crests became taller and more elaborate. There also seem to be differences in the shape of the crest between what might be males and females, but this theory is more difficult to prove.

Teeth by the hundred
Most reptiles—and many other animals—have only a single row of teeth. But the jaws of *Lambeosaurus*, and those of other hadrosaurs, contained many rows of teeth that were stacked up on top of each other. There were between 45 and 60 tooth positions in each row, and each one of these had several replacement teeth stacked in sequence beneath them. So the jaws could contain as many as 700 teeth at any one time. This special arrangement of teeth is known as a dental battery. The surface of the battery was very rough, with many tough ridges of enamel, the material that makes up the hard outer layer of teeth. As a result, *Lambeosaurus* could grind up even the toughest plants with ease.

Below: *Hadrosaur teeth were arranged in "batteries" that could contain many hundreds of teeth. The teeth are arranged in vertical rows, and those teeth at the top of the row became heavily worn as they ground down plant food. When these teeth were almost completely worn down, they fell out of the jaws and were replaced by new, unworn teeth from below.*

Below: *The crest of* Lambeosaurus *is very distinctive. Note the flat, hatchet-like blade at the front of the crest and the smaller prong that juts out from the back of the skull.*

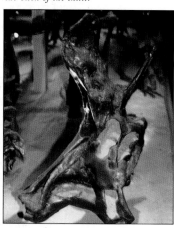

FACT FILE

Genus: *Lambeosaurus*

Classification: Ornithopoda; Euornithopoda; Iguanodontia; Hadrosauridae

Length: Up to 50 ft (15 m)

Weight: 7 tons

Lived: Late Cretaceous period, about 80-73 million years ago

Found in: Canada, U.S.A., Mexico

Left: *Despite being much bigger than a living elephant,* Lambeosaurus *was in great danger from fearsome attacks by packs of the small but vicious meat-eater* Saurornitholestes. *A lone* Lambeosaurus *would have had little chance against these pack hunters, though it might have been able to use its heavy tail for defense.*

Above: Lambeosaurus *fossils have been found in Canada, the United States and Mexico. Herds of* Lambeosaurus *must have roamed all over western North America during the late Cretaceous period.*

CRETACEOUS

JURASSIC

TRIASSIC

70
80
90
100
110
120
130
140
150
160
170
180
190
200
210
220
230
240

Huge herds of duck-billed dinosaurs, such as Lambeosaurus, roamed the landscape during the late Cretaceous period. Scientists have found that some of these herds contained hundreds of individuals.

Parasaurolophus
Beside the lizard crest

One of the rarest of the duck-billed dinosaurs, *Parasaurolophus* was also one of the most advanced of those plant-eating giants. Early ideas about *Parasaurolophus* had it standing upright, using its crest as a weapon and its tail as a swimming aid. But further research showed that not one of those hypotheses is true. Its most distinctive feature is its crest, which has been the source of most of the confusion among scientists. Many unusual ideas have been put forward as to what it was used for.

The crest—a huge pipelike structure extending back from the top of the head to reach over the neck and shoulders—was once thought to have been used for battling against rival males in fights for mates. Another suggestion was that it was used as a "snorkel" in swimming, because hollow tubes within the crest connected to the nasal passages. But there is no hole at the end of the crest. Another idea is that the crest was used in making noises to communicate with other *Parasaurolophus*. Models have been made of the crest, and, when air is blown through the tubes, it makes a noise rather similar to that of a trombone.

Standing four-square
For many years, scientists portrayed *Parasaurolophus* as standing upright on its two hind legs, with its neck held straight up and its heavy tail on the ground helping to support its great weight. Paleontologists now know that this could not have been so. It seems that *Parasaurolophus* had a downward bend in its neck just like bison of today. And its huge bones show that, although *Parasaurolophus* could walk on two legs as well as on all fours, it held its back horizontally, rather than vertically as in the old reconstructions. And its huge tail did not drag along the ground.

Swimming duckbills?
It was once thought that *Parasaurolophus* used its powerful tail in swimming, beating it from side to side to push itself through the water. But *Parasaurolophus* fossils are found in rocks that suggest it lived in a dry, land environment, rather like the habitats in which elephants live today. And the manner in which the bones of the tail are connected to each

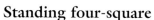
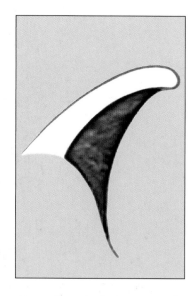

Above: *Some scientists have suggested that the* Parasaurolophus *crest might have supported a flap of skin that was connected to the back of the neck. This skin flap could have been brightly colored. But although this is an intriguing idea, there is no evidence to support it at present.*

other shows that they were not capable of making big and powerful sideways movements. It seems that this duck-billed dinosaur did not live and swim in the rivers and lakes of the late Cretaceous period like a gigantic duck after all. It probably lived on dry land, where it fed on the tough plants that were adapted to grow in such conditions.

FACT FILE

Genus: *Parasaurolophus*

Classification: Ornithopoda;
   Euornithopoda; Iguanodontia;
   Hadrosauridae

Length: Up to 33 ft (10 m)

Weight: 5 tons

Lived: Late Cretaceous period, about
   83-65 million years ago

Found in: Canada and U.S.A.

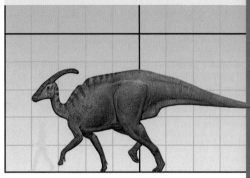

Left: *The crest of* Parasaurolophus *was over 3 ft (1 m) long. Despite early ideas that it was used as a weapon or a snorkel, it is now thought to have been used for sound production or species identification.*

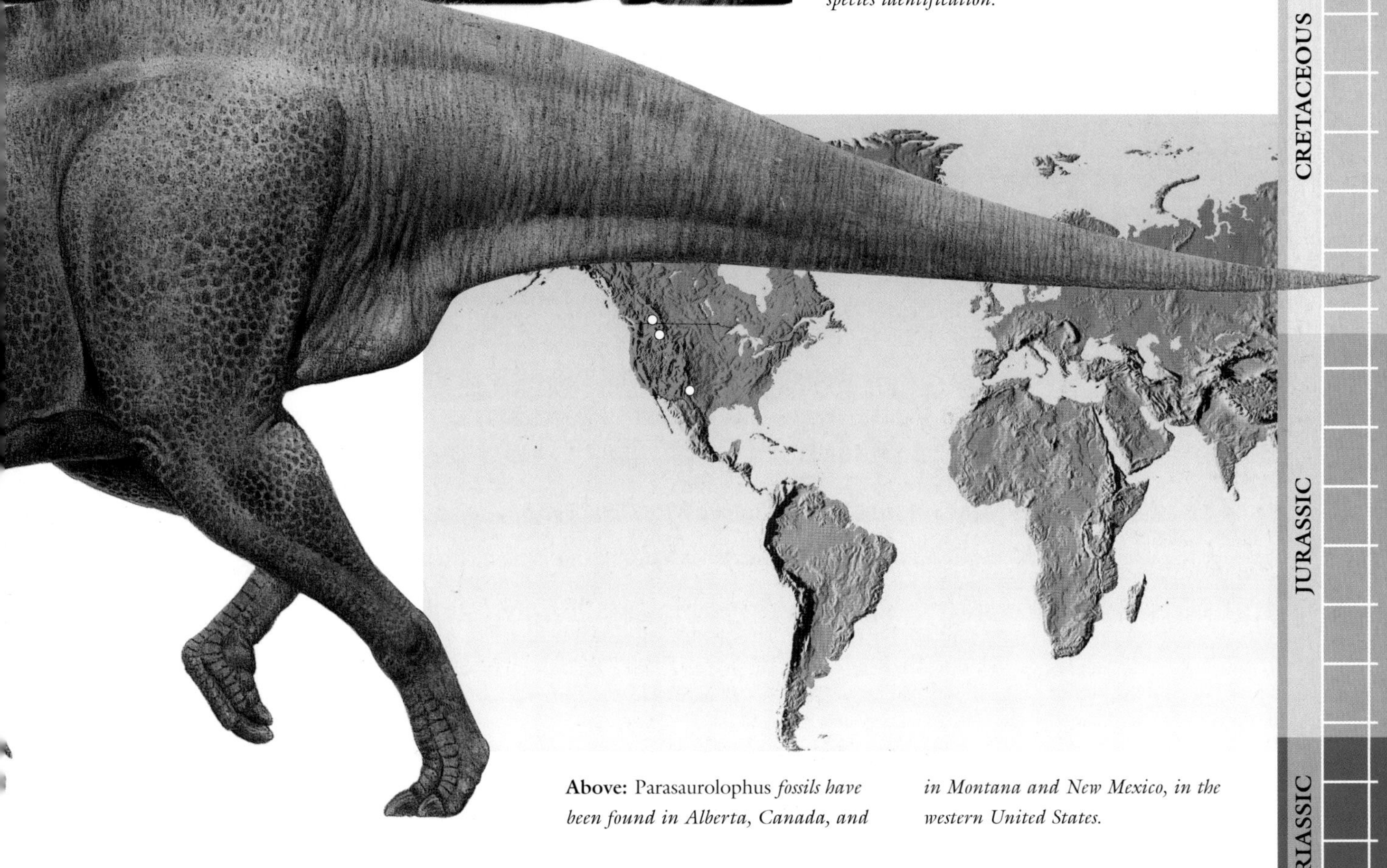

Above: Parasaurolophus *fossils have been found in Alberta, Canada, and* in Montana and New Mexico, in the western United States.

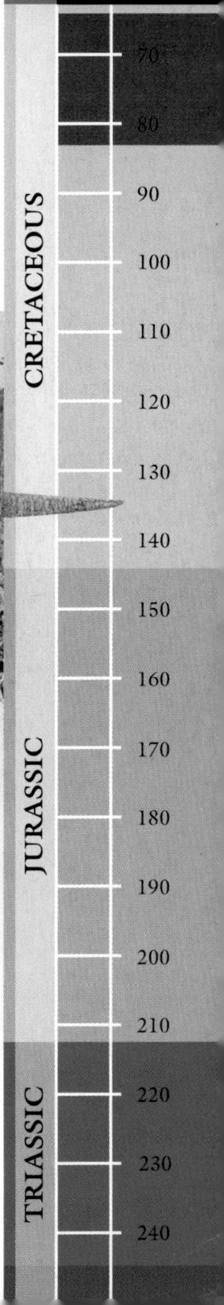

CRETACEOUS

JURASSIC

TRIASSIC

70
80
90
100
110
120
130
140
150
160
170
180
190
200
210
220
230
240

Lizard-hipped dinosau

Saurischia

This family tree shows the relationships of the many different kinds of saurischian (lizard-hipped) dinosaurs to each other. The Saurischia splits into two major groups, known as the Theropoda and the Sauropodomorpha.

The Theropoda includes bipedal, meat-eating dinosaurs and the birds. Theropods first appeared in the late Triassic period and survived until the end of the Cretaceous period. They were the most important large predators on land during the Mesozoic era.

Sauropodomorphs were large-bodied herbivores with long necks and tails and large barrel-shaped bodies. The group is split into the Prosauropoda and the Sauropoda. Prosauropods lived during the late Triassic and early Jurassic periods, while sauropods first appeared in the early Jurassic. Sauropods were most abundant in the late Jurassic, and remained as important herbivores in South America, Europe and India during the Cretaceous period.

Baptornis
Archaeopteryx
Iberomesornis
Velociraptor
Deinonychus
Troodon
Therizinosaurus
Caudipteryx
Oviraptor
Pelecanimimus
Compsognathus
Sinosauropteryx
Struthiomimus
Tyrannosaurus

AVES
MANIRAPTORA
COELUROSAURIA

MAJOR SUBGROUPS

■	Prosauropoda
■	Sauropoda
■	Ceratosauria
■	Tetanurae
■	Coelurosauria
■	Maniraptora
■	Not in major subgroup

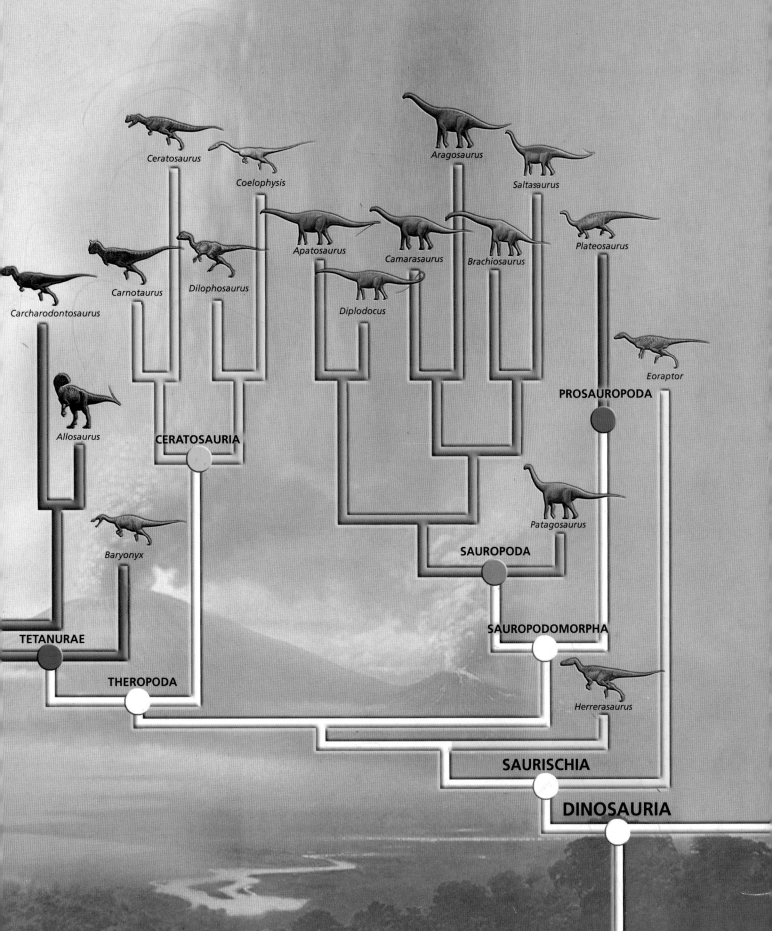

Ceratosaurus

Coelophysis

Aragosaurus

Saltasaurus

Carcharodontosaurus

Carnotaurus

Dilophosaurus

Apatosaurus

Camarasaurus

Brachiosaurus

Plateosaurus

Diplodocus

Allosaurus

Eoraptor

CERATOSAURIA

PROSAUROPODA

Baryonyx

Patagosaurus

SAUROPODA

TETANURAE

SAUROPODOMORPHA

THEROPODA

Herrerasaurus

SAURISCHIA

DINOSAURIA

Eoraptor
Dawn thief

FACT FILE

Genus: *Eoraptor*

Classification: Saurischia; Theropoda?

Length: 3 ft (1 m)

Weight: 20 lb (10 kg)

Lived in: Late Triassic period, about 231-225 million years ago

Found in: Northwestern Argentina

About 225 million years ago, in what is now a remote region of Argentina, South America, a new group of animals began to evolve. These were the dinosaurs, and their presence on earth would change the face of the planet forever. *Eoraptor* is not the ancestor of all other dinosaurs, but it may be a very primitive dinosaur or a very close relative of dinosaurs. Its remains help scientists to work out how dinosaurs first evolved.

Right: Eoraptor *was not a large animal—its skull is only about 5 inches (12 cm) long. The different types of teeth can be seen lining the jaws.*

Eoraptor was discovered only in 1993 by a team of American and Argentinian paleontologists. It was a small, bipedal (two-legged) meat-eating animal. It possessed certain dinosaurian characteristics, such as modifications of the ankle, hind legs and hip. These features enabled dinosaurs to stand with their legs directly beneath their bodies. On the other hand, it lacked some dinosaurian features, such as the structures of the skull, wrist, hand and pelvis.

Where does it belong?

Along the jaws, curved and serrated theropod-like teeth sit side by side with more leaf-shaped teeth, like those seen in the most primitive prosauropods. Hollow limb bones and elongated hands ending in

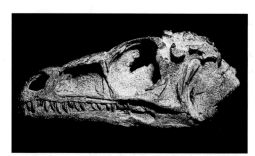

curved, grasping and raking claws seem to place *Eoraptor* within the theropods. However, lack of a flexible hinge in the lower jaw suggests that *Eoraptor* is at the very bottom of the theropod family tree—or perhaps not a theropod at all. The anatomy of *Eoraptor* suggests that dinosaurs evolved from a small, bipedal, carnivorous reptile, at some time in the middle Triassic period.

Above: Eoraptor *was found in a place called the Valley of the Moon, in northwestern Argentina, South America. It is known from a single skeleton.*

70
80
90
100
110
120
130
140
1
160
170
180
190
200
210
220
230
240

CRETACEOUS

JURASSIC

TRIASSIC

Herrerasaurus

Herrera's lizard

One of the earliest meat-eating dinosaurs, *Herrerasaurus* lived during the late Triassic period in what is now northwestern Argentina. Although it reached only a few feet in length, it was one of the largest bipedal animals in the world at that time. Its mixture of primitive and advanced features has made it very difficult to place in any particular group of dinosaurs. Recent discoveries suggest that *Herrerasaurus* was a either a theropod or a very close relative of dinosaurs.

FACT FILE

Genus: *Herrerasaurus*

Classification: Saurischia; Theropoda?; Herrerasauridae

Length: 10-15 ft (3-4.5 m)

Weight: 550-660 lb (250-300 kg)

Lived: Late Triassic period, about 231-225 million years ago

Found in: Northwestern Argentina

Herrerasaurus was one of the top predators of its time. Like those of theropods, its limb bones were long and hollow. The individual vertebrae of its tail were locked together, making it very stiff, a feature that added stability during running and jumping. Powerful hands, with three enlarged fingers, ended in long, curved, grasping claws. It might have preyed upon the piglike rhynchosaur, a large plant-eating reptile abundant during the late Triassic period. Rhynchosaur remains have actually been found inside the ribcage of a *Herrerasaurus* skeleton. Healed bite marks on the skull of one *Herrerasaurus* specimen show that even members of the same species were

at risk of attack from other *Herrerasaurus*. Animals such as *Eoraptor* and *Herrerasaurus* retain the carnivorous habits of the close relatives of dinosaurs. Though some scientists conclude that they were true theropods, others conclude that the animals had carnivorous habits but were not true dinosaurs.

Below: Herrerasaurus *had an elongated skull, with jaws full of curved serrated teeth. At the back were large spaces for the attachment of powerful jaw-closing muscles.*

Below: Herrerasaurus *remains are found in a place known as the Valley of the Moon, in northwestern Argentina, South America.*

CRETACEOUS

70
80
90
100
110
120
130
140
150
160

JURASSIC

170
180
190
200
210

TRIASSIC

220
230
240

Plateosaurus
Flat lizard

In comparison with the giant sauropods of the Jurassic period, *Plateosaurus* was a medium-size animal. But during the late Triassic it was one of the largest dinosaurs on earth, and one of the first really big dinosaurs. *Plateosaurus* was a member of the Prosauropoda, a small group of dinosaurs closely related to the later sauropods. Prosauropods flourished during the late Triassic, but they became extinct at the end of the early Jurassic period.

In the early 1800s, more than 100 skeletons of a large extinct reptile were discovered in a single quarry in central Germany. They were very well preserved, and ten complete skulls were recovered. These fossils were named *Plateosaurus* by the German scientist Hermann von Meyer in 1837. This preceded the invention of the term "dinosaur" by five years, and it was not until sometime later that *Plateosaurus* was recognized as a dinosaur.

Powerful limbs

Like other prosauropods, *Plateosaurus* had a long neck, a small head and an elongated, barrel-like body. Its limbs were strong and stoutly constructed, and its tail was very long and heavy. In life, the limbs and tail would have been equipped with powerful muscles. The hind limbs were very long, and it appears that *Plateosaurus* was capable of walking bipedally. It would also have been able to rear up onto its hind legs. In combination with the long neck, this would have allowed *Plateosaurus* to feed on branches 10-13 feet (3-4 m) above ground level. Its arms were quite short, but its broad hands would have been able to support a lot of weight. This

suggests that *Plateosaurus* usually chose to walk on all fours.

Meat on the menu?

Plateosaurus is usually thought of as a plant-eating dinosaur. But large claws on its thumb and on the second toe of the foot have led some scientists to suggest that it might occasionally have eaten meat. Its teeth show a combination of features that would have been useful in both chopping up plant food and catching small prey. *Plateosaurus* might have used its claws for tearing up roots, the carcasses of dead animals, and insect mounds. The claws could also have been used to defend against attack from large predators.

FACT FILE

Genus: *Plateosaurus*

Classification: Sauropodomorpha; Prosauropoda; Plateosauridae

Length: Up to 30 ft (9 m)

Weight: Up to 4 tons

Lived: Late Triassic period, about 221-219 million years ago

Found in: Germany, France, Switzerland and Greenland

Below: Plateosaurus *could have used its long neck to reach up into trees in search of food. The heavy tail counterbalanced the neck. Prosauropods* had very elongated chests and bellies in comparison with other dinosaurs. This probably indicates that they had very long guts.

Below: *Since the huge finds in Germany in the 1800s, remains of* Plateosaurus *have also been unearthed in Switzerland and France and more recently in Greenland.*

CRETACEOUS
70
80
90
100
110
120
130

JURASSIC
150
160
170
180
190
200
210

TRIASSIC
220
230
240

Apatosaurus
Deceptive lizard

This colossal sauropod is one of the most familiar of all dinosaurs and is often referred to as *Brontosaurus. Apatosaurus* was a close relative of *Diplodocus* and lived in the same areas of North America during the late Jurassic period. Like *Diplodocus*, it had a long whiplash tail and short forelimbs. It was much more sturdily built than *Diplodocus*, although not quite so long. Scientists have made many mistakes in their studies of *Apatosaurus*, including giving it the wrong name and even the wrong head!

The name *Apatosaurus* (deceptive lizard) is very appropriate, as it was associated with one of the biggest blunders in dinosaur science. Professor Othniel Marsh studied a few fossil bones of a new dinosaur in 1877 and gave it the name *Apatosaurus*. Two years later, he examined another collection of fossil bones. Thinking these were from a new sauropod species, he named this dinosaur *Brontosaurus* (thunder lizard). Later, it was realized that all these fossils came from the same type of animal, and that *Brontosaurus* was, in fact, *Apatosaurus!* Because *Apatosaurus* was the first name to be proposed, it must be the official name for this creature.

Below: *The vertebrae of many sauropods are hollowed out, making them lighter. The hollow areas contain a few thin struts and plates of bone that impart great strength to a vertebra despite its lightness.*

Below: *The long, low, flat skull of* Apatosaurus *was well adapted for stripping leaves and soft foliage from branches and plants. Only two skulls of* Apatosaurus *have ever been discovered.*

Losing its head

The skulls of the plant-eating sauropods are very rarely preserved, probably because they were lightweight, flimsy structures. So scientists do not know what the skulls of many sauropods looked like, even though they might have found all the other parts of the animal's skeleton. In one quarry, an *Apatosaurus* skeleton was found very close to a *Camarasaurus* skeleton and a skull. At the time of the discovery, it was not known what the head of either animal looked like. Scientists thought the skull might belong to *Apatosaurus*, as it lay slightly closer to this skeleton than to that of *Camarasaurus*. For many years, skeletons of *Apatosaurus* were displayed in museums with a model of this skull attached to them. But new discoveries showed that the skull actually belonged to *Camarasaurus*. As a result, *Apatosaurus* remained headless until scientists discovered a new skeleton with the proper skull attached.

Reaching high to feed

Apatosaurus had forked spines attached to the top of the bones of its neck and the front part of its back. These spines were small but important, because they supported a large cablelike ligament that in turn helped support the neck and tail. Ligaments, found in the bodies of all backboned animals, attach muscles to bones. In contrast, the spines attached to the hipbones were not forked, but were very long. They had massive back muscles attached to them, which might have enabled *Apatosaurus* to rear up on its hind legs. If it did this, its tail was probably used as a "third leg" to prop it up. In this way, *Apatosaurus* could reach high up into the trees in search of particularly juicy leaves and shoots.

FACT FILE

Genus: *Apatosaurus*

Classification: Sauropoda; Diplodocoidea; Diplodocidae

Length: Up to 90 ft (27 m)

Weight: Up to 35 tons

Lived: Late Jurassic period, about 156-144 million years ago

Found in: Colorado, Utah, Oklahoma and Wyoming

Left: Apatosaurus *had a comblike arrangement of long peglike teeth at the front of its mouth. These teeth are heavily worn, suggesting that they could have been used to nip small pieces off plants in addition to stripping branches.*

Above: *Remains of* Apatosaurus *have been found in the United States.*

CRETACEOUS

70
80
90
100
110
120
130
140

JURASSIC

160
170
180
190
200
210

TRIASSIC

220
230
240

Brachiosaurus
Arm lizard

Brachiosaurus was once thought to be the largest dinosaur of all. Some scientists estimated that it weighed as much as 80 tons, making it heavier than the combined weight of 20 adult elephants! Most scientists now accept a figure of about 50 tons—still much heavier than any land animal alive today.

Below: *The skull of* Brachiosaurus *has a long snout and many stout, chisel-like teeth. The large, curved bar of bone in front of the eyes marks the position of the animal's nostrils.*

Below: *This skeleton of* Brachiosaurus, *in the Humboldt Museum, Berlin, is the tallest mounted dinosaur skeleton on display anywhere in the world.*

The name *Brachiosaurus* refers to the very long arms of this sauropod. *Brachiosaurus* was the only dinosaur with arms that were much longer than its hind limbs, a feature that raised the chest and shoulder region of this animal to perhaps 8 feet (2.5 m) above ground level. However, these long limbs were surprisingly slim—not strong enough for *Brachiosaurus* to run or even to walk too quickly. The long arms might have been useful in stepping over large obstacles, or they could have been an adaptation for feeding on tall trees.

High-level feeding

The neck also contributed to this high-level feeding strategy. It was made up of 12 individual vertebrae, each of which could be over 28 inches (70 cm) long. This gave the neck a total length of about 30 feet (9 m). Add this to the height of the shoulders, and it would be reasonable to suggest that *Brachiosaurus* could reach plants up to 36 feet (11 m) above ground level while standing on all fours. Few other sauropods could reach these levels, so *Brachiosaurus* was able to feed with little disturbance.

Getting blood to the brain

When *Brachiosaurus* held its neck upright, it would have been very difficult for the heart to pump blood all the way up to the brain, unless there was some way to boost circulation. This problem could have been solved in several ways. The heart might have been capable of keeping the blood pressure very high, so that blood could always reach the brain. But then, when *Brachiosaurus* bent down to drink, the high blood pressure could cause many of the fragile blood vessels in the brain to burst. Giraffes solve this problem with elastic, muscular arteries that keep blood flowing, and a protective network of capillaries behind the brain to prevent blood from flooding it when the head is lowered. Did the problem of pumping blood to the head prevent *Brachiosaurus* from raising its head above shoulder height? If this were the case, why should *Brachiosaurus* and the other sauropods have developed such long necks?

Air sacs

The vertebrae of all advanced sauropod dinosaurs had holes in their sides known as pleurocoels. These often became so large that the vertebrae were reduced to a honeycomb structure of struts and bars. These were filled with air sacs that made the vertebrae very light but strong enough to support the animal's weight.

FACT FILE

Genus: *Brachiosaurus*

Classification: Sauropoda;
Titanosauromorpha; Brachiosauridae

Length: Up to 92 ft (28 m)

Weight: About 50 tons

Lived: Late Jurassic period, about
156-144 million years ago

Found in: Colorado and Utah, Tanzania
and possibly Portugal

Left: *This* Brachiosaurus *skeleton shows its enormous arm bones and its deep chest region. The hand bones are very long, making up about one-fifth of the total length of the arm.*

☐ Confirmed finds
☐ Possible finds

Above: Brachiosaurus *fossils have been found in the western United States and Tanzania. Some remains from Portugal have also been attributed to this animal. The presence of* Brachiosaurus *in North America and Africa is evidence that a land connection existed between these two regions during the late Jurassic period.*

CRETACEOUS

70
80
90
100
110
120
130
140
150
160
170
180
190
200
210
220
230
240

JURASSIC

TRIASSIC

123

Camarasaurus
Chambered lizard

Camarasaurus was the most abundant dinosaur in North America during the late Jurassic period. Herds of these animals roamed through the open conifer forests that covered the western United States at this time. Although *Camarasaurus* reached a length of about 66 feet (20 m), it is actually one of the smaller sauropod dinosaurs. Its relatively small size and abundance probably made it a target for large predators such as *Allosaurus*.

Below: *The broad, strong teeth of* Camarasaurus *were used to slice through tough vegetation. They became very heavily worn as they continually cut against each other and rubbed past twigs and branches.*

Below: *The foot of* Camarasaurus *was very stout and strongly constructed. Note the large claw, which might have been useful in digging nests for its eggs or in hunting for buried roots or water.*

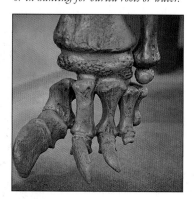

Most species of sauropod dinosaur are known from only one or two skeletons, and even these may be damaged or have many missing parts. The skulls of these huge animals are particularly rare, and only a few complete skulls have ever been discovered. *Camarasaurus*, however, is one of the few sauropods for which scientists have a large number of good skeletons and several skulls in good condition. As a result, scientists know a great deal about the anatomy of *Camarasaurus*. Skeletons from all age groups are known, from babies up to fully grown adults.

Well-chewed food

It used to be thought that sauropods did not chew their food very much, but just used their teeth to nip off leaves and fruits before allowing their very long guts to do all of the hard work involved in digestion. However, detailed studies on the teeth and jaws have shown that *Camarasaurus* could have chewed its food at least somewhat. The teeth are broad and robust, and they locked together as the jaws were closed. This allowed *Camarasaurus* to make short work of even the toughest plants. To many, it seems remarkable that the small heads of sauropods could have eaten enough food to maintain their size and growth.

Stiff neck

The neck of *Camarasaurus* is relatively short by sauropod standards. It is made up of 12 individual neck bones, or vertebrae. These were connected to each other by large ball-and-socket joints at the bottom, and by smaller peglike joints at the top. These joints allowed a considerable amount of up-and-down movement, and the head of *Camarasaurus* could probably reach up to 23-26 feet (7-8 m) above ground level when the neck was raised. But the neck was not particularly flexible from side to side. Long, overlapping ribs along the sides of the neck prevented large sideways movements.

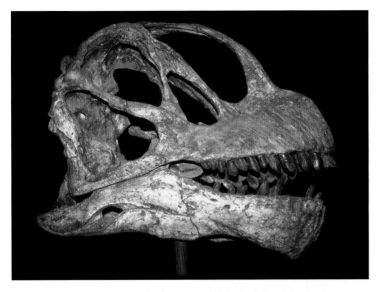

FACT FILE

Genus: *Camarasaurus*

Classification: Sauropoda;
Titanosauromorpha; Camarasauridae

Length: Up to 66 ft (20 m)

Weight: Up to 20 tons

Lived: Late Jurassic period, about
156-144 million years ago

Found in: Western U.S.A. and possibly
in Zimbabwe

Above and Right: *The front of the
skull has a narrow muzzlelike region
that would have allowed* Camarasaurus
*to poke its snout into narrow gaps in
the dense treetops in search of food.*

☐ Confirmed finds
☐ Possible finds

Above: Camarasaurus *fossils have been
found in the western United States. It
used to be thought that* Camarasaurus
also lived in what is now Portugal, but
*this idea is no longer accepted. A few
bones in Zimbabwe have been
identified as* Camarasaurus, *but this
discovery has yet to be confirmed.*

CRETACEOUS

JURASSIC

TRIASSIC

70
80
90
100
110
120
130
140
150
160
170
180
190
200
210
220
230
240

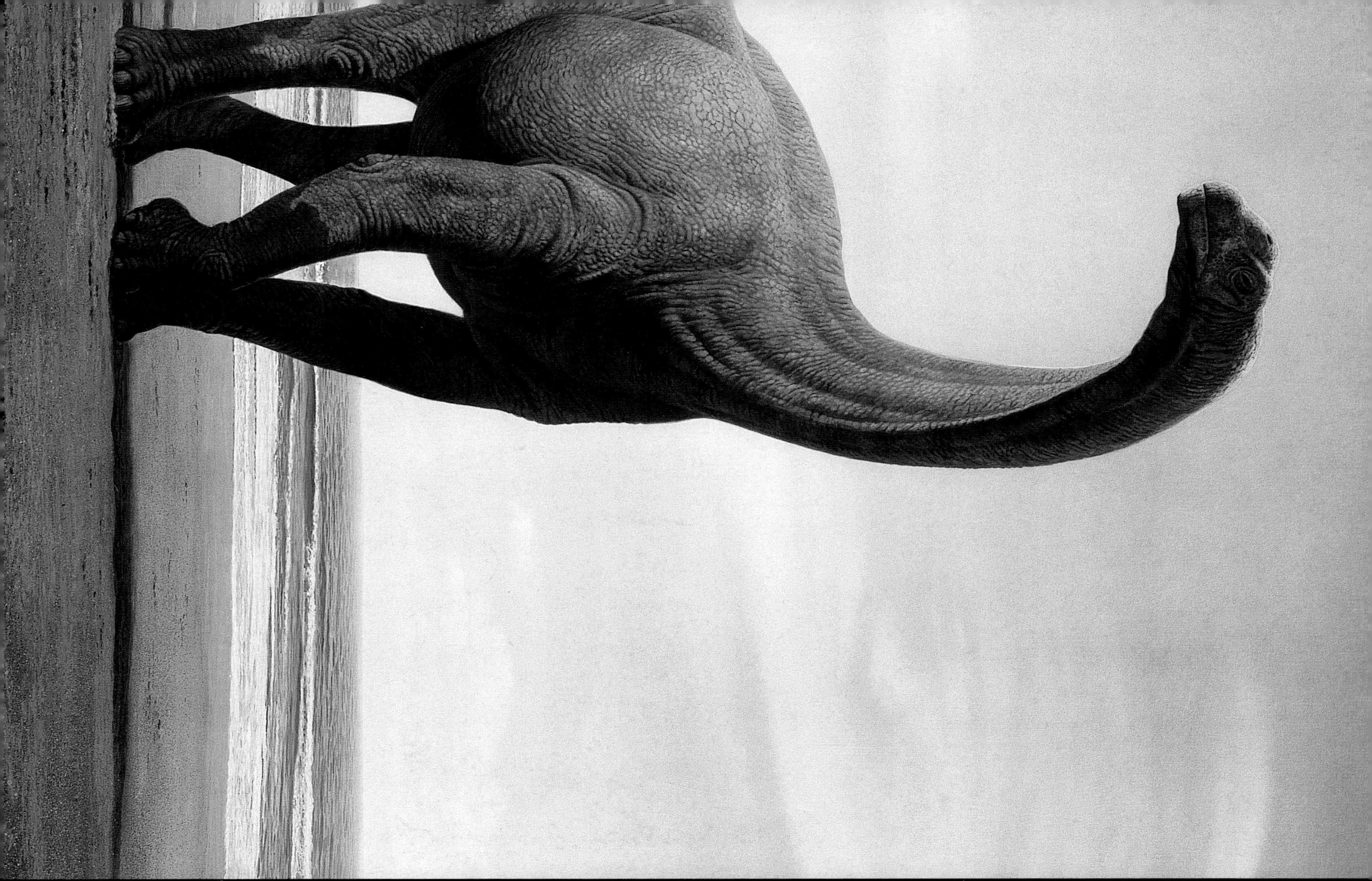

Camarasaurus was the commonest dinosaur in North America during the late Jurassic period.
It was one of the smaller sauropod dinosaurs, but still reached a length of about 66 feet (20 m).

Diplodocus
Double-beam

Diplodocus is one of the most familiar of all dinosaurs, but in some ways it is highly unusual. Although it has the long neck, tiny head and huge body seen in all other sauropods, it differs from its relatives in several respects. The most important differences are found in the way that *Diplodocus* used its teeth, jaws and neck to reach, and eat, a wide variety of plant foods.

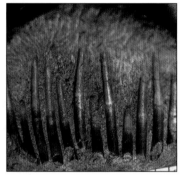

Above: *The tips of these teeth were worn away as they made contact with branches and stems during feeding.*

Below: Diplodocus *had a comblike arrangement of teeth at the front of the skull. The nostrils were in an odd position. They merged into a single opening in between the eyes rather than at the tip of the snout, as in most other animals.*

The teeth of *Diplodocus* are tall, slim and pencil-like. Rather than running for the entire length of the jaws, they are confined to the front of the mouth, where they form a comblike or rakelike arrangement. Such teeth are unsuitable for chewing tough plant food, and the wear on their tips suggests they cannot have been locked together to cut through leaves and stems.

These features have caused some debate among scientists. Some thought that the teeth could be used to pull bark from trees, others that the rakelike arrangement might have been useful in straining weeds or mussels from ponds and rivers. It is now known, however, that the teeth were used to rake leaves and fruits from the branches of trees and shrubs. They could also have been used to pluck ferns and horsetails from closer to ground level.

Up, down or sideways?

Until recently, it was thought that the long neck of *Diplodocus* meant that it ate leaves from the tops of trees and rarely ate food at lower levels. But computer modeling and detailed studies of the individual neck bones have shown that the neck could move in a number of different ways. It seems that most of the time—when *Diplodocus* was walking or standing at rest, for example—the neck was held horizontally. It could be lifted up to reach the treetops, but it is likely that *Diplodocus* could not have held the neck in this position for long periods of time. Special joints between the neck bones allowed the neck to be moved from side to side as well as up and down. This flexible neck would have allowed *Diplodocus* to feed on food from a variety of heights above ground level. Another clue that suggests *Diplodocus* sometimes fed on low-growing vegetation comes from its forelimbs. The front legs are very short for an animal of this kind, and as a result, the front of the body, including the head, is held closer to the ground.

Whiplash weapon?

Diplodocus might have used its tail as a powerful weapon against marauding meat-eaters, such as *Allosaurus*. The end of the tail is very thin and could be swung from side to side at great speed by massive muscles at the front end of the tail. This "whiplash" could be flicked at predators and would strike a severe blow. Some scientists have suggested that the tail moved so fast that it even sounded like a cracking whip.

FACT FILE

Genus: *Diplodocus*

Classification: Sauropoda; Diplodocoidea; Diplodocidae

Length: Up to 90 ft (27 m)

Weight: Up to 20 tons

Lived: Late Jurassic period, about 156-144 million years ago

Found in: Western U.S.A.

Left: *The massive hipbones provided an anchor for many of the powerful muscles that moved the hind legs. It has been suggested that* Diplodocus *could have reared up onto its hind legs from time to time in order to reach the succulent leaves at the tops of trees.*

Above: *Remains of* Diplodocus *have been found in the western United States, in Utah, Colorado and Wyoming.*

CRETACEOUS	70
	80
	90
	100
	110
	120
	150
JURASSIC	160
	170
	180
	190
	200
	210
TRIASSIC	220
	230
	240

Diplodocus

Reaching a length of about 90 feet (27 m), Diplodocus was one of the longest of all dinosaurs. The long neck would have enabled it to feed from the tops of very tall trees.

FACT FILE

Genus: *Aragosaurus*

Classification: Sauropoda;
Titanosauromorpha; Camarasauridae

Length: 60 ft (18 m)

Weight: Up to 15 tons

Lived: Early Cretaceous period, about
125-123 million years ago

Found in: Spain

Aragosaurus
Aragon lizard

Although dinosaur remains had been found in Spain before the discovery of *Aragosaurus*, the gigantic bones of this sauropod represented the first new species of dinosaur to be described from that country. It is also one of the very few sauropods that are known from the early Cretaceous period. Only a few fragmentary remains have been unearthed. But enough of the skeleton is preserved to show that *Aragosaurus* is closely related to the North American sauropod *Camarasaurus*.

Right: *A model of*
Aragosaurus *in a Spanish park gives a good idea of the size of this animal.*

Below: Aragosaurus *fossils are found in the region of Aragon, in Spain. Fossils of close relatives have been found as far away as the United States.*

Like *Camarasaurus, Aragosaurus* probably had a short, compact skull and a moderately long neck. The teeth were large and wide, and would have been useful for slicing through the leaves and branches of tall conifer trees. The forelimbs were only a little shorter than the hind limbs, and the tail was long and muscular.

Continental clues

Close relatives of *Aragosaurus* lived nearby in what is now Portugal, as well as in what are now the United States and eastern Africa. The discovery of these widely dispersed fossils from closely related dinosaurs has helped scientists to reconstruct the positions of the continents as they were many millions of years ago. As sauropods could not have swum across wide oceans, *Aragosaurus* and its relatives must have walked to the different areas of the earth in

which their fossilized remains have been found. If these animals could walk from the United States to Europe to Africa, these continents must have been connected back in the late Jurassic and early Cretaceous periods (see maps, page 25).

70
80
90
100
110
120
130
140
150
160
170
180
190
200
210
220
230
240

CRETACEOUS

JURASSIC

TRIASSIC

Patagosaurus

Patagonian lizard

FACT FILE

Genus: *Patagosaurus*

Classification: Sauropoda; Cetiosauridae

Length: Up to 60 ft (18 m)

Weight: Up to 16 tons

Lived: Middle Jurassic period, about 169-163 million years ago

Found in: Argentina

This is one of the earliest sauropods for which scientists have reasonably complete remains. *Patagosaurus* belonged to a group of sauropods known as the cetiosaurids, which also includes *Cetiosaurus* (whale lizard) from the middle Jurassic rocks of England. These two animals tell us almost all we know about sauropod biology and evolution during that period. They were primitive sauropods, lacking many of the features seen in their more advanced relatives, such as *Diplodocus* and *Brachiosaurus*.

Its neck, though quite short for a sauropod, was still considerably longer than that of any other group of dinosaurs, and would have enabled *Patagosaurus* to feed on leaves and shoots up to 16-20 feet (5-6 m) above ground level. A complete skull has yet to be found, but a few individual skull bones show that it was tall, but not very long, and that the jaws were lined with broad slicing teeth. Its nostrils were situated farther forward than in most other sauropods. The system of hollowed-out vertebrae and air sacs found in many advanced sauropod dinosaurs was poorly developed in *Patagosaurus* and *Cetiosaurus*. *Patagosaurus* shared its environment with the large predatory dinosaur *Piatnitzkysaurus*. Its large size probably helped the adult *Patagosaurus* to defend itself from attack, but its young would have been vulnerable to this expert hunter.

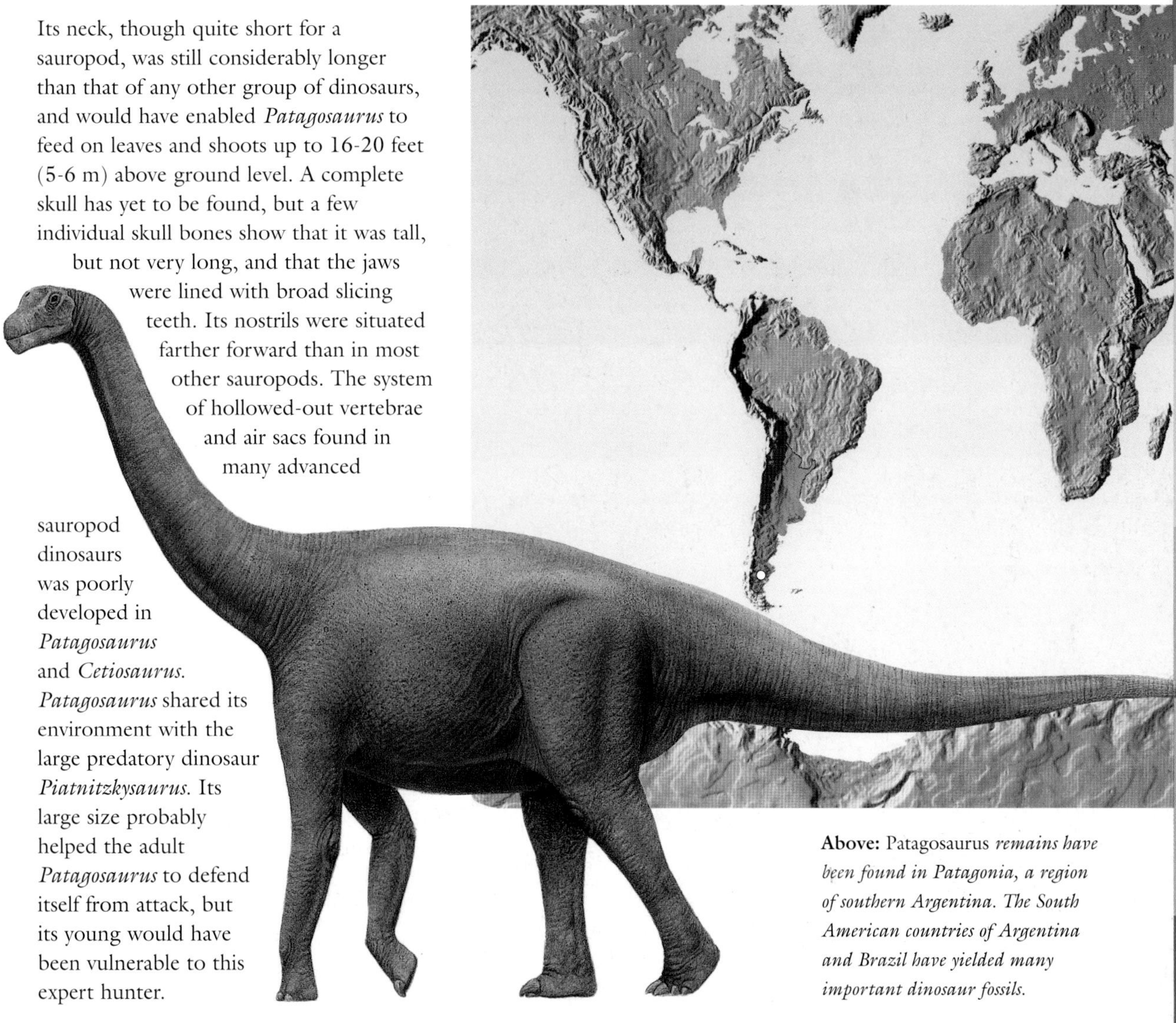

Above: Patagosaurus *remains have been found in Patagonia, a region of southern Argentina. The South American countries of Argentina and Brazil have yielded many important dinosaur fossils.*

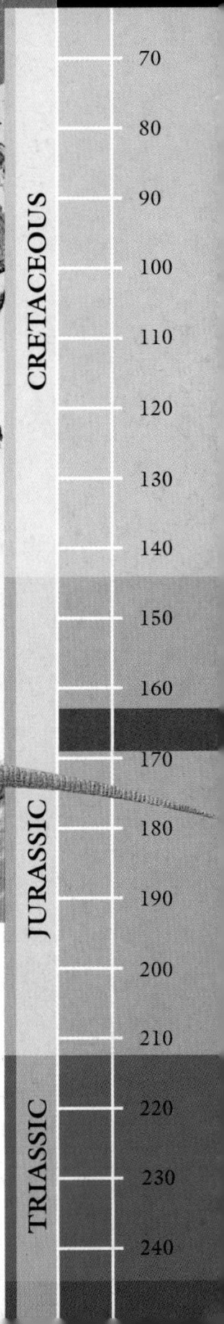

70
80
90
100
110
120
130
140
150
160
170
180
190
200
210
220
230
240

CRETACEOUS

JURASSIC

TRIASSIC

133

Saltasaurus

Salta lizard

This dinosaur, a four-legged plant-eater, might have been the largest armored animal of all time. The fossil bones of *Saltasaurus* were found in the remote Salta region of Argentina. *Saltasaurus* was not very big for a sauropod, being less than half the length of *Apatosaurus*. It was an extremely rare sauropod. It had a series of small lumpy bones on its back that served it well as a suit of armor, a feature seen in only a few other sauropod species.

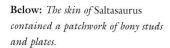

Below: *The skin of* Saltasaurus *contained a patchwork of bony studs and plates.*

Saltasaurus might have been rare, but it was a pretty typical sauropod dinosaur in most respects. As with all sauropods, it had a bulky body, an extremely long tail and a long neck. *Saltasaurus* belongs to a group of sauropods called the titanosaurids. It was one of the very last sauropods to exist. It lived during the last few million years of the Age of the Dinosaurs. Almost all of the sauropods from the late Cretaceous period are titanosaurids that were closely related to *Saltasaurus*.

The mysterious titanosaurids

The fossil remains of many titanosaurids are rather fragmentary, and this makes them difficult to study. Indeed, most titanosaurid species are known from only one or two partial skeletons, and no complete skull of any titanosaurid has ever been discovered. A few isolated skull bones tell us that the skulls of titanosaurids were short and compact, and a little like that of *Camarasaurus*. All titanosaurids had long, peg-shaped teeth, similar to those of *Diplodocus*. These were used to strip branches of their leaves and to nip off small fruits and pinecones. The necks of titanosaurids were rather short for sauropods, though they were still much longer than the necks of any other type of dinosaur. Their legs were also slightly shorter and much more thickly set than those of other sauropods, and their body

was slightly broader. Because of these features, *Saltasaurus* and other titanosaurids could not rear up on their hind legs to reach high into the trees like *Diplodocus*. But its long neck probably gave *Saltasaurus* a maximum reach of about 20 feet (6 m) above ground level—still pretty high.

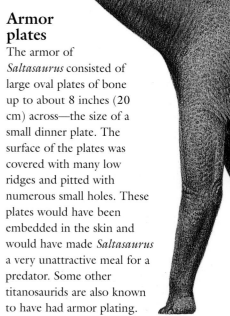

Armor plates

The armor of *Saltasaurus* consisted of large oval plates of bone up to about 8 inches (20 cm) across—the size of a small dinner plate. The surface of the plates was covered with many low ridges and pitted with numerous small holes. These plates would have been embedded in the skin and would have made *Saltasaurus* a very unattractive meal for a predator. Some other titanosaurids are also known to have had armor plating.

FACT FILE

Genus: *Saltasaurus*

Classification: Sauropoda;
    Titanosauromorpha; Titanosauridae

Length: Up to 40 ft (12 m)

Weight: 25 tons

Lived: Late Cretaceous period, about
    73-65 million years ago

Found in: Argentina

Left: *All sauropods were thought to lack armor until eight fragments of bony armor were discovered close to a skeleton of* Saltasaurus. *Initially, scientists thought the armor must belong to an ankylosaur, but detailed study showed that the fragments did indeed come from* Saltasaurus.

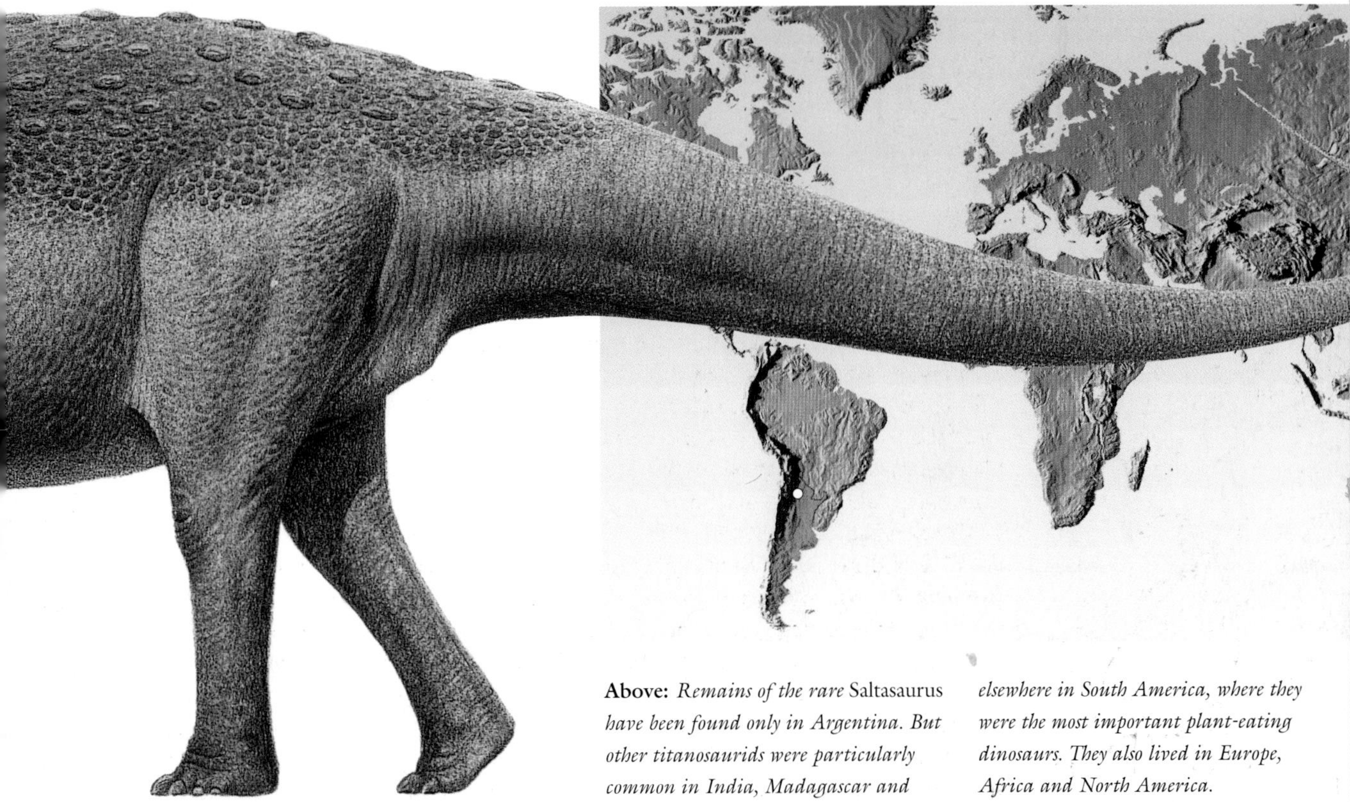

Above: *Remains of the rare* Saltasaurus *have been found only in Argentina. But other titanosaurids were particularly common in India, Madagascar and elsewhere in South America, where they were the most important plant-eating dinosaurs. They also lived in Europe, Africa and North America.*

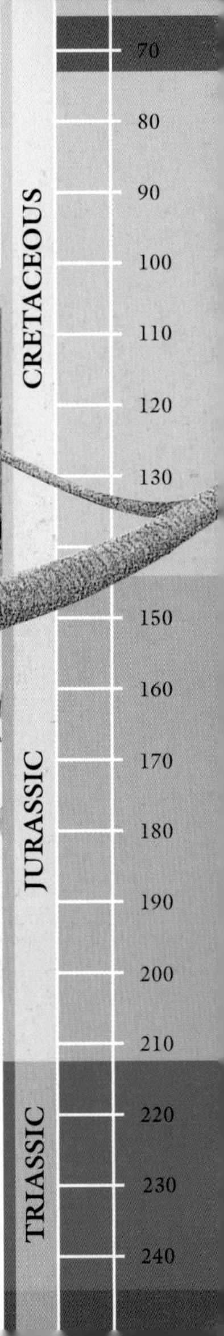

CRETACEOUS

JURASSIC

TRIASSIC

70
80
90
100
110
120
130
150
160
170
180
190
200
210
220
230
240

Coelophysis
Hollow form

During the late Triassic period, North America was a warm, dry place. Among the few giant conifers and low-lying ferns existed an early theropod called *Coelophysis*. This dinosaur was not the top predator of its time. That was a role reserved for creatures called phytosaurs and rauisuchids, both large reptiles and distant cousins of the dinosaurs. But speed and agility enabled *Coelophysis* to feed on a wide range of small animals, including fish and insects.

With long and slender hind limbs, *Coelophysis* was a fast runner. Its arms were fairly short, ending in three fingers tipped with deep, narrow claws. A fourth finger, lacking a claw, also remained, as well as a fifth, a tiny nubbin with no useful purpose. *Coelophysis* had many small, strongly curved, sharp teeth with serrated edges.

Cannibals?

Several hundred *Coelophysis* skeletons have been discovered, and these represent all stages of life. Inside the ribcage of two adult *Coelophysis* were found the bones of young *Coelophysis*. It was originally thought these were the skeletons of hatchlings that had emerged from their eggs inside the mother before birth. But the bones are too big and too well developed to be newborns. The only other conclusion is that these young *Coelophysis* were the victims of cannibalism—eaten by a member of their own species!

☐ Confirmed finds
☐ Possible finds

Above: *Most* Coelophysis *remains come from a place called Ghost Ranch in New Mexico. The animals preserved there appear to be the victims of a single catastrophic event.*

Dinosaur in space!

In a strange turn of events, *Coelophysis* was awarded the honor of being the first dinosaur in space. In 1998, a *Coelophysis* skull was taken aboard the Endeavor Space Shuttle on a mission to the Mir Space Station. It returned unharmed.

70
80
90
100
110
120
130
140
150
160
170
180
190
200
210
220
230
240

CRETACEOUS

JURASSIC

TRIASSIC

Ceratosaurus
Horned lizard

FACT FILE

Genus: *Ceratosaurus*

Classification: Theropoda; Ceratosauria

Length: 15-20 ft (4.5-6 m)

Weight: 0.5-1 ton

Lived: Late Jurassic period, about 156-144 million years ago

Found in: Utah and Colorado

This was a two-legged, meat-eating dinosaur from the late Jurassic period of North America. It is marked by a single small horn situated on the top of its snout, just behind the nostrils. Fossils of *Ceratosaurus* are sometimes found alongside those of another large theropod dinosaur, *Allosaurus*. But, although these two animals shared the same environment, *Ceratosaurus* was a much rarer inhabitant of this late Jurassic North American landscape.

It is unusual to find two large predatory animals in the same environment. Such a discovery suggests that each animal had a slightly different feeding strategy. Whereas *Allosaurus* could be up to 45 feet (14 m) in length, *Ceratosaurus* reached no more than 20 feet (6 m). So perhaps *Allosaurus* tackled larger prey, such as *Stegosaurus* and the sauropods *Diplodocus* and *Apatosaurus*. The abundance of *Allosaurus* fossils also suggests that this animal may have been a group hunter. In contrast, *Ceratosaurus* could prey upon small ornithopods and other smaller reptiles. *Ceratosaurus* fossils are rather rare, suggesting that it was a lone hunter.

Left: *The horn on its snout was too thin to have been used as a weapon, but probably helped* Ceratosaurus *in recognizing one another. A small crest rises in front of each eye.*

Not closely related

The body of *Ceratosaurus* was supported by large pillarlike hind limbs. Its forelimbs, although shorter, were robust and strong. They would have been useful tools during prey capture and feeding. The head is large, and balanced by a long, heavy tail. But the skull is not particularly strong. And the neck is quite short and stout for a meat-eating theropod. Although the skeletons of *Ceratosaurus* and *Allosaurus* look quite similar, *Ceratosaurus* has four fingers on its hand, as opposed to the three fingers of *Allosaurus*. This feature, among others, shows that these two dinosaurs are not particularly closely related.

Above: Ceratosaurus *has been found in several spectacular fossil assemblages, such as the Cleveland Lloyd Quarry in Utah, and at several other localities in Colorado.*

CRETACEOUS	70
	80
	90
	100
	110
	120
	130
	140
	150
JURASSIC	160
	170
	180
	190
	200
	210
TRIASSIC	220
	230
	240

Dilophosaurus
Two-crested reptile

This is one of the earliest known, large meat-eating dinosaurs. *Dilophosaurus* fossils have been recovered from early Jurassic rocks in the deserts of northern Arizona. It was the largest predatory animal in North America at this time and probably fed upon small plant-eating dinosaurs such as the ornithischian *Scutellosaurus* and the prosauropod *Ammosaurus*. Its skull is notable for two curious crests that extend upward from the nostrils and run back along the top of the head.

The skull of *Dilophosaurus* is so unusual that when the skeleton of this animal was first discovered the crests were not recognized as such. They were explained away as a result of crushing suffered during fossilization. Only later, when a better-preserved skull was unearthed, were these strange features appreciated.

The crests are paired, and extend away from each other and from the head in a V-shaped pattern, leaving a large gap between them. They are made from bone, but are too thin to offer any protection for the skull. So it is likely that they were used for signaling to other *Dilophosaurus*. Another purpose might have been for attracting mates. A discovery of two *Dilophosaurus* skeletons in the same place suggests that these animals might, at least for some of their time, have lived in groups.

A formidable predator

Dilophosaurus might have participated in group hunting, but it had many features that would have enabled it to hunt alone. Long, powerful hind limbs indicate the ability to run fast. The toes are tipped by long claws to grip the ground and to pin down unfortunate prey. The first finger on the hand could function like a thumb, giving *Dilophosaurus* a grasping hand useful for capturing and holding on to prey. And the jaws were lined with large, bladelike teeth.

Chinese cousin?

Another dinosaur, very similar to *Dilophosaurus*, has been found in China, in rocks dating from the early Jurassic period. This animal may actually be another species of *Dilophosaurus*. Indeed, the skull has the same paired crests running along the top surface. On the other hand, there are certain features that distinguish this animal from its American relative. The two dinosaurs differ in the number and shape of teeth, and in the sizes, shapes and positions of the various holes in the skull that housed the jaw muscles and glands. And similar skull crests have now been identified in other theropod dinosaurs that were not so closely related to *Dilophosaurus*. So scientists are still debating whether this Chinese animal is *Dilophosaurus*.

Below: *The characteristic crests of* Dilophosaurus *extend along the top of the skull. The skull is lightly constructed, and the tip of the snout is flexibly connected to the rest of the upper jaw. The teeth at the front of the snout were probably used for plucking and tearing at flesh rather than hard biting, a task that was reserved for the stronger teeth farther back in the jaws.*

FACT FILE

Genus: *Dilophosaurus*

Classification: Theropoda; Ceratosauria;

Length: 20-23 ft (6-7 m)

Weight: 660-990 lb (300-450 kg)

Lived: Early Jurassic period, about 206-194 million years ago

Found in: U.S.A. (Arizona) and possibly southern China

Left: *As in many other meat-eating dinosaurs, the skull of* Dilophosaurus *is large relative to the size of the body. Its neck is unusually long, but is stabilized by muscles connecting to the back and the ribs. Each hand has four fingers, unlike the hands of many later theropods, which had three fingers or fewer. This feature places* Dilophosaurus *in a group of dinosaurs called ceratosaurs.*

□ Confirmed finds
◌ Possible finds

Above: Dilophosaurus *is known from the western United States and possibly from southern China.*

139

CRETACEOUS

JURASSIC

TRIASSIC

70
80
90
100
110
120
130
140
150
160
170
180
190
200
210
220
230
240

Carnotaurus
Meat-eating bull

During the Jurassic period, a large ocean separated the northern and southern continents of the world. Dinosaurs at different ends of the earth began to evolve into a number of different forms. At the end of the Jurassic period, about 144 million years ago, South America became separated from the rest of the southern continents. This isolation resulted in the evolution of special types of South American dinosaurs, including the meat-eating *Carnotaurus.*

Below: Carnotaurus *had four fingers on each hand whereas most other theropods had three. From the shapes of the arm bones, it appears that the palm faced upward, instead of the usual downward position. The reason for this is unknown.*

Below: *The shape of the* Carnotaurus *skull is different from that of most other meat-eating theropods. The snout is short, yet the skull is much taller. In contrast, the lower jaw is shallow and hinged half-way down to allow the front part of the jaws to move more than the back. The horns project outward and upward above the eye sockets.*

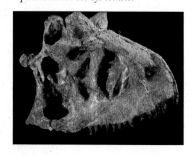

Carnotaurus shares some characteristics with dinosaurs from the Northern Hemisphere, such as the sharp, narrow curved teeth seen in all other meat-eating theropods. It has very short arm bones, similar to those of the tyrannosaurs from North America and Asia. In contrast, other features, such as the horns, are unique to *Carnotaurus.*

The horns are made from bone and extend upward and outward from the rear corners of the skull. Other large theropods such as *Allosaurus* can have bony prominences over the eyes, but not as large as in *Carnotaurus.* The horns might have been used for display. But, as so few *Carnotaurus* skeletons have been discovered, we do not know whether only the males had horns or whether females also had them.

Hunting ability

The snout of *Carnotaurus* is very narrow, but beneath the horns the skull gets much wider, with eyes facing forward slightly. As a result, *Carnotaurus* might have had binocular vision, in which the fields of vision of the left and right eye are able to cross. This is also a feature of human eyesight, and enables an animal to estimate distances accurately. And its agile build suggests that *Carnotaurus* could chase down prey.

Small prey

But what did *Carnotaurus* eat? Most dinosaurs with short arms, such as the tyrannosaurs, have very strong, enlarged heads that served as the main killing machine. But, because of its shape and flexibility, the skull of *Carnotaurus* was quite weak. It could have got twisted and bent, particularly in struggles with large animals. This suggests that *Carnotaurus* did not often attack animals of the same size or larger than itself, as its skull could not withstand such forces. Instead, it might have preyed upon smaller, more agile animals, using its specialist vision and bursts of high-speed running to catch them.

FACT FILE

Genus: *Carnotaurus*

Classification: Theropoda; Ceratosauria; Abelisauridae

Length: 25 ft (7.5 m)

Weight: Up to 1 ton

Lived: Mid-Cretaceous period, about 113–91 million years ago

Found in: Argentina

Left: Carnotaurus *has an impressive skeleton. Note the very large breastbones situated at the front of the chest.*

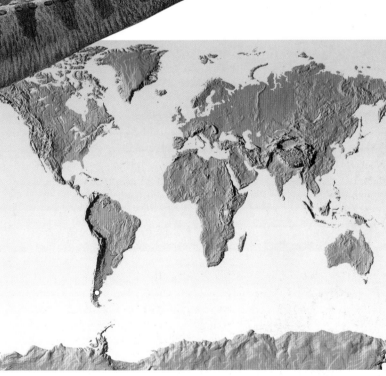

Above: *So far,* Carnotaurus *has been discovered only in the South American continent, in a region called Patagonia, in Argentina.*

CRETACEOUS

70
80
90
100
110
120
130
140

JURASSIC

150
160
170
180
190
200
210

TRIASSIC

220
230
240

141

Allosaurus
Strange lizard

Allosaurus was the top predatory dinosaur of the late Jurassic period in North America. It is one of the most scientifically important of all theropod dinosaurs because experts know much more about its anatomy, appearance and lifestyle than any other large meat-eating dinosaur.

Allosaurus is best known from finds in the western United States. It was named by Othniel Marsh in 1877 on the basis of an incomplete skeleton from Colorado. Additional remains of *Allosaurus* have been discovered in South Dakota, Utah, Montana, Wyoming and New Mexico. Many complete skeletons, several complete skulls and hundreds of individual bones are now known. One of the most spectacular finds was made at a site in Utah, where hundreds of *Allosaurus* bones were found mixed with the bones of the sauropods *Camarasaurus* and *Apatosaurus*.

Finding and eating food

Like almost all other theropods, *Allosaurus* was a flesh-eater. The commonest North American dinosaurs at this time were the gigantic plant-eating sauropods (see pages 120-131). *Allosaurus* was not big enough to threaten adult sauropods, but could probably prey upon those that were young, sick or very old. The large size of *Allosaurus* suggests that it was not a particularly fast runner, but speed was not necessary to hunt sauropods, as they were very slow-moving animals. Smaller plant-eating dinosaurs, such as *Camptosaurus* and *Stegosaurus,* would have formed an important part of an *Allosaurus* diet, and small theropods, lizards and mammals might also have been taken. As *Allosaurus* could not outrun any of these creatures, it probably lay in ambush, waiting for unsuspecting prey to pass by. *Allosaurus* might also have eaten the carcasses of dead animals.

Unusual feature

One of the most distinctive features of *Allosaurus* is the presence of a ridge of bone, or crest, just in front of each eye. In some skulls, these crests are large and pointed, whereas in others they are smaller and rounded. The function of the crests is not known, but some experts have suggested that the differences in crest size and shape might reflect the different sexes of the animals. An *Allosaurus* with large pointed crests might have been male, one with smaller crests female, or vice versa. Alternatively, the crests might have had a special function, such as housing glands near to the eye.

Above: *The backward curvature of the teeth allowed* Allosaurus *to dig them into the flesh of its prey and hold it firmly, even when the victim was trying to escape. Tiny serrations on the teeth, like those along the side of a steak knife, helped it cut through even the toughest hide.*

Above: *The three-fingered hands were capable of gripping and holding tightly on to any animal unfortunate enough to get too close. Each finger was tipped with a sharp, curved claw.*

FACT FILE

Genus: *Allosaurus*

Classification: Theropoda; Tetanurae; Allosauridae

Length: Up to 45 ft (14 m)

Weight: Up to 3.6 tons

Lived: Late Jurassic period, about 156-144 million years ago

Found in: Western U.S.A. and Portugal and possibly Australia

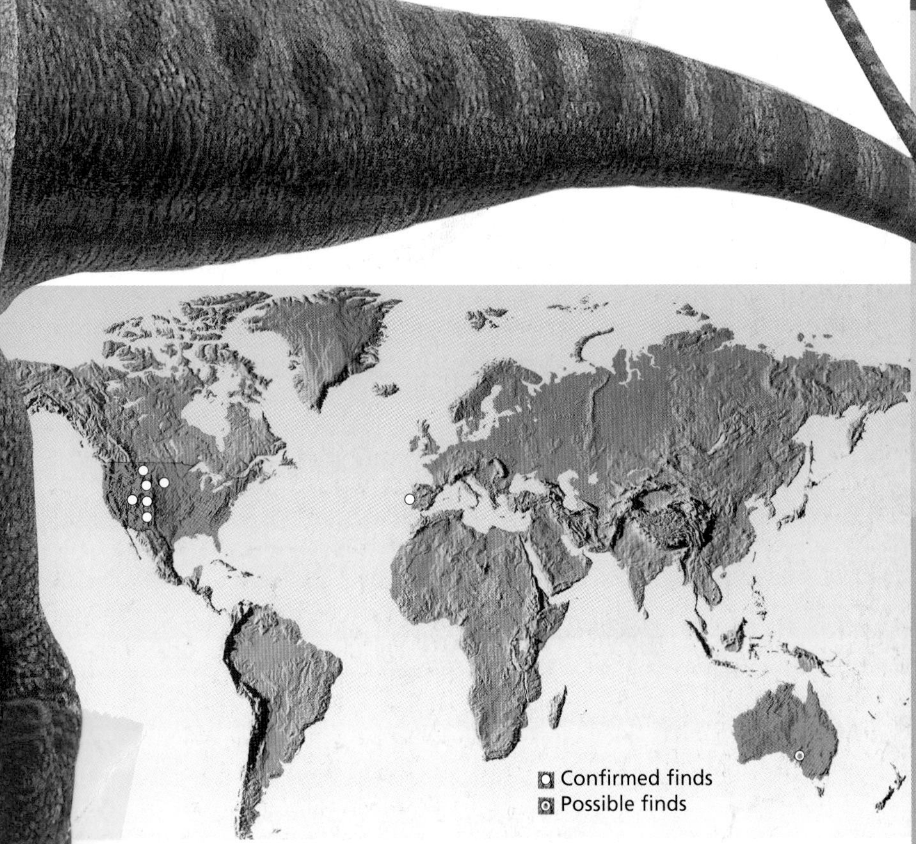

Above: *The skull of* Allosaurus *had powerful jaws that were ideally suited to slicing through flesh. Its neck was also very strong, and helped it hold on to violently struggling prey. Note the pointed crests situated just in front of the eye sockets.*

▢ Confirmed finds
◎ Possible finds

Above: *Although most remains of* Allosaurus *have been found in the United States, recent discoveries from late Jurassic rocks in Portugal suggest that it also lived in Europe, which was situated close to North America at the* time. *More controversially,* Allosaurus *has also been identified from fossils of the early Cretaceous period in Australia, although this discovery has yet to be confirmed.*

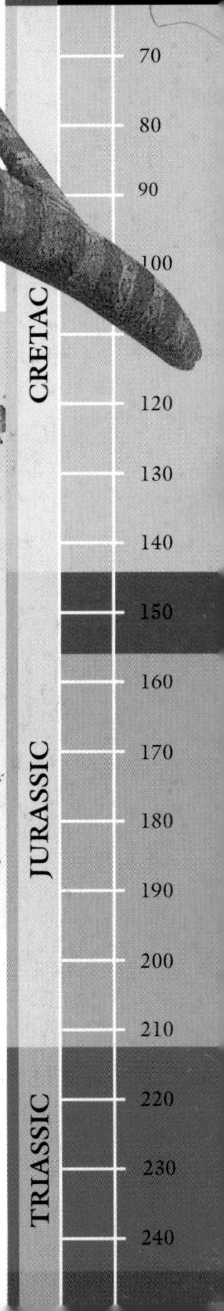

CRETAC

JURASSIC

TRIASSIC

70
80
90
100
120
130
140
150
160
170
180
190
200
210
220
230
240

Baryonyx
Heavy claw

Baryonyx was discovered in 1983 in a quarry in southern England. It was a surprising and important find, as paleontologists had collected fossils from these rocks for many years but had not found any evidence of this dinosaur before. In addition, *Baryonyx* is very different in shape from most other meat-eating dinosaurs and had a very different diet.

The skull of *Baryonyx* is very long, low and narrow. The nostrils, instead of being at the tip of the skull as they are in most other theropods, are placed about 4 inches (10 cm) back along the snout. The teeth are wider, with finer serrations, than the bladelike "steak knife" teeth of other meat-eaters, making them more efficient stabbers than slashers. At the ends of the jaws, the teeth are larger in size and stand out from the bone in a circular "rosette" pattern. These types of skull adaptations can be seen in the modern fish-eating crocodilian, the gavial of southern Asia, and strongly suggest that *Baryonyx* lived on a diet of fish.

as 10 feet (3 m) in length, inhabited these waters. The partly digested remains of some of these fish, including scales and teeth, were found preserved in the stomach region of *Baryonyx* as the fossil was excavated.

Another interpretation?
Some features of the hand and skull suggest that *Baryonyx* was also a scavenger—that is, it fed on dead animals. Its strong arms and claws might have been used to rip open carcasses. And the position of its nostrils would have enabled it to feed with its snout deep inside a carcass, while still being able to breathe. Remains of a young *Iguanodon* were also found close to the belly region of *Baryonyx,* supporting the idea that it ate not only fish but other animals too.

Feeding on fish
The teeth of *Baryonyx* could pierce soft flesh, and their rosette structure helped it grip and hold slippery fish. As its nostrils were placed farther back, it could hold its snout in water and breathe at the same time. The arms are very strong and end in large claws used to hook fish out of the water. Complete with horny sheath, the biggest claw is nearly 1 foot (0.3 m) long.

Baryonyx lived during a time when the south of what is now England enjoyed a subtropical climate. It lived on a large river delta, or floodplain, very close to the sea. Large fish, some of which reached as much

Above: *The low, narrow shape of the skull allowed it to move quickly through water with little resistance. There are twice the number of teeth in the lower jaw than there are in the upper jaw. This enabled* Baryonyx *to gain a firm grip on its fishy prey. On the other hand,* Baryonyx *was not well adapted for attacking and killing large land-living animals, because its long skull would have been prone to bending.*

146

Below: Baryonyx *was a large animal, and the fish it ate were probably quite large too. Note the stout, short arm bones. Instead of using its jaws,* Baryonyx *probably used its powerful claws to tear prey items into chunks small enough to eat comfortably.*

FACT FILE

Genus: *Baryonyx*

Classification: Theropoda; Spinosauroidea; Spinosauridae

Length: 33 ft (10 m)

Weight: 1.5-2 tons

Lived: Early Cretaceous period, about 125-119 million years ago

Found in: Southeast England and Spain

Above: *Although close relatives have been found in northern Africa and* South America, Baryonyx *is known only from southern England and Spain.*

CRETACEOUS
JURASSIC
TRIASSIC

70
80
90
100
110
120
130
140
150
160
170
180
190
200
210
220
230
240

Baryonyx

Baryonyx was one of the few dinosaurs that lived on a diet of fish. It plucked fish from the water using its sharp claws and long snout.

Carcharodontosaurus
Shark-toothed lizard

Carcharodontosaurus

FACT FILE

Genus: *Carcharodontosaurus*

Classification: Theropoda; Tetanurae; Allosauridae

Length: 25-45 ft (8-14 m)

Weight: 7-8 tons

Lived: Mid-Cretaceous period, about 113-97 million years ago

Found in: Northern Africa

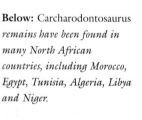

Below: Carcharodontosaurus *remains have been found in many North African countries, including Morocco, Egypt, Tunisia, Algeria, Libya and Niger.*

The theropod dinosaur *Carcharodontosaurus* was unlucky enough to suffer two extinctions. After its natural demise sometime in the late Cretaceous period, some of its fossil remains were destroyed during a bombing raid on a German museum in World War II. Luckily, recent expeditions to northern Africa have uncovered exciting new *Carcharodontosaurus* material. These latest discoveries revealed that it was one of the largest land-based predators ever to walk the earth.

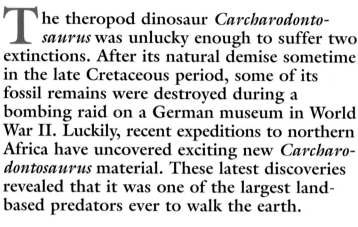

Below: *The enormous skull of* Carcharodontosaurus *dwarfs that of a human. It measured 5 feet (1.6 m) across, longer even than the skull of* Tyrannosaurus.

Where the Sahara now stretches across northern Africa, a lush, green environment once existed during late Cretaceous times. *Carcharodontosaurus* could be found along the banks of large rivers, searching the land for its next meal. Its skull is even longer than that of the huge North American theropod *Tyrannosaurus rex*. Another enormous theropod, *Giganotosaurus* from South America, was similar in size to *Carcharodontosaurus*. These two animals are closely related, and it seems that large body size evolved in a common ancestor. But large body size evolved independently in the more distantly related *Tyrannosaurus*. All of these animals were the top predators in their environments, able to catch the largest prey and to feast on the kills of others. They used their sheer size to scare away all other competitors for food.

Recognizing remains
Thanks to the unique shape of its teeth, the remains of *Carcharodontosaurus* can easily be recognized, even when there are only fragments of skeleton. The telltale signs are little grooves running from the characteristic theropod serrations across the surface of the tooth. They were created from wrinkles in the tooth enamel. These wrinkles sometimes stretch across the whole tooth.

Compsognathus

Elegant jaw

First discovered in Germany during the 1850s, *Compsognathus* is one of the smallest dinosaurs known. From head to tail it measured no more than 3 feet (1 m), and its bones were small and fragile. Luckily for scientists, *Compsognathus* lived close to the shore of a calm lake. After death, the animal's body sank to the bottom of the lake, and the calm waters ensured that the bones were not broken up before the process of fossilization could begin.

Compsognathus was a bipedal animal. Long, slender hind legs indicate it was built for speed. Its bones were hollow and its tail long and flexible. Its arms were also elongated and slender, and the hand had three fingers, but the third finger was reduced to nothing more than a stump. *Compsognathus* could have used its hands as effective hooks or raking tools when capturing prey.

Small prey

Features of its skull give clues to the diet of *Compsognathus*. The teeth are sharp and pointed, but the lower jaws and the skull are quite slender and not particularly strong. Small vertebrates, such as lizards and mammals, as well as insects would have been the first choices on the menu. The skeleton of a small lizard is preserved within the body cavity of the German specimen of *Compsognathus*. Its presence suggests that *Compsognathus* was an agile, fast-moving predator, capable of pinpointing and dispatching even small, darting prey such as lizards.

Above: Compsognathus *had hollow limb bones, a light skull and a long thin tail extending straight out behind it.*

FACT FILE

Genus: *Compsognathus*

Classification: Theropoda; Coelurosauria; Compsognathidae

Length: 2-3 ft (0.6-1 m)

Weight: 5 lb (2.5 kg)

Lived: Late Jurassic period, about 156-150 million years ago

Found in: Bavaria (Germany) and southern France

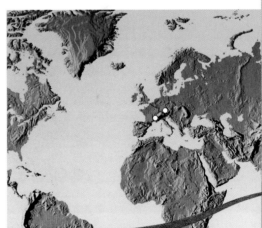

Above: *Two* Compsognathus *skeletons are known—from Bavaria, in Germany, and from southern France. The French specimen was discovered in 1972.*

CRETACEOUS

70
80
90
100
110
120
130
140
150
160

JURASSIC

170
180
190
200
210

TRIASSIC

220
230
240

151

Sinosauropteryx
Chinese lizard wing

Above: *This beautifully preserved skeleton of* Sinosauropteryx *provides a great deal of detailed information. In addition to the downlike covering, it also shows other rarely fossilized features, such as stomach contents.*

Above: *This is a close-up of some of the downlike structures that are preserved with the skeleton of* Sinosauropteryx. *Note the large number of long, hairlike filaments.*

Recent discoveries in China are adding greatly to our knowledge of theropod dinosaurs and early birds. *Sinosauropteryx* was one of the first of these spectacular new animals to come to light. The *Sinosauropteryx* fossils preserve the remains of small, hairlike features that appear to be growing from out of the skin of the animal. These features are probably the remains of a fluffy coating made up of small, downy structures.

Overwhelming evidence suggests that birds are the direct descendants of small, meat-eating dinosaurs, and that, among the theropods, animals such as *Deinonychus* and *Velociraptor* are the closest relatives of birds. This view is based on the large number of detailed similarities found in the skeletons of birds and of dinosaurs and which are not found in the skeletons of any other animals. For example, birds and some theropod dinosaurs have three-fingered hands with very flexible wrist joints. Both groups also have many holes in their vertebrae that housed air-filled sacs, which were parts of the lungs. The discovery of *Sinosauropteryx* in 1996 showed that dinosaurs and birds shared yet another important feature—a downy covering.

Feathers
The downy structures on the skin of *Sinosauropteryx* are not true flight feathers. They are simple structures from which feathers might have evolved. True flight feathers are complicated structures that have a thick central rib, called a quill, which attaches the feather to the animal. Attached to the quill are the vanes, which make up most of the body of the feather. Each vane is made up of many smaller filaments, called barbs, which are closely packed together. The downy structures of *Sinosauropteryx* do not have barbs or vanes, but are simple, almost hairlike, structures.

But the structures in *Sinosauropteryx* share some similarities with a type of feather that is found on the bodies of living birds. These feathers, called down feathers, are not involved in flying but help to keep the birds warm. Baby birds lack flight feathers but are covered in a layer of fluffy down. When the arrangement of these down feathers is compared with the way in which the downlike structures of *Sinosauropteryx* are placed on its body, many similarities can be seen between the two. This evidence suggests that the downy

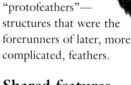

structures of *Sinosauropteryx* are "protofeathers"— structures that were the forerunners of later, more complicated, feathers.

Shared features
Sinosauropteryx shares many features with the small theropod *Compsognathus*, and it seems they were very closely related. These two animals are not as closely related to birds as some other theropods, such as *Velociraptor*. So the presence of fine down on the skin of *Sinosauropteryx* shows that featherlike structures evolved in theropod dinosaurs well before the origin of birds. It also suggests that *Compsognathus* might have had a downy covering, too.

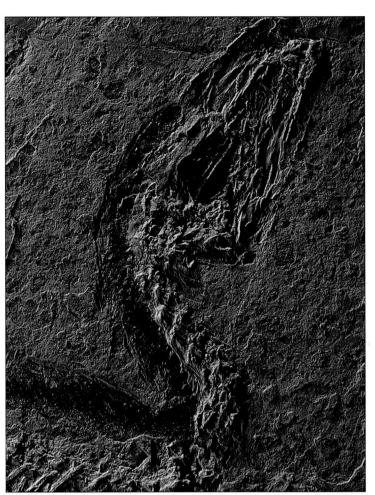

FACT FILE

Genus: *Sinosauropteryx*

Classification: Theropoda; Coelurosauria;
Compsognathidae

Length: Up to 50 in (1.25 m)

Weight: 22 lb (10 kg)

Lived: Early Cretaceous period, about
125-119 million years ago

Found in: Northeastern China

Left: *The narrow snout of*
Sinosauropteryx *is lined with many
small, sharp teeth, suggesting that it
was a meat-eater. Note the thick layer
of down that covers the head and neck.*

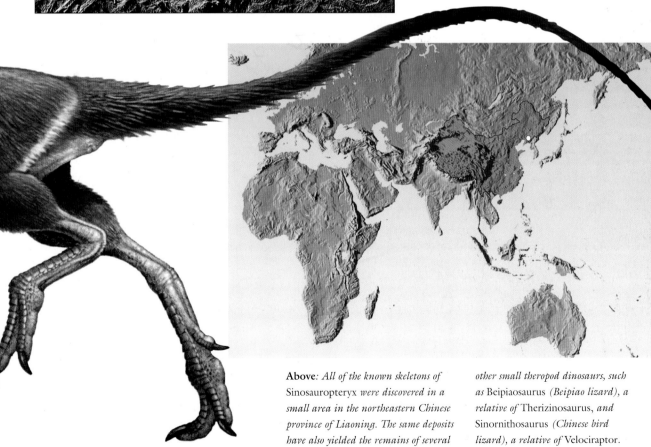

Above: *All of the known skeletons of*
Sinosauropteryx *were discovered in a
small area in the northeastern Chinese
province of Liaoning. The same deposits
have also yielded the remains of several* other small theropod dinosaurs, such
as Beipiaosaurus (Beipiao lizard), a
relative of *Therizinosaurus, and*
Sinornithosaurus (Chinese bird
lizard), a relative of *Velociraptor.*

CRETACEOUS

JURASSIC

TRIASSIC

70
80
90
100
110
120
130
140
150
160
170
180
190
200
210
220
230
240

Tyrannosaurus
Tyrant lizard

When the first reasonably complete skeleton of *Tyrannosaurus* was uncovered in 1902, scientists realized they had discovered one of the most important and one of the most fearsome dinosaurs yet known. Its huge head was over 5 feet (1.5 m) in length, and its large teeth were razor-sharp conical spikes up to 8 inches (20 cm) long. For nearly a hundred years, we regarded *Tyrannosaurus* as the largest meat-eating animal ever known. But carnivorous dinosaurs discovered recently in South America and Africa have proved to be even larger.

Above: *The skull of* Tyrannosaurus *is quite flexible in places. Mobile connections between some of the bones may have helped to absorb the shocks created during impact into prey.*

Above: *Large, heavy legs ended in three broadly spaced toes. These were tipped by sharp claws that would have served to hold down prey.*

In contrast to the relatively light skull of animals such as *Allosaurus,* the skull of *Tyrannosaurus* is made of thick, heavy bone. The back of the head is very wide, providing space for large jaw-closing muscles. Most of the teeth are much wider than those of other meat-eaters and are serrated along the front and back edges. But teeth at the front of the snout are narrower.

Bite marks

Thanks to the distinctive nature of the teeth, paleontologists have been able to identify *Tyrannosaurus* bite marks on a number of fossil bones that belong to herbivorous dinosaurs. *Tyrannosaurus* teeth functioned less like the slashing weapons of *Allosaurus* and more like large spikes, used to pierce and grip food. Powerful neck muscles aided the ripping away of large chunks of meat from its prey. Bones of the herbivorous dinosaur *Edmontosaurus* have been found covered in deep gashes created during this 'puncture and pull" method of feeding. The narrow front teeth were probably used to reach into awkward gaps and tug out pieces of flesh.

Bone crusher?

Other evidence tells us that *Tyrannosaurus* was able to crush and break bone. A *Triceratops* hipbone, covered in *Tyrannosaurus* bite marks, has had a large chunk removed—it was probably bitten away. And fossilized *Tyrannosaurus* dung was found to be full of the broken bones of a young *Edmontosaurus.* A recent study has shown that the bite of *Tyrannosaurus* was three times as powerful as the bite of a lion.

Scavenging

Aided by its keen sense of smell, *Tyrannosaurus* also perhaps scavenged from the bones of animals that were already dead. Being the largest predator of its time, it was able to scare away other feeding animals and dine on its stolen prey in peace, unless disturbed by another, larger *Tyrannosaurus.*

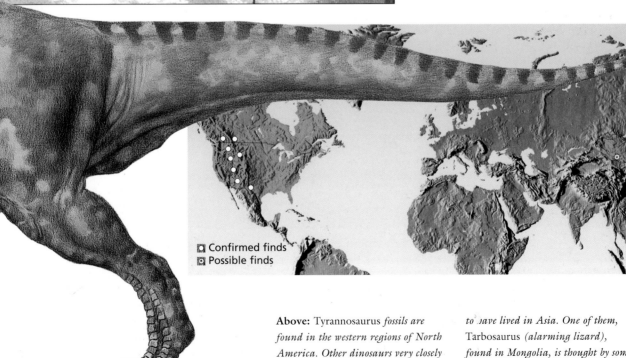

FACT FILE

Genus: *Tyrannosaurus*

Classification: Theropoda; Coelurosauria; Tyrannosauridae

Length: 33–46 feet (10–14 m)

Weight: 4.5–7 tons

Lived: Late Cretaceous period, about 68–65 million years ago

Found in: Canada, U.S.A. and possibly Asia

Left: *With its long legs and powerful leg muscles,* Tyrannosaurus *enjoyed swift acceleration and probably ambushed its prey. Its forearms are tiny and end in only two fingers. Its hands could not even reach its mouth, yet surprisingly the arms were quite powerful.*

☐ Confirmed finds
◉ Possible finds

Above: Tyrannosaurus *fossils are found in the western regions of North America. Other dinosaurs very closely related to* Tyrannosaurus *are known* to have lived in Asia. One of them, Tarbosaurus *(alarming lizard), found in Mongolia, is thought by some to be a species of* Tyrannosaurus.

CRETACEOUS

70
80
90
100
110
120
130
140
150
160
170
180
190
200
210
220
230
240

JURASSIC

TRIASSIC

Tyrannosaurus

Like many other large meat-eating animals, Tyrannosaurus probably spent most of its time hunting alone. But recent evidence suggests that it might also have hunted in packs.

Oviraptor
Egg thief

Around 80 million years ago, the area now smothered by the sands and stony wastes of Mongolia's desert, the Gobi, was home to a large number of dinosaurs and mammals. Abundant in this environment were the hornless *Protoceratops*, the meat-eating *Velociraptor* and several types of ankylosaurs. Skeletons were also discovered of a very unusual dinosaur—*Oviraptor*, a small theropod with a short domed skull, a toothless beak and a bizarre head crest.

The crest was probably covered by a horny sheath, as is a similar-looking crest in a living bird, the cassowary (see page 35). Cassowaries move quickly on land, and the crest helps them pass through dense undergrowth by pushing leaves and branches aside as they run. It has been suggested that the crest of *Oviraptor* might have functioned in a similar fashion. But the Mongolian environment was quite arid, and there may not have been much dense undergrowth. It is possible that the crest functioned as a display and recognition structure instead.

Oviraptor described

The skull of *Oviraptor* is very unusual. It is full of openings and in some places it is composed of only very thin struts of bone. The snout is very short, the skull is deep and there are no teeth in the jaws. Instead, the roof and the floor of the mouth are expanded to provide a wide bony surface. When the animal was alive, this area would have been covered by a wide horny beak with sharp edges. The single crest rises from above the nostrils and stretches backward to a point just in front of the eye sockets. It is also full of openings and air chambers.

    Oviraptor possessed a wishbone, or furcula, that is very similar to the structure found in modern birds. Its arms are long and thin, and a crescent-shaped bone in the wrist permitted twisting of the hand. The first finger is much shorter than the other two, yet each finger terminated in a large, narrow claw. The hind limbs are long

and slender and the tail is short. These features suggest that *Oviraptor* was agile and fast-moving.

The discovery of *Oviraptor*

In the early 1920s, a party of researchers from the American Museum of Natural History in New York, set off on an expedition to Mongolia with the aim of finding fossils of the earliest human beings. They did not discover any human fossils, but they did uncover a wealth of dinosaur and small mammal fossils. *Protoceratops* fossils were very abundant, as were nests full of dinosaur eggs, which were assumed to belong to *Protoceratops*. Found on top of one of these nests was the partial skeleton and skull of a unique new theropod, apparently fossilized in the act of feasting on *Protoceratops* eggs. This animal was named *Oviraptor philoceratops*, meaning "ceratopsian-loving egg thief." Joint Polish-Mongolian and Soviet-Mongolian expeditions in the 1970s discovered more *Oviraptor* material, providing scientists with further information about the skeleton and appearance of this dinosaur.
(continued on page 160)

Below: *A short, high snout with a deep curved jaw, a wide horny beak and large spaces for bulging jaw muscles all suggest that* Oviraptor *had a powerful bite.* Oviraptor *might have eaten small mammals and lizards that it would have crushed in its beak, although some scientists have suggested that it fed upon shellfish or plants.*

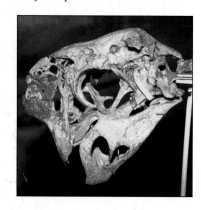

FACT FILE

Genus: *Oviraptor*

Classification: Theropoda; Coelurosauria; Oviraptorosauria

Length: 5-8 feet (1.5-2.5 m)

Weight: About 55-77 lb (25-35 kg)

Lived: Late Cretaceous period, about 80-73 million years ago

Found in: The Gobi region of Mongolia and China

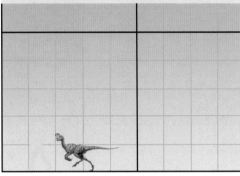

Left: *The open nature of the skull can be seen in this drawing. The enlarged eye socket suggests that* Oviraptor *had large eyes and keen vision. The elongated nostrils extend backward into the crest, which itself is full of openings. These holes were probably filled with air pockets, to lighten the skull.*

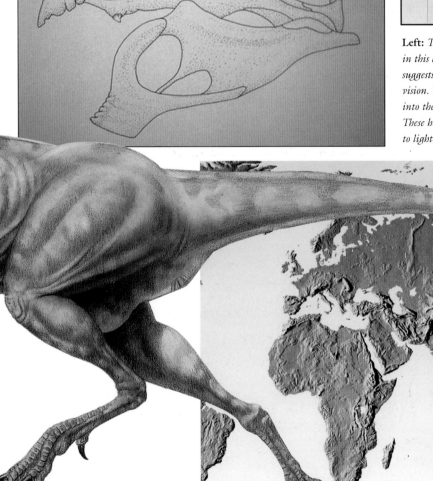

Above: *The remains of* Oviraptor *have been found in the Gobi region of eastern Asia.*

159

CRETACEOUS
70
80
90
100
110
120
130
140
150

JURASSIC
160
170
180
190
200
210

TRIASSIC
220
230
240

Oviraptor reanalyzed

In 1993, a baby *Oviraptor* was found within a fossilized egg. The egg was part of a nest that had originally been thought to belong to *Protoceratops,* but the baby *Oviraptor* proved otherwise. The *Oviraptors* found on top of the nests were not stealing eggs, as had been thought originally, but were brooding them. It appears that the mother *Oviraptor* had perished on top of the nest while protecting her eggs during a sudden slumping of sand dunes.

Was *Oviraptor* feathered?

The types of rocks in which *Oviraptor* skeletons are found very rarely preserve soft tissues. But it is possible that *Oviraptor* had some kind of fuzzy or feathery covering over its body, as other closely related theropods are known to have these features. Feathers, particularly along the arms, might have helped in incubation or in shading the eggs from the harsh midday sun.

Above: *The discovery of these eggs and nests, made by members of the Central Asiatic Expeditions from the American Museum of Natural History in the 1920s, was the first real evidence that dinosaurs laid eggs.*

Oviraptor sat on top of its nest and brooded its eggs like a modern bird, with its arms bent backward on either side in order to envelop and protect the eggs.

Caudipteryx
Winged tail

The discovery of two beautifully preserved specimens of *Caudipteryx* caused much excitement among scientists. Detailed study of these skeletons showed that *Caudipteryx* was a theropod dinosaur, but one that possessed true feathers. Until this discovery, it was thought that true feathers were found only in birds. Several other theropod dinosaurs, such as *Sinornithosaurus*, are now known to have possessed true feathers, too.

The feathers of *Caudipteryx* share many similarities with the feathers of living birds. Each of the feathers has vanes, made up of many individual barbs, and a quill. Such feathers are much more complex than the hairlike down seen in *Sinosauropteryx*. But although the feathers of *Caudipteryx* are very birdlike, it is not closely related to the birds.

Various features of the *Caudipteryx* skeleton show that it is most closely related to animals such as *Oviraptor*, and that *Caudipteryx* was a ground-dwelling, fast-running animal. This indicates that true feathers appeared in theropod dinosaurs well before the origin of birds and before the origin of flight.

In living birds, feathers have many functions other than flight. They help to keep a bird warm, by trapping heat produced by the body close to the surface of the skin. Feathers may also be used in display—to attract mates or to warn enemies. The tail of *Caudipteryx* carried a large fan of long feathers, a structure that would have made a very impressive display. The rest of the body seems to have been covered in much shorter feathers, which would have helped to keep *Caudipteryx* warm. A few large feathers were present on the arms, and these might have been involved in display. The large fan of tail feathers might also have acted as a stabilizer. This would have kept *Caudipteryx* balanced as it turned quickly during spells of fast running.

Caudipteryx and the other feathered theropods show that feathers probably first appeared for either insulation or display— they were not used for flight. In birds, the feathers first seen in theropod dinosaurs became modified so that they could be used for flight.

Diet and digestion

The fossilized skeletons of *Caudipteryx* contained lots of small stones, which were concentrated in the region where the animal's stomach would have been. These stones, called gastroliths, would have been used to help grind up the animal's food (see page 53). Almost all other land-living animals with gastroliths are herbivores, and it seems likely that *Caudipteryx* lived on a diet of leaves, fruits and seeds. The stones probably did almost all of the work in grinding the food—*Caudipteryx* had teeth, but they were small and weak. Plant-eating theropods are rare. All other plant-eating theropods, such as *Therizinosaurus*, are quite closely related to *Caudipteryx*.

Below: *This is a close-up of feathers from the arm of* Caudipteryx. *The preservation of the fossil is so good that many of the small, individual barbs can be seen. Some of the feathers even show evidence of coloration.*

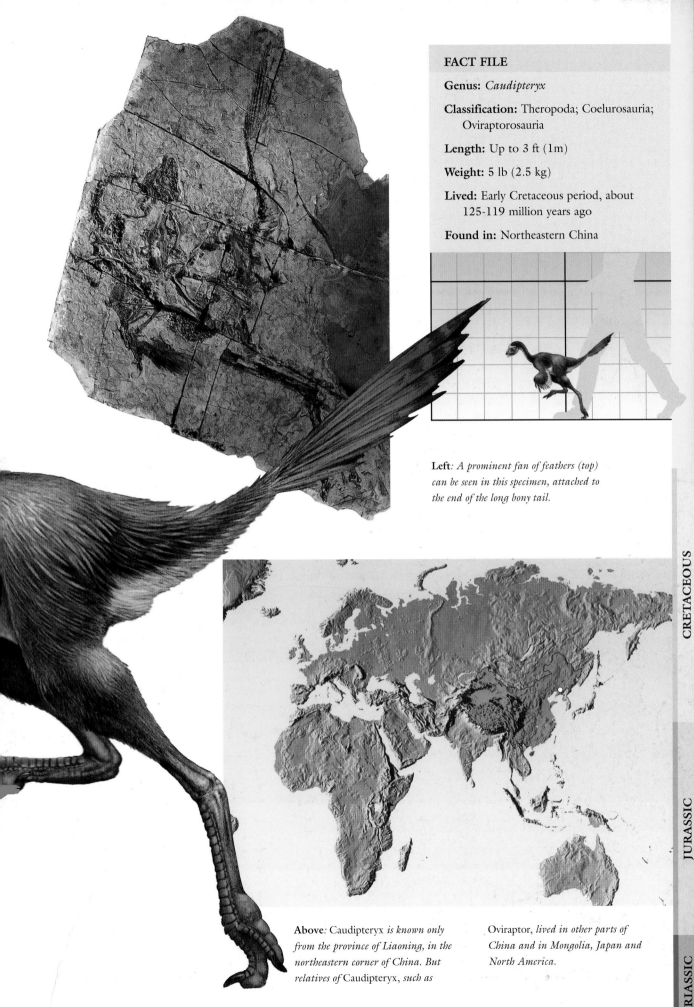

FACT FILE

Genus: *Caudipteryx*

Classification: Theropoda; Coelurosauria; Oviraptorosauria

Length: Up to 3 ft (1m)

Weight: 5 lb (2.5 kg)

Lived: Early Cretaceous period, about 125-119 million years ago

Found in: Northeastern China

Left: *A prominent fan of feathers (top) can be seen in this specimen, attached to the end of the long bony tail.*

Above: Caudipteryx *is known only from the province of Liaoning, in the northeastern corner of China. But relatives of* Caudipteryx, *such as* Oviraptor, *lived in other parts of China and in Mongolia, Japan and North America.*

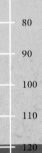

CRETACEOUS

70
80
90
100
110
120
130
140

150
160
170
180
190
200
210

JURASSIC

TRIASSIC

220
230
240

Therizinosaurus
Scythe lizard

The biggest claws of any animal that has ever lived belonged to the mysterious *Therizinosaurus*. Its name refers to the gigantic, sickle-shaped claws found on the hand. The best specimen of this animal consists of an enormous arm and shoulder blade that were found in rocks in the desert of central Mongolia, the Gobi. The limited number of remains available to scientists makes deduction of this animal's behavior extremely difficult.

The first claws of *Therizinosaurus* were discovered in 1948 by a joint Russian-Mongolian scientific expedition. Initially, they were thought to be the remains of a huge turtle. But later finds included several teeth, incomplete forelimbs, a large claw, a few fragments of hind limbs and a distinctive four-toed foot. These specimens showed that the mighty claws were actually those of a dinosaur. The question of what type of dinosaur was more difficult, and this matter was debated among scientists for many years. Eventually, in the 1990s, it was decided that *Therizinosaurus* was a theropod dinosaur. But it was so unlike any other theropod that it was put into a group of its own.

Mighty muscles
Most theropod dinosaurs had relatively small claws on their hands, and their arms were not usually very powerful. But the claws of *Therizinosaurus* were about a quarter the length of the arm— 2-foot (0.6-m) claws on an 8-foot (2.5-m) arm. The bones of the arm are massive, and show lumps and scars where extremely powerful muscles would have been attached. There appears to have been a mighty set of shoulder muscles, too. As a result, this monster must have possessed a huge pair of muscular arms.

What did it look like?
As scientists have so few bones of *Therizinosaurus*, its overall appearance is much more of a mystery. Some scientists think that it looked a bit like the early prosauropod dinosaur *Plateosaurus*, with a medium-length neck and a small head. Others think that it had shorter hind limbs and a shorter tail. These features would have caused *Therizinosaurus* to adopt a strange posture when standing—it would have looked as if it were sitting down with its back held very straight, even though it was standing up.

Close relatives?
Many of the bones of *Therizinosaurus* look very similar to those of two other dinosaurs that were found in rocks of about the same geological age in the same region of Mongolia. These dinosaurs are *Segnosaurus* and *Erlikosaurus*, and all three of these animals appear to be very closely related to each other. A well-preserved skull of *Erlikosaurus* gives some useful clues to the lifestyle of *Therizinosaurus*. *Erlikosaurus* had a long, low, lightweight skull with a horny beak at the front of the snout. The small, leaf-shaped teeth show that this animal was mainly herbivorous, though it might have preyed occasionally on small lizards and mammals. *Therizinosaurus* probably had a similar diet, despite its massive claws. The claws might have been used to grasp on to plants. Plant-eating is extremely rare among theropods, adding yet another unusual feature to our understanding of this bizarre animal.

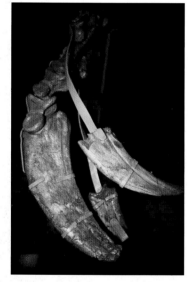

Above: *This huge claw of* Therizinosaurus *is not very curved, suggesting it was not used for grasping struggling prey. Instead, it might have been used to rip open the fleshy trunks of plants or even termite hills. The claws might also have been used as a defense against large meat-eating dinosaurs.*

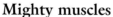

FACT FILE

Genus: *Therizinosaurus*

Classification: Theropoda; Coelurosauria; Therizinosauroidea

Length: Unknown, but large—maybe up to 36 ft (11 m)

Weight: Up to 6 tons

Lived: Late Cretaceous period, about 70-65 million years ago

Found in: Mongolia, China (northern)

Left: *The curved shape of these huge* Therizinosaurus *arms shows how muscular they were in life. Why these arms needed to be so powerful is still a mystery.*

Below: *Fossils of* Therizinosaurus *and its relatives have been found only in the deserts of Mongolia and northern China.*

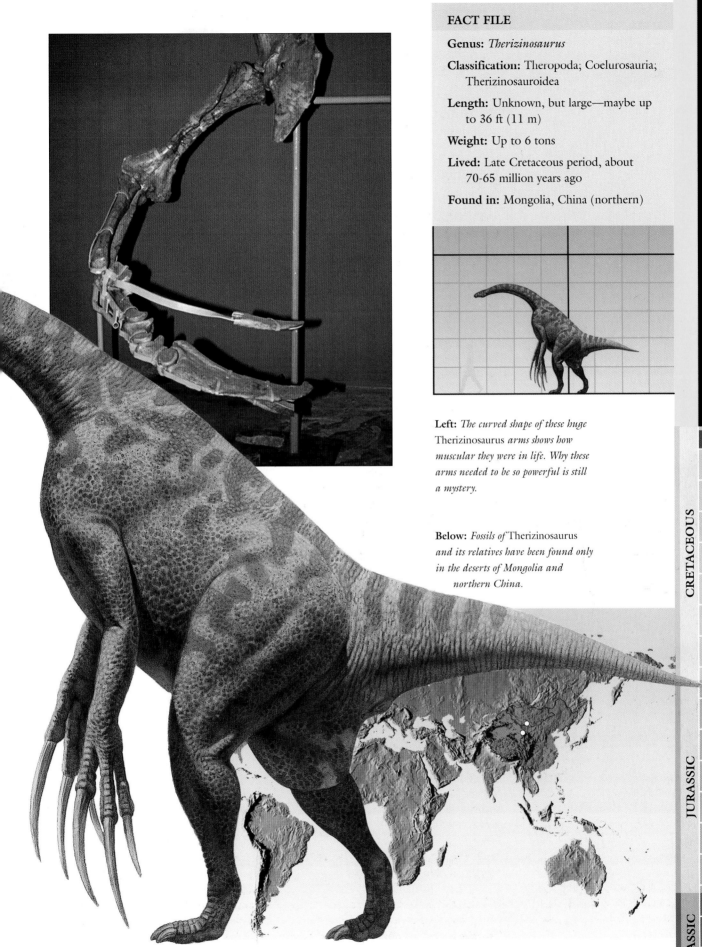

165

Pelecanimimus

Pelican mimic

Pelecanimimus was the earliest "ostrich dinosaur," or ornithomimosaur. It is known from a single skeleton that, although only partially complete, includes a beautifully preserved skull and a number of skin impressions. It is the only unquestionable ostrich dinosaur to have been found in Europe. It occurs in rocks that are significantly older than those that have yielded the remains of other types of ornithomimosaurs.

The skull of *Pelecanimimus* is long and narrow and has an elongated, sharply pointed beak. In most other ornithomimosaurs, the skull lacks teeth and the jaws are lined with a hard, horny beak. But in *Pelecanimimus* the front of the mouth is packed with about 220 tiny, spikelike teeth. The lack of teeth in other ornithomimosaurs has led to the suggestion that these animals were omnivores—that they ate both plants and other animals. The teeth of *Pelecanimimus* are lined with a few tiny serrations that would have been useful in both cutting through the flesh of small animals and slicing up the leaves and fruits of plants.

Skin impressions

Impressions of the skin of *Pelecanimimus* were found about the skeleton in the area of the throat, the neck, the shoulder and the upper part of the arm. Another skin impression was found just behind a small pointed crest of bone at the back of the skull. The patches of skin below the throat look a little like the fleshy pouch found on the throat of a living pelican, and it was this feature that gave *Pelecanimimus* its name.

Mysterious pouch

Although pelicans use their pouch for catching and storing fish, the function of the pouch in *Pelecanimimus* is unknown. Study of the rocks in which the skeleton was found shows that *Pelecanimimus* lived next to a large lake, so it is possible that it was used in fishing. Alternatively, the

pouch might have been brightly colored or inflatable so that it could be used in display.

The top predator?

No remains of large carnivores or herbivores have been found in the deposits from which the skeleton of *Pelecanimimus* was recovered, although the remains of *Iguanodon*, sauropods and large theropods have been discovered at other nearby fossil sites. However, small animals, such as lizards, turtles and even birds, are found in the same rocks as *Pelecanimimus*. This might suggest that the local environment in which these smaller animals were living was not good enough to support the food demands of large animals. If this were the case, then *Pelecanimimus*, at only 6 feet (2 m) in length, would have been the top predator! Alternatively, the geological processes that allowed the fossilization of the small animals may in some way have prevented the preservation of large animal bones, hiding the fact that bigger animals might also have lived in this area. More study of the fossil site is necessary in order to choose between these competing ideas.

Below: *This close-up of the snout shows some of the many tiny teeth that lined the jaws of* Pelecanimimus. *Although teeth can be found along the entire length of the lower jaw, those in the upper jaw are limited to the front.*

Below: *Several small bony crests are present on the skull of* Pelecanimimus. *A small ridge of bone is situated over each eye, and a small pointed crest arises from the back of the skull. The functions of these structures are unknown.*

FACT FILE

Genus: *Pelecanimimus*

Classification: Theropoda; Coelurosauria; Ornithomimosauria

Length: Up to 6 ft (2 m)

Weight: Up to 55 lb (25 kg)

Lived: Early Cretaceous period, about 125-119 million years ago

Found in: Spain

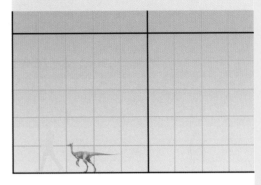

Left: *The only known skeleton of* Pelecanimimus *includes the skull, neck, shoulders, part of the chest and one complete arm. It was found on a single large slab of limestone.*

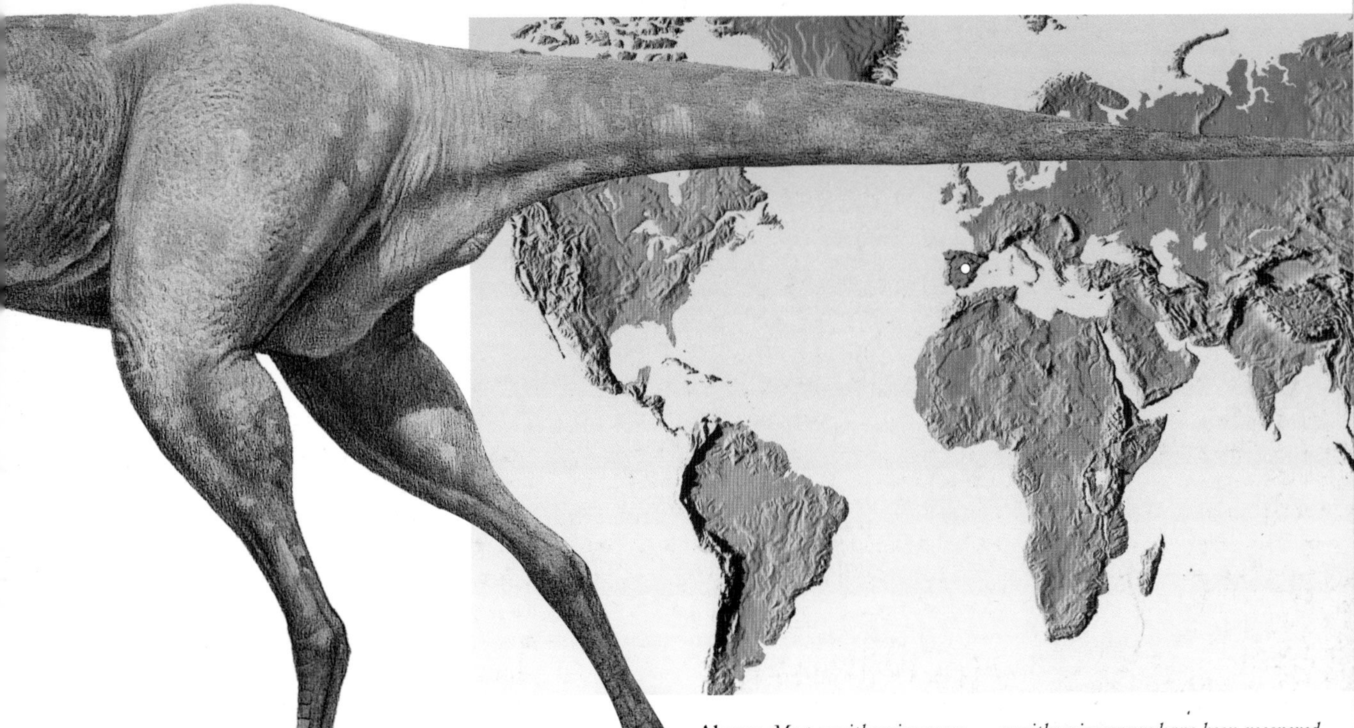

Above: *Most ornithomimosaur fossils have been found in the late Cretaceous rocks of North America and eastern Asia. A few fragmentary bones that look very similar to those of ornithomimosaurs have been recovered from late Jurassic deposits in southern England, but they cannot be identified with confidence. The single skeleton of* Pelecanimimus *comes from the Las Hoyas site in central Spain.*

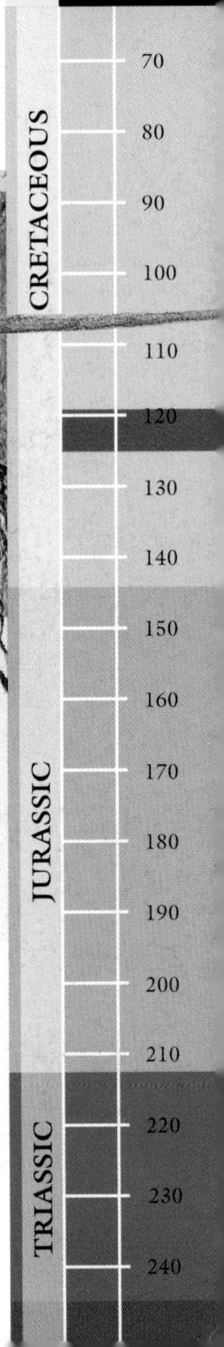

CRETACEOUS
70
80
90
100
110
120
130
140
150
160
JURASSIC
170
180
190
200
210
TRIASSIC
220
230
240

Struthiomimus
Ostrich mimic

Struthiomimus owes its name to its strong similarity to the living ostrich. It is the best known of the so-called ostrich dinosaurs, which are also known as ornithomimosaurs ("bird-mimics").

Below: *This long-legged and light-framed dinosaur was built for speed.* Struthiomimus *was probably one of the fastest-running animals of all time.*

Struthiomimus stood on its two long hind legs and had a short, deep body that was well balanced over its hips. The neck was elongated and slender, and was counterbalanced by a lengthy, muscular tail. Its long hind legs allowed *Struthiomimus* to make long strides and run very swiftly. The legs were powered by huge thigh muscles that were attached to the hip and to the base of the tail. These muscles gave *Struthiomimus* legs that looked like giant chicken "drumsticks" and made it a tasty meal for a roaming meat-eater. But its speed enabled *Struthiomimus* to make a quick getaway when danger threatened. It may also have sought safety in numbers by living in herds.

The narrow, toothless beak of *Struthiomimus* was very useful for feeding on small food items such as tiny reptiles, seeds, insects and plant material. But it was no good as a defensive weapon. The arms and slim hands of *Struthiomimus* were probably very good at grasping and picking up small pieces of food. Its long neck was probably used like that of birds such as ostriches, where the head is darted out quickly and the beak picks up the food.

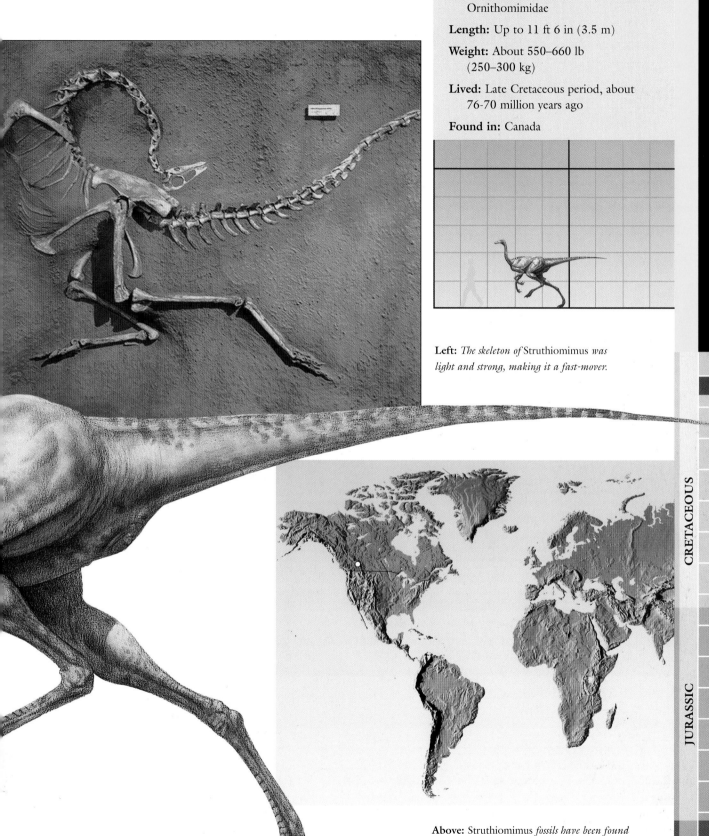

FACT FILE

Genus: *Struthiomimus*

Classification: Theropoda; Coelurosauria; Ornithomimidae

Length: Up to 11 ft 6 in (3.5 m)

Weight: About 550–660 lb (250–300 kg)

Lived: Late Cretaceous period, about 76-70 million years ago

Found in: Canada

Left: *The skeleton of* Struthiomimus *was light and strong, making it a fast-mover.*

Above: Struthiomimus *fossils have been found in Alberta, Canada. Close relatives lived in Mongolia, China and the U.S.A.*

CRETACEOUS

JURASSIC

TRIASSIC

70
80
90
100
110
120
130
140
150
160
170
180
190
200
210
220
230
240

169

Troodon
Wounding tooth

The late Cretaceous dinosaur *Troodon* appears to have led a double life. On the one hand, it was a fierce meat-eater, adequately equipped to terrorize small reptiles and mammals. On the other hand, it appears to have been a caring and attentive parent, dedicated to brooding its young. *Troodon* was also an intelligent dinosaur. Of all known dinosaurs, it appears to have had the biggest brain relative to body size. And a light body and long legs enabled it to run very fast.

Troodon teeth were first discovered in the 1850s. But only when scientists found skull material that was more complete, many years later, did they realize they had unearthed a new and distinctive dinosaur. The teeth are very curved and flattened, with rough serrations along the back edge, used for ripping through meat. A flexible wrist and a thumb able to move independently of the other two fingers gave it a strong grasping hand. Together with its speed, these adaptations enabled *Troodon* to catch small fast-moving prey such as mammals and lizards.

An intelligent hunter

Brain size needs to be compared with body size to gain an accurate idea of an animal's intelligence. The relative brain size of *Troodon* suggests that it was about as intelligent as a parrot. This may not sound very bright, but parrots are extremely clever birds.

In *Troodon*, the parts of the brain involved in sight are enlarged and well developed. The eyes were its primary hunting tool, and enlargement of other regions of the brain would have given it more control over movement and balance when moving quickly. Its intelligence might have enabled it to coordinate its attacks with other individuals and work as a pack-hunter to bring down large prey.

A caring parent

Crocodiles and birds are the closest living relatives of dinosaurs. As both groups of animals lay their eggs in nests and look after these eggs to some degree, it is not surprising that dinosaurs behaved in a similar way. Fossilized *Troodon* nests have been found in Montana, at a famous fossil locality called Egg Mountain. Some nests contain complete eggs, and a few eggs even contain baby *Troodon* skeletons. Sometimes, adult *Troodon* bones are found along with nests, suggesting that *Troodon* sat on top of the eggs to keep them warm in the same way as modern birds do.

Above: Troodon *had very large eyes compared with the size of its head. Large eyes can absorb more light in dark or dimly lit environments. Perhaps this helped* Troodon *hunt for nocturnal prey, such as mammals, throughout the night. The eyes also faced forward, giving* Troodon *binocular vision, which enabled it to pinpoint prey more accurately.*

FACT FILE

Genus: *Troodon*

Classification: Theropoda; Coelurosauria; Troodontidae

Length: 10 ft (3 m)

Weight: 110 lb (50 kg)

Lived: Late Cretaceous period, about 76-70 million years ago

Found in: United States (Montana, Wyoming and possibly Alaska) and Alberta, Canada

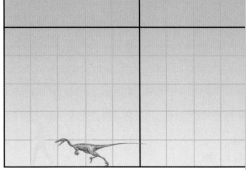

Left: *The size of the brain and the eye sockets can clearly be seen in this side view of the skull. Note also the sharp, serrated meat-eating teeth.*

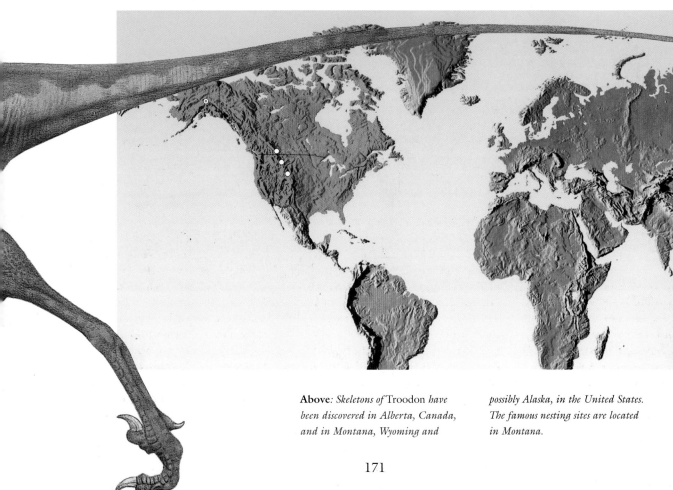

Above: *Skeletons of* Troodon *have been discovered in Alberta, Canada, and in Montana, Wyoming and possibly Alaska, in the United States. The famous nesting sites are located in Montana.*

CRETACEOUS

JURASSIC

TRIASSIC

70
80
90
100
110
120
130
140
150
160
170
180
190
200
210
220
230
240

Deinonychus
Terrible claw

FACT FILE

Genus: *Deinonychus*

Classification: Theropoda; Coelurosauria; Dromaeosauridae

Length: 8-11 ft (2.5-3.5 m)

Weight: 110-150 lb (50-70 kg)

Lived: Mid Cretaceous period, about 119-97 million years ago

Found in: Western U.S.A., in Montana, Oklahoma, Wyoming and Utah

Although not large, *Deinonychus* was a ferocious meat-eating dinosaur. Its discovery in the 1960s introduced paleontologists to a whole new method of dinosaur attack and feeding. Instead of relying on a large head with powerful jaws, like most of the bigger carnivores, *Deinonychus* used long arms to hold its prey, with legs and toes delivering the all-important killing strike. It probably hunted in packs, rather like wolves do today.

Deinonychus and its close relatives, such as *Velociraptor,* shared a peculiar feature of the foot—they walked only on the third and fourth toes. Attached to the tip of the second toe was a huge, curved claw, twice as long as the claws on toes three and four. One of the joints on the second toe flexed against the others in a way opposite to normal joints, so that the rest of the toe and its great claw were always held off the ground, as in Troodontids. The claw was covered by a huge, sharp, horny sheath like those of birds and cats. Its arms were relatively long and powerful, and three long fingers each ended in a sharp, curved claw. *Deinonychus* probably leapt at prey with arms and legs extended, its long, bony tail aiding balance. While the arms gripped the prey, the legs kicked backward and the sicklelike claws sprang into action. Recent fossil discoveries of featherlike structures in close relatives of *Deinonychus* suggest it might have had a featherlike covering, too.

Left: Deinonychus *was a small to medium, meat-eating dinosaur that appears to have hunted in packs. Teamwork meant that* Deinonychus *could hunt large, plant-eating dinosaurs such as* Tenontosaurus.

Above: Deinonychus *fossils come from the western U.S.A. They have been found at the same sites as skeletons of the ornithopod* Tenontosaurus. *It is likely that packs of* Deinonychus *preyed upon this unarmored herbivore.*

Deinonychus

CRETACEOUS

70
80
90
100
110
120
130
140
150
160

JURASSIC

170
180
190
200
210

TRIASSIC

220
230
240

Velociraptor
Swift robber

Velociraptor gave its nickname to the vicious predators in *Jurassic Park* that were called "raptors." In fact, those movie monsters were closer in size to *Deinonychus*. And the term "raptor" is normally used by ornithologists to describe eagles, hawks and their relatives, which swoop down on their prey and grab them with their sharp, curved talons.

Velociraptor was closely related to *Deinonychus* and had many of the same features—notably, the enormous second claw of the foot that made such a formidable weapon. Like *Deinonychus,* it also had a long tail that was reinforced along its length by an unusual feature. The bony arches above and below the central column of tail bones were flattened and elongated into thin rods that extended forward and backward along many vertebrae. These rods formed bundles above and below each side of the central column of tail bones. They supported the tail and held it straight but also had some flexibility. As a result, the muscles of the tail could be reduced, whereas in most reptiles they are large to help pull back the legs in walking and running. Here, the tail was more independent of the legs.

Another interesting feature of *Deinonychus, Velociraptor,* and their relatives was an unusual joint in the wrist. In most animals, the wrists hinge up and down because, like the foot bones, the hand bones are used in walking. But in these bipeds, the wrists were also able to move from side to side, in the same way that a bird can flex its wrists. This is not surprising, because these animals are the closest known relatives of the first birds. The sideways motion of these long hands, which helped *Velociraptor* and its relatives trap prey, was later used by birds as an important part of the flight stroke.

Killer claws

Of all the features that made *Velociraptor* such an efficient killer, the most important was the sharply curved claw on the second toe. When *Velociraptor* was walking, its claws were pulled back and held clear of the ground to prevent them becoming blunt. When *Velociraptor* attacked, a claw could be flicked forward and downward by kicking out powerfully with one leg. In this way, the claw worked like a switchblade knife. It could cut a long wound in the prey, which would probably then bleed to death.

Below: Velociraptor *had a long, low skull with slim jaws that were lined with sharp teeth. The teeth were curved backward to hold prey firmly. The skull had lots of window-like openings for the attachment of powerful jaw muscles.*

FACT FILE

Genus: *Velociraptor*

Classification: Theropoda; Coelurosauria; Dromaeosauridae

Length: Up to 6 ft (1.8 m)

Weight: Up to 33 lb (15 kg)

Lived: Late Cretaceous period, about 80-73 million years ago.

Found in: Mongolia and China

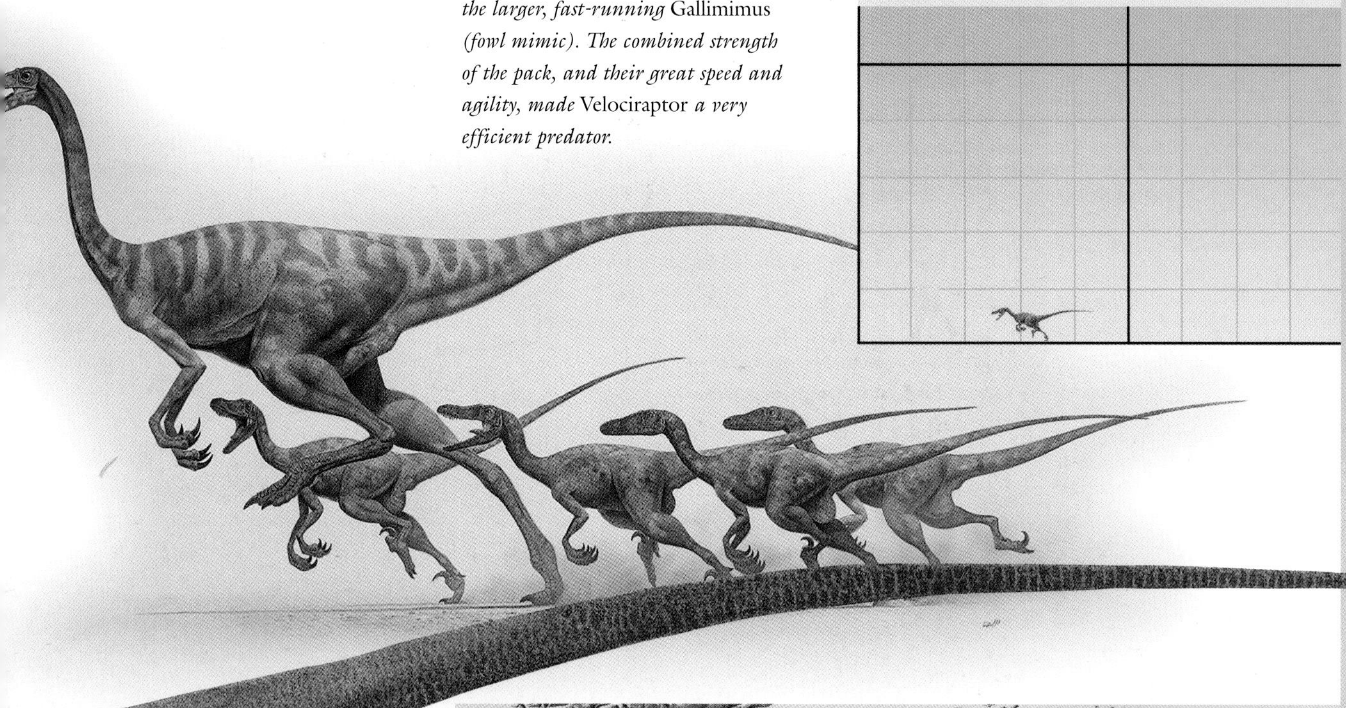

Below: *A pack of* Velociraptor *hunt the larger, fast-running* Gallimimus *(fowl mimic). The combined strength of the pack, and their great speed and agility, made* Velociraptor *a very efficient predator.*

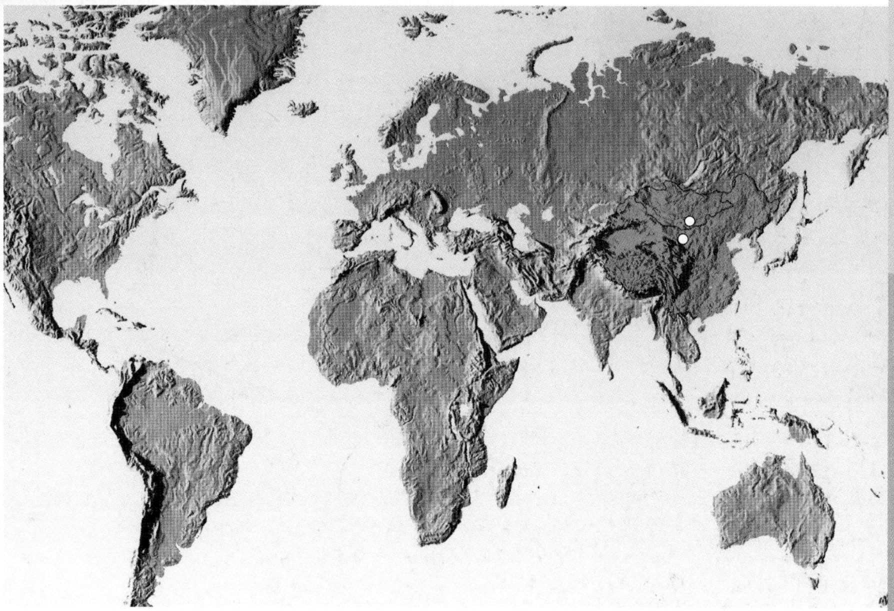

Above*: Velociraptor remains are found in Mongolia and China, having first been unearthed there by the American expeditions to the Gobi in the 1920s.*

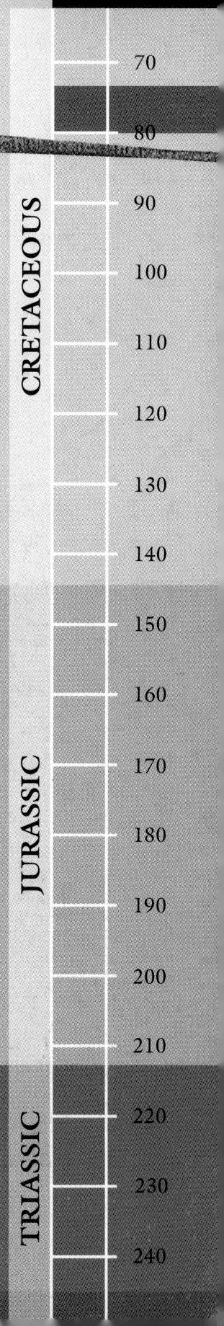

CRETACEOUS

JURASSIC

TRIASSIC

70
80
90
100
110
120
130
140
150
160
170
180
190
200
210
220
230
240

Archaeopteryx
Ancient wing

Archaeopteryx is recognized as the earliest known bird. It existed during the late Jurassic period in Germany. It is one of the most scientifically interesting fossils because it gives important evidence supporting the theory that birds evolved from a dinosaur ancestor. The unusual mixture of birdlike and reptilelike features in *Archaeopteryx* has led scientists to the conclusion that it was a "missing link" between dinosaurs and birds.

The first evidence of this ancient bird was found in the limestone quarries about the small town of Solnhofen, in southern Germany. A single feather was found in 1860 by quarrymen and named by scientists in 1861. *Archaeopteryx* is now known from seven skeletons—of which five are almost complete. Some of these skeletons have the fossilized impressions of feathers about the wing bones. This feature helped scientists to recognize that *Archaeopteryx* was a bird—other features of the skeleton were more similar to those of theropods.

Lagoon habitat
Because all eight specimens of *Archaeopteryx* come from the same place, many scientists have studied the Solnhofen limestones to discover something about the habitat that it lived in. It seems to have flown through the skies above a salty lagoon that was separated from warm tropical seas by a coral reef.

Fish not on the diet
Unlike modern birds, which have a horny beak and no teeth, *Archaeopteryx* had long, slim jaws lined with sharp teeth that curved slightly backward. It was about the same size as a modern magpie, so it probably fed in a similar way and ate almost anything that was small enough to be swallowed. Insects probably made up much of its diet. But although *Archaeopteryx* lived close to the sea, it is unlikely that it ate fish. There are two main reasons for this. First, the

lagoon was too salty for fish to live in. And second, the sea beyond the reef was too rough to allow *Archaeopteryx* to swoop down and catch fish swimming beneath the surface. The fossil skeletons show that *Archaeopteryx* was probably not as good at flying as a modern bird is. So it might not have been able to fly with enough skill to pluck fish out of the sea.

"Wishbone"
An unusual feature of *Archaeopteryx* is the presence of a birdlike "wishbone." In living birds, the wishbone is made from the joined-up collarbones that lie across the upper part of the chest. In birds, this is an important area for the attachment of the strong muscles that power the wings. Many theropod dinosaurs, including oviraptorids, velociraptors, allosaurs and even tyrannosaurs, also had a wishbone, which was probably used for the attachment of powerful arm muscles. Other features of *Archaeopteryx,* besides its teeth and wishbone, show its intermediate status between typical theropods and living birds. It has a long bony tail with feathers along the sides. The bones of its hands and feet are not fused together as they are in living birds. And its three fingers, identical to those of other theropods, are also separate, not fused as in today's birds.

Below: *The big toe of* Archaeopteryx *faced in the opposite direction to the two other toes. This allowed it to perch on branches or rocks. A moon-shaped bone in its wrist suggests that it is closely related to the theropod dinosaurs—some of which also had this feature.*

CRETACEOUS

70
80
90
100
110
120
130
140
150

JURASSIC

180
190
200
210

TRIASSIC

220
230
240

FACT FILE

Genus: *Archaeopteryx*

Classification: Theropoda; Aves; Archaeopterygidae

Length: 12-20 in (30-50 cm)

Weight: 1 lb (500 g)

Lived: Late Jurassic period, about 156-150 million years ago

Found in: Southern Germany

Left: *The impressions of the feathers of* Archaeopteryx *show that they were very similar to those of living flying birds. The arms were as long as the legs, so the wings provided plenty of surface area for flight. But the flight muscles might have been strong enough only for limited flight.*

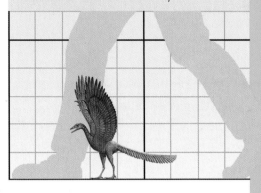

Above: *All eight discoveries of* Archaeopteryx *to date have been made at the same site, in the* limestone deposits around Solnhofen, *a small town in Bavaria, southern Germany.*

Baptornis

Diving bird

A specialized diving bird, *Baptornis* lived in the shallow seas covering central North America during the late Cretaceous period. Unlike any modern bird, the jaws of *Baptornis* were lined with small, sharp teeth. These teeth would have been useful in gaining a firm hold on the fish that made up most of its diet.

Baptornis was a large bird and had an unusually long neck that would have enabled it to dart its sharp beak out at fish as they swam by. It is closely related to another diving bird from the late Cretaceous period of North America called *Hesperornis* (western bird). Both of these birds must have been in constant danger from the large marine reptiles, such as mosasaurs, that lived beneath the surface of the sea. The famous dinosaur expert Othniel Charles Marsh first described the fossil skeletons of these birds in the late 1870s. Along with *Archaeopteryx*, these were the first bird fossils to be known to science. But unlike *Archaeopteryx*, neither *Baptornis* nor *Hesperornis* was capable of flight.

Right: Baptornis *swam using its huge webbed hind feet—its tiny wings were of no use at all—and it was a skilled underwater predator. It could twist and turn quickly as it chased down its prey.*

Diving and swimming

The body of *Baptornis* was superbly designed for diving. It was shaped like a torpedo and streamlined for easy movement through the water. *Baptornis* had tiny wings that would have been useless for flying in the air. They were so small that they would also not have been of any use in propelling the animal forward while swimming. Indeed, the flat breastbone shows that the muscles that operated the wings were small and weak. But its wings might have been useful in steering as *Baptornis* swam underwater.

Webbed feet

Baptornis had huge, webbed feet that would have provided almost all of the forward propulsion as it swam. Living diving birds, such as loons and grebes, use a similar strategy today, though these modern birds have large wings and are capable of flight.

Living in the sea

The feet of *Baptornis* were set so far back on the body that it would have been difficult to move on land. *Baptornis* probably spent most of their time in, or bobbing on the surface of, the sea. In addition, *Baptornis* fossils are found in chalk, a rock type that usually forms some way from the shore. This supports the idea that these birds spent most of their time on the open sea. They probably came onto land only to lay their eggs and raise their young.

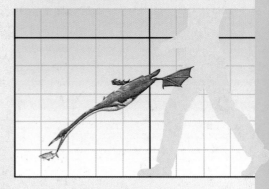

FACT FILE

Genus: *Baptornis*

Classification: Theropoda; Aves; Ornithurae; Hesperornithiformes

Length: 3 ft (1 m)

Weight: 15 lb (7 kg)

Lived: Late Cretaceous period, about 83-80 million years ago

Found in: Kansas

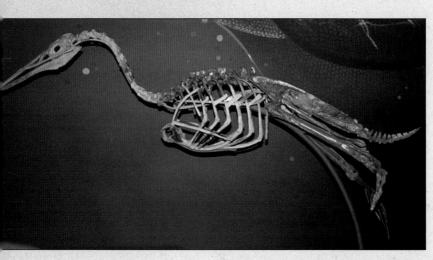

Left: *This is a reconstruction of the skeleton of* Baptornis. *As* Baptornis *is known from only a few isolated specimens, the skeleton of its close relative* Hesperornis *was used as a blueprint for the missing parts. Note the tiny wings and large paddlelike feet.*

Right: Baptornis *is known from only a few scattered bones, all of which have been recovered from the late Cretaceous chalk deposits of Kansas. No complete skeleton has ever been discovered.*

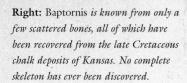

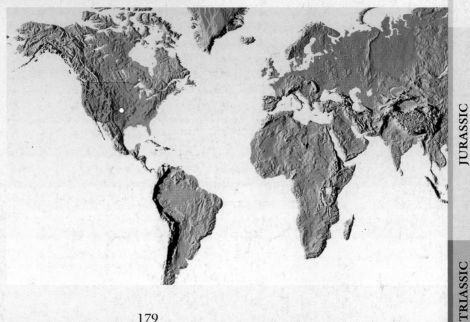

CRETACEOUS

JURASSIC

TRIASSIC

70
80
90
100
110
120
130
140
150
160
170
180
190
200
210
220
230
240

Iberomesornis
Intermediate Spanish bird

Some of the most spectacular bird fossils come from a remarkable fossil-bearing site in central Spain. This is the famous Las Hoyas locality, with rocks that date from the early Cretaceous period. It has yielded specimens of the early birds *Iberomesornis, Concornis* and *Eoalulavis*. Fossil bird skeletons are rare, and Las Hoyas provides a significant window onto the early history of this important group.

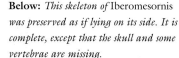

The rocks at Las Hoyas show that *Iberomesornis* lived along the margins of a big, shallow lake that was home to crocodiles, turtles and a large variety of fish. The dinosaurs *Iguanodon* and *Pelecanimimus* walked along the shoreline accompanied by many different types of lizards and other small animals. *Iberomesornis* itself was a sparrow-size bird that was an adept flyer. Its fossils are of great importance to scientists because the skeletons of this bird possess an intriguing set of features. Some of these features are seen in modern birds, but in other respects *Iberomesornis* is more primitive than the birds we are familiar with today.

Pygostyle—the parson's nose

Iberomesornis was a more advanced bird than *Archaeopteryx*. Its tail is not long and bony like that of *Archaeopteryx*. It developed into a shorter structure called a pygostyle. This is actually that part of a cooked chicken or turkey that is sometimes referred to as "the parson's nose" because of its pointed shape. The pygostyle is a very short, bony rod formed from lots of little tail bones that have become fused together. *Iberomesornis* is the earliest bird known to have possessed this structure. This early bird probably had a fanlike display of tail feathers making up most of the length of its tail, just like the tail structure in living birds.

Perching feet

When birds such as sparrows, blackbirds and pigeons perch on trees today, we can see how the toes of their feet are designed to do this. Three of the toes point forward, and one toe points backward. This arrangement enables the foot to keep a firm grip on a branch. In *Iberomesornis*, the big-toe bone was reversed to point backward, and its main three toe bones still faced to the front. It was one of the very first perching birds.

A good flier

The arm bones of *Iberomesornis* are very similar to those of modern birds. In addition, there is a well-developed wishbone that supported the muscles of the flying apparatus. These features show that *Iberomesornis* could undoubtedly fly very well.

Missing parts

The wonderful preservation of the fossils from Las Hoyas often includes feathers and some traces of internal organs. However, despite this fine detail, the specimen of *Iberomesornis* lacks the skull, the front part of the neck, and the hand. Because the skull is missing, it is difficult to decide what this animal ate, though it might have eaten insects like other small birds do today.

Below: *This skeleton of* Iberomesornis *was preserved as if lying on its side. It is complete, except that the skull and some vertebrae are missing.*

FACT FILE

Genus: *Iberomesornis*

Classification: Theropoda; Aves;
  Ornithothoraces

Length: 4 in (10 cm)

Weight: 1 oz (25 g)

Lived: Early Cretaceous period, about
  125-119 million years ago

Found in: Spain

Left: *Although* Iberomesornis *had a pygostyle and perching feet, its hipbones were not like those of modern birds, but were more similar to those of* Archaeopteryx. *Details such as these show how* Iberomesornis *fits in between* Archaeopteryx *on the one hand and more advanced birds on the other.*

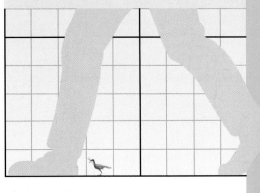

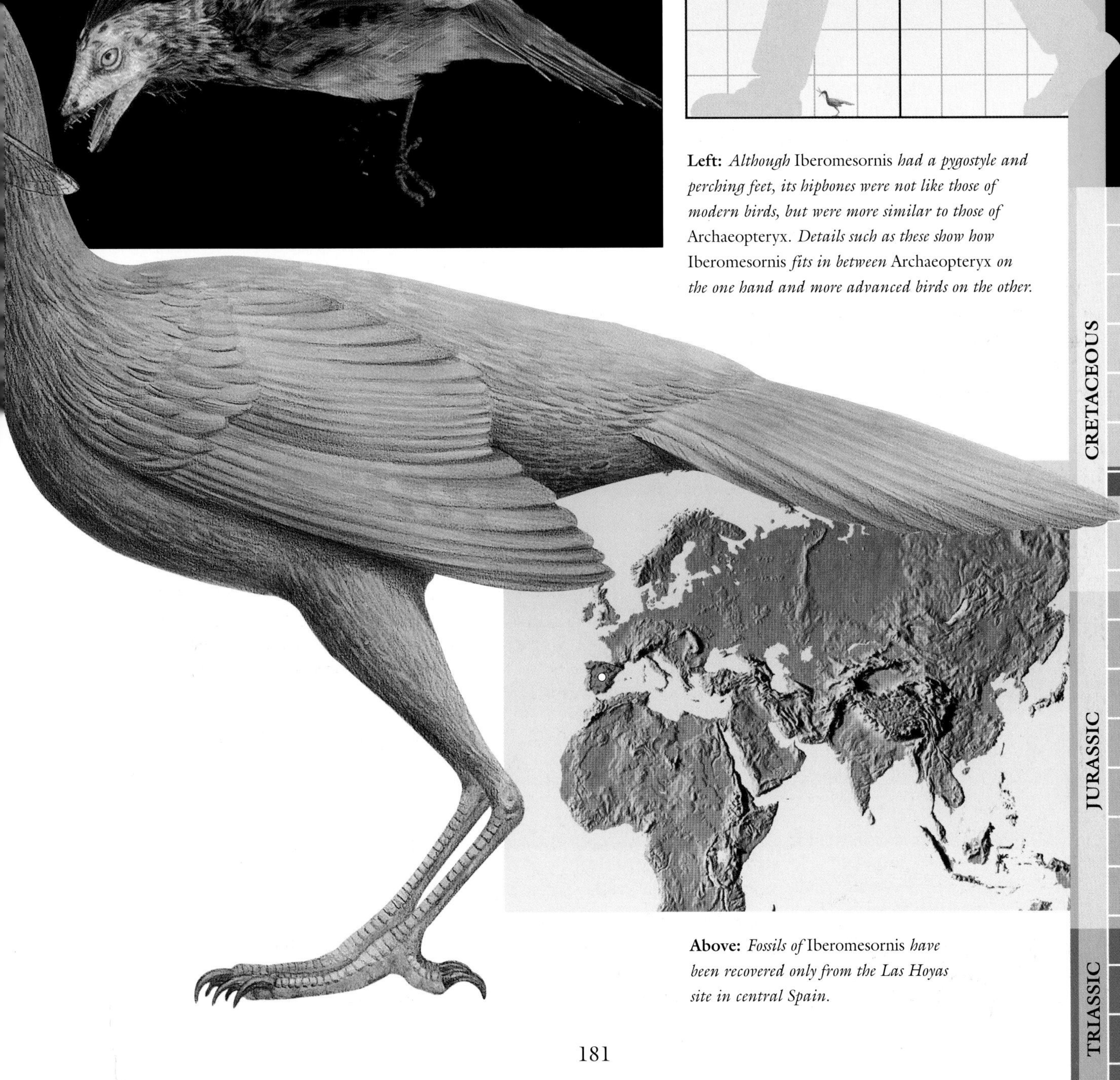

Above: *Fossils of* Iberomesornis *have been recovered only from the Las Hoyas site in central Spain.*

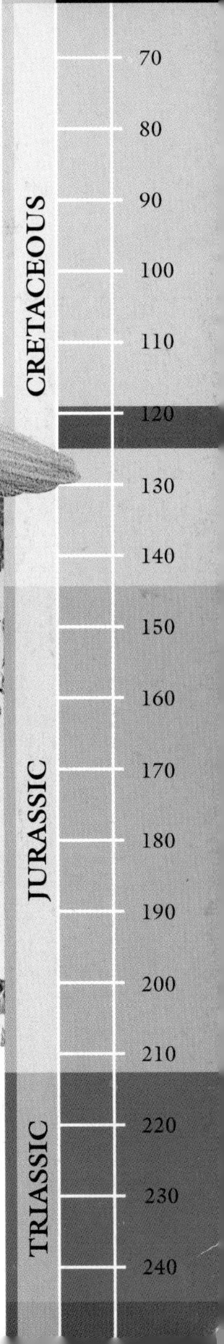

CRETACEOUS

70
80
90
100
110
120
130
140
150

JURASSIC

160
170
180
190
200
210

TRIASSIC

220
230
240

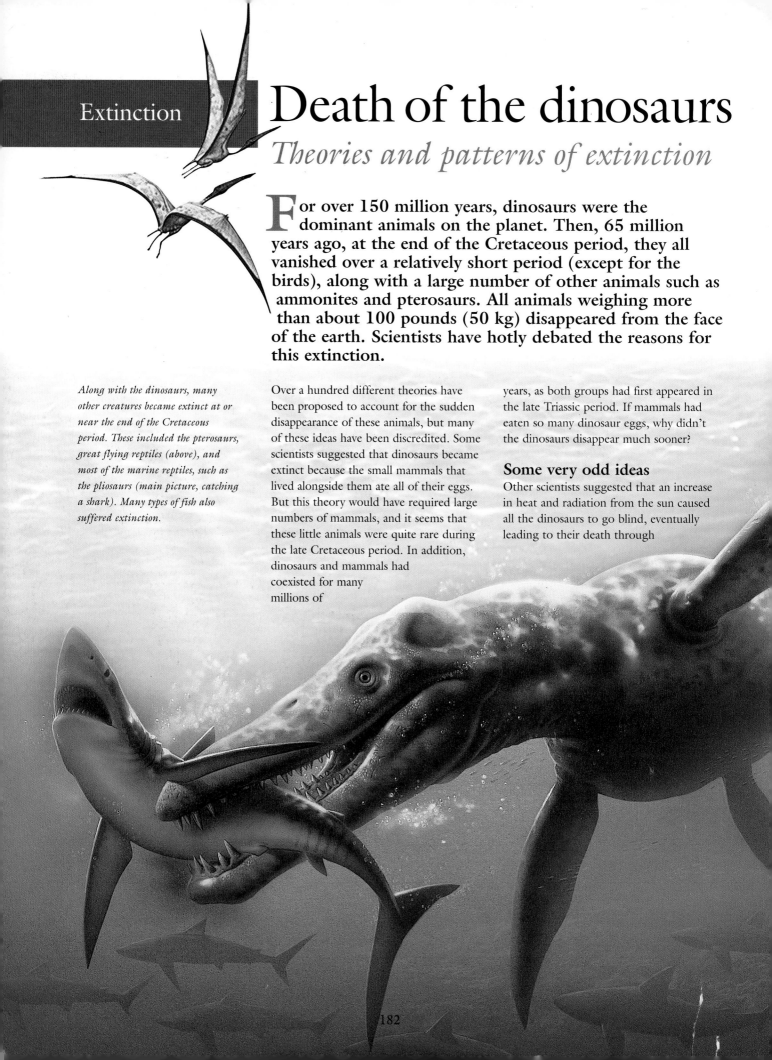

Death of the dinosaurs

Theories and patterns of extinction

For over 150 million years, dinosaurs were the dominant animals on the planet. Then, 65 million years ago, at the end of the Cretaceous period, they all vanished over a relatively short period (except for the birds), along with a large number of other animals such as ammonites and pterosaurs. All animals weighing more than about 100 pounds (50 kg) disappeared from the face of the earth. Scientists have hotly debated the reasons for this extinction.

Along with the dinosaurs, many other creatures became extinct at or near the end of the Cretaceous period. These included the pterosaurs, great flying reptiles (above), and most of the marine reptiles, such as the pliosaurs (main picture, catching a shark). Many types of fish also suffered extinction.

Over a hundred different theories have been proposed to account for the sudden disappearance of these animals, but many of these ideas have been discredited. Some scientists suggested that dinosaurs became extinct because the small mammals that lived alongside them ate all of their eggs. But this theory would have required large numbers of mammals, and it seems that these little animals were quite rare during the late Cretaceous period. In addition, dinosaurs and mammals had coexisted for many millions of

years, as both groups had first appeared in the late Triassic period. If mammals had eaten so many dinosaur eggs, why didn't the dinosaurs disappear much sooner?

Some very odd ideas

Other scientists suggested that an increase in heat and radiation from the sun caused all the dinosaurs to go blind, eventually leading to their death through starvation, accidents and an inability to find mates. But there is no firm evidence of changes in the sun's activity at this time. Disease has also been proposed as a cause of death, but it is difficult to imagine a disease that could have killed all the different types of dinosaurs while leaving other animals unharmed. Other even more bizarre theories have been proposed. Some people think that the dinosaurs were killed by aliens, whereas others have suggested that the evolution of flowering plants led to the dinosaurs dying of constipation! Neither of these odd ideas has any basis in scientific fact.

Extinction of other animals

Most of these theories fail to account for the fact that many other animals also became extinct at the end of the Cretaceous period. In the sea, many types of fish, shellfish and corals disappeared, along with most marine reptiles and many microscopic animals called foraminiferans. On land, pterosaurs and various other kinds of reptiles suffered too. Any theory that tries to account for the extinction of dinosaurs must also explain how these other animals were affected at around the same time.

Patterns of extinction

Scientists have noticed several other patterns in the fossil record around the time of the final Cretaceous extinction. No animals that weighed over about 100 pounds (50 kg) survived this event. This suggests there was a worldwide breakdown in food chains and environments that particularly affected large land animals requiring a lot of food. And not all of these animals became extinct at exactly the same time. Some groups, such as marine reptiles, had disappeared a few million years before the end of the Cretaceous period, whereas others, such as dinosaurs and ammonites, can be found in rocks that were deposited at the very end of the Age of Dinosaurs. Additionally, the number of different dinosaur species seems to have been declining for several million years before they finally became extinct. At the very end of the Cretaceous period, there were only a few types of dinosaur left, including *Tyrannosaurus* and *Triceratops* and possibly some early forms of birds, such as loons, that had evolved from dinosaurs.

How can all of these facts be fitted together to form an explanation for the extinctions? Until recently, most scientists have looked for a single cause for this event. But it is more likely that several different factors caused the decline and eventual extinction of the dinosaurs and of many of the other animals that shared their world. The debate continues on page 184.

LAST OF THE DINOSAURS

Here are some of the dinosaurs that were living in the late Cretaceous period, at the time of the great extinction. One of them, Parasaurolophus, had been around for nearly 20 million years.

Ankylosaurus

Pachyrhinosaurus

Saltasaurus

Tyrannosaurus

Pachycephalosaurus

Triceratops

Therizinosaurus

Parasaurolophus

The debate continues
Catastrophes and gradual changes

For over 150 million years, dinosaurs were the dominant animals on the planet. Then, 65 million years ago, at the end of the Cretaceous period, they all vanished over a relatively short period (except for the birds), along with a large number of other animals such as ammonites and pterosaurs. All animals weighing more than about 100 pounds (50 kg) disappeared from the face of the earth. Scientists have hotly debated the reasons for this extinction.

As the great landmass broke up and the continents drifted apart from each other and started moving toward the positions they occupy today, changes in the ocean currents and wind patterns began a steady cooling of the earth's climate. Flowering plants began to dominate the forests and plains, replacing the conifers and ferns that had existed there previously. In geological terms, this was a rapid series of events, and might have led to the decline in the number of dinosaur species that occurred during the last few million years of the Cretaceous period. But this kind of gradual change cannot account for the sudden extinction of the remaining dinosaurs and other creatures at the end of the Cretaceous period. Two world catastrophes probably sealed their fate—the impact of a large meteor and the eruption of a "supervolcano."

Death from above

The earth is continually bombarded with small particles of rock and dust from outer space. These objects usually burn up in the atmosphere before reaching the earth's surface. Occasionally, however, they are large enough to survive and land on the earth as meteorites. Most meteorites are quite small—no larger than a tennis ball. But some meteorites are huge, and can cause massive devastation. Evidence of this destruction comes from the enormous craters produced as these heavy lumps of rock and iron hit the earth. Meteorites contain large quantities of a rare metal called iridium. The discovery of large amounts of this element in layers of clay that were deposited at the very end of the

Cretaceous period alerted scientists to the possibility that a large meteorite impact had helped to cause the extinction at the end of the Cretaceous period. The discovery of a vast meteor crater, several hundreds of miles across—partly on the Yucatán Peninsula in Mexico, but mostly under the sea—confirmed this idea.

Death from below

At around the same time, a series of immense volcanic eruptions was taking place in what is now central India. These eruptions produced billions of tons of ash and lava, and continued over a period of several million years. The lava and ash formed a series of rocks called the Deccan Traps, which are many miles thick. This "supervolcano" would have thrown up a mass of dust and gas many miles into the atmosphere, where it would have blocked out the heat of the sun, causing a sharp drop in the temperature of the earth. The meteor impact would have had a similar effect, as it would have thrown up immense amounts of rock and soil that would stay in the atmosphere for years.

The dust settles

As the earth cooled, plants died and large herbivores quickly ran out of food to eat. They began to starve to death. As the herbivores became rarer, the carnivores also began to run out of food, and they, too, started to die out. It would take only a few months for all of the plant life to die and for all of the large animals to become extinct. By the time the dust had settled and plant life had regenerated, the dinosaurs had disappeared from the face of the earth.

Right: *Volcanic eruptions lasting several million years marked the end of the Cretaceous period. These, together with the impact of a huge meteorite, would have sent up such a mass of material into the atmosphere that the sun's warmth would have been blocked out. The larger animals—those at the top of the food chain—including the dinosaurs, could not have survived these twin catastrophes. Smaller creatures could have lived on dead vegetation until the regeneration of plant life. But there would not have been enough food around for the dinosaurs and other large animals.*

Dinosaur movies
Fact or fiction?

Dinosaurs have always captured the imagination of Hollywood moviemakers, as they possess all of the ingredients needed for a classic villain—they are strong, fierce and frightening. The first movies that portrayed dinosaurs included such classics as the 1925 *The Lost World* (based on the 1910 story by Sir Arthur Conan Doyle) and *Gertie the Dinosaur* (a short cartoon that thrilled American audiences in 1914). Some movies give a reasonable picture of dinosaurs as living animals, but most of them twist the facts to make them more sensational.

Below: *In the 1961 British film* Gorgo, *the special effects are pretty bad. The larger-than-life dinosaur monster Gorgo is obviously a man dressed in a rubber suit!*

Below: *Although the story is pure fantasy, the depictions of dinosaurs in the original version of* King Kong *(1933) are similar to the scientific reconstructions of the time.*

Many movies, such as the 1966 live action film *One Million Years BC*, show tribes of cavemen living alongside dinosaurs. The cavemen live in fear of being attacked and eaten by these menacing creatures, and often have to fight them off in order to protect themselves and their families. But this is a scientific impossibility. Cavemen and dinosaurs could not have existed side by side. Dinosaurs became extinct 65 million years ago, whereas the ancestors of humans did not appear for another 64 million years. Several other movies, such as *The Lost World*, suggest that dinosaurs might have survived in some remote region of the world, waiting to be discovered by modern explorers. But it is most unlikely that animals as large as the dinosaurs depicted could have survived without having been discovered by now. Recent movies, especially the 1993 *Jurassic Park* and its 1997 sequel *The Lost World*, are based on the idea that it might be possible to bring dinosaurs back to life using genetic engineering. Although this is an intriguing thought, most scientists dismiss it, as the genetic material does not survive the fossilization process.

Movie monsters
Dinosaurs are often portrayed in movies

Right: *The special effects used in* One Million Years BC *were considered revolutionary when this movie was released in 1966. However, the moviemakers show early humans living with dinosaurs, a scientific impossibility.*

as gigantic monsters, the size of skyscrapers. They may be given amazing powers, like the ability to breathe fire, or incredible physical strength. But there is no scientific evidence to support such reconstructions. Although dinosaurs were large, no known dinosaur was over 165 feet (50 m) long. The *Velociraptors* in *Jurassic Park* were portrayed as far larger than the real animals, probably to make them seem even scarier. The idea of fire-breathing dinosaurs probably comes from medieval stories of mythological monsters such as dragons. Dragons, like dinosaurs, were large and reptilian—but dinosaurs were real, whereas dragons were not.

Accurate portrayal

A few movies have tried to give an accurate portrayal of dinosaur behavior. Filmmakers of Walt Disney Pictures' animated *Dinosaur* movie in 2000 and the makers of *Jurassic Park* and *The Lost World*, for example, consulted with dinosaur experts to strive to make the appearance and the behavior of their dinosaur film stars both believable and scientifically accurate.

Above: *Many of the reconstructions used in* Jurassic Park *depict dinosaurs as living animals, with the help of the latest scientific research and information. This scene, of a hatching* Velociraptor, *is based on recent discoveries of dinosaur eggs and babies.*

Below: *In* Dinosaur, *Disney has created wonderful reconstructions using the latest techniques in computer animation. But they sometimes have to sacrifice scientific accuracy for the sake of a good story. This scene, for example, shows Jurassic and Cretaceous dinosaurs living together.*

Glossary of terms

air sacs Hollow, air-filled structures that are present in bird bones. It is thought that some dinosaurs also had air sacs.

ammonites Extinct shellfish, related to the living octopus and squid. They had beautiful coiled shells, and are very common fossils in Mesozoic rocks.

ankylosaurs (Ankylosauria) One of the five main groups of ornithischian (bird-hipped) dinosaurs. Ankylosaurs were plant-eaters and walked on all fours. They were covered in a coating of bony armor plates. They are split into two groups (Ankylosauridae and Nodosauridae), and lived during the Jurassic and Cretaceous periods.

Aves The scientific group name for birds.

binocular vision The ability to focus both eyes on the same object. This allows an animal to judge distances accurately. Humans, monkeys, many other mammals and birds have this ability. Some dinosaurs might have had binocular vision too.

biology The science of life and all of its aspects, such as structure and growth of animals and plants.

biped An animal that walks only on its two hind legs.

bone-bed A layer of rock that contains a very large number of fossil bones. They often record the mass death of large herds of animals. Many bone-beds were formed when floods or volcanic eruptions quickly overwhelmed herds.

carnivore An animal that eats mainly meat. Theropods were carnivorous dinosaurs. Cats and dogs are examples of living carnivores.

catastrophe A disaster. Several catastrophes at the end of the Cretaceous period (the impact of a meteorite and massive volcanic eruptions) led to the extinction of the dinosaurs.

ceratopsians (Ceratopsia) One of the five main groups of ornithischian (bird-hipped) dinosaurs. All ceratopsians were plant-eaters, and most walked on all fours. The majority of ceratopsians had a neck frill and a parrotlike beak. Some had horns. The Ceratopsia includes *Psittacosaurus* and two other groups—the Protoceratopsidae and Ceratopsidae (horned dinosaurs). Ceratopsians lived during the Cretaceous period.

collagen An important building material for many parts of an animal's body. It is especially important in skin and bones.

conifers Evergreen trees, such as firs and pines, with cones and needlelike leaves. Conifers were the most common types of trees during the Mesozoic era and were very important sources of food for plant-eating dinosaurs.

coprolites Fossilized dung. Examination of coprolites can give information about the food eaten by dinosaurs.

crest A projection made from bone or skin that sticks out from a bone or from a part of the body. Dinosaur skulls are often adorned with a bony crest. The most spectacular crests were found among the hadrosaurs (duck-billed dinosaurs), which had a variety of large crests on top of their head.

cycads Plants with a short, pineapple-shaped stem and large fanlike leaves. They are not particularly common today, but they were very important plants during the Mesozoic era.

dental battery An arrangement of closely packed, stacked teeth found in the jaws of hadrosaurs (duck-billed dinosaurs) and ceratopsids (horned dinosaurs). Each dental battery can contain several hundred teeth.

Dinosauria The word "dinosaur" was invented by the English scientist Sir Richard Owen in 1842. It means "terrible lizard." The dinosaurs, or Dinosauria, make up a group of extinct reptiles that lived during the Mesozoic era, from the late Triassic period to the end of the Cretaceous period. They ranged from small, agile meat-eaters that ran on two legs to massive plant-eaters that walked on all fours.

embryo The name given to a baby animal before it hatches or is born.

era A major division in geological time. Dinosaurs lived during the Mesozoic era (245-65 million years ago).

extinct A term used to describe animals or plants that have died out. There are many different reasons why a species may become extinct, including changes in the climate, environmental disasters, or overhunting by humans. Dinosaurs became extinct 65 million years ago. The reasons for their extinction are not fully understood, but a meteor impact, massive volcanic eruptions and changes in the weather might all have been to blame.

food chain A chain of animals and plants that are dependent on each other for food. A simple food chain would be: grass (at the bottom of the chain), which is eaten by antelope, which are eaten by lions (at the top of the chain).

fossil The remains of an ancient animal or plant preserved in rock.

gastrolith A stomach stone. These stones were swallowed by some dinosaurs to help grind up food in the stomach.

geologist A scientist who studies the earth and how it was formed and has changed.

hadrosaurs (Hadrosauridae) Duck-billed dinosaurs. Hadrosaurs are members of the group Ornithopoda. They were plant-eaters and walked on their hind legs. Some hadrosaurs had a spectacular crest on the top of the skull. Hadrosaurs lived during the Cretaceous period.

herbivore An animal that eats mainly plants. Antelope, sheep and rabbits are examples of living herbivores. Ornithischians, sauropods and prosauropods were herbivorous dinosaurs.

ichnite The scientific name for a fossilized footprint.

ichthyosaurs (Ichthyosauria) Marine reptiles that were common during the Mesozoic era and were especially abundant in the Jurassic period. Ichthyosaurs had a fish-shaped body, a long snout full of teeth and a large, crescent-shaped tail.

invertebrate Animal that lacks a backbone—e.g., worms, jellyfish, shellfish.

keratin The substance from which fingernails, hair, claws, feathers and the sheaths that cover horns are made. A horny beak made of keratin was found at the front of the jaws in some dinosaurs and is also found in living birds and turtles.

land bridge A small strip of land linking two larger landmasses. When the continents were closer together, as they were during the Mesozoic era, they were connected to each other by land bridges. This allowed dinosaurs and other animals to roam all over the earth.

ligaments Tough, ropelike strands of tissue that connect bones to each other. Ligaments are made out of collagen, but in some dinosaurs turned into bone. *See also* **tendons.**

marine Relating to the sea and the animals and plants that live there.

meteor A piece of space rock hurtling through the atmosphere, usually seen as a bright streak in the night sky. Meteors come in many shapes and sizes, ranging from tiny dust particles to asteroids many miles across. What is left of a meteor that has landed on earth is known as a meteorite.

mosasaurs Large marine lizards that lived during the Cretaceous period. They ate fish, ammonites and other marine reptiles. They are closely related to living monitor lizards.

omnivore An animal that eats a mixture of plants and meat. Pigs and badgers are examples of living omnivores. Ornithomimosaurs are examples of omnivorous dinosaurs.

ornithischians (Ornithischia) Bird-hipped dinosaurs. Ornithopods, ankylosaurs, stegosaurs, pachycephalosaurs and ceratopsians all belong to this group of dinosaurs. All ornithischians were plant-eaters.

ornithomimosaurs (Ornithomimosauria) A group of theropod dinosaurs. They lacked teeth and had a sharp, horny beak. They were omnivores and walked on long hind legs. The neck was long and graceful. They are often called "ostrich dinosaurs" because of their strong similarity to living ostriches. Ornithomimosaurs were among the fastest runners of all time. They lived during the Cretaceous period.

ornithopods (Ornithopoda) One of the five main groups of ornithischian (bird-hipped) dinosaurs. Ornithopods were plant-eaters and walked on their hind legs, though they could walk on all fours from time to time. They include hypsilophodontids (such as *Hypsilophodon*), iguanodontids (such as *Iguanodon*) and hadrosaurs (duck-billed dinosaurs). Ornithopods had powerful jaws and special teeth for chewing up plants, and lived during the Jurassic and Cretaceous periods.

pachycephalosaurs (Pachycephalosauria) One of the five main groups of ornithischian (bird-hipped) dinosaurs. Pachycephalosaurs were plant-eaters and walked on their hind legs. Their most distinctive feature is their skull, which is topped by a huge dome made of solid bone. They lived during the Cretaceous period.

paleontologist A scientist who studies fossils.

Pangaea During the Triassic and Jurassic periods, all the continents were grouped together into a single large landmass that scientists call Pangaea. Pangaea means "all earth." During the Cretaceous period, Pangaea began to split apart, and the shapes and positions of the continents began to look more similar to the way they appear today.

period A division of geological time. The Mesozoic era is divided into three periods: the Triassic period (245-213 million years ago), Jurassic period (213-144 million years ago) and Cretaceous period (144-65 million years ago).

plesiosaurs (Plesiosauria) Marine reptiles that were very common during the Mesozoic era. Most plesiosaurs had a short, barrel-shaped body, four paddlelike flippers, a very long neck and a small head.

pliosaurs Marine reptiles that were abundant during the Jurassic period. Pliosaurs are very closely related to plesiosaurs (see above), but had a short neck and massive head. Some pliosaurs were the largest marine predators of all time.

predator An animal that hunts other animals for food.

prehistoric Meaning "before history." The period of time (making up most of earth's history) that occurred before the invention of written records.

prey Animals that are hunted and eaten by other animals.

prosauropods (Prosauropoda) One of the three main groups of saurischian (lizard-hipped) dinosaurs. Prosauropods had a long neck and a barrel-shaped body. Some prosauropods walked on all fours, but others walked on the hind legs only. They ate plants and were the first of the large-bodied dinosaurs to appear on earth. Prosauropods lived during the late Triassic and early Jurassic periods.

pterosaurs (Pterosauria) Flying reptiles that were very abundant during the Mesozoic era. Pterosaurs had long wings made from thin flaps of skin. They ranged from sparrow-size to the size of small airplanes, and ate a variety of foods, including insects and fish. Pterosaurs were close relatives of dinosaurs.

pygostyle A small bony structure, made out of several joined vertebrae, found in birds and some theropod dinosaurs in place of a long bony tail.

quadruped An animal that walks on all fours.

saurischians (Saurischia) Lizard-hipped dinosaurs. Theropods, sauropods and prosauropods all belong to this group of dinosaurs.

sauropods (Sauropoda) One of the three main groups of saurischian (lizard-hipped) dinosaurs. Sauropods had a very long neck and tail and a barrel-shaped body. They walked on all fours, ate plants and were the largest of all the dinosaurs. Sauropods lived during the Jurassic and Cretaceous periods.

scavengers Animals that eat the food other animals leave behind. They feed on the carcasses (dead bodies) of animals that they find.

sedimentary rocks Rocks that are formed from deposits of sands, muds and clays. Fossils are found in sedimentary rocks.

serration A structure with a sawlike or knifelike edge. The teeth of dinosaurs have different kinds of serrations. Theropods have teeth with many small serrations that are useful for slicing flesh. Ornithischian teeth have large serrations that can easily cut through plants.

species A distinct kind of animal or plant.

stegosaurs (Stegosauria) One of the five main groups of ornithischian (bird-hipped) dinosaurs. Stegosaurs were plant-eaters and walked on all fours. They had a series of bony plates and spines running along the back. Stegosaurs lived during the Jurassic and Cretaceous periods.

tail club A solid club of bone found on the end of the tail in some ankylosaurs and sauropods. Tail clubs were probably used as a defense against large meat-eating dinosaurs.

tendons Tough, ropelike strands of tissue that connect muscles to bones. Tendons are made of out collagen but in some dinosaurs turned into bone. *See also* **ligaments.**

theropods (Theropoda) One of the three main groups of saurischian (lizard-hipped) dinosaurs. Theropods walked upright on their two hind legs and were the only meat-eating dinosaurs. They lived during the late Triassic and the Jurassic and Cretaceous periods.

trackway A series of individual footprints made by a dinosaur in motion. Fossil trackways provide information about dinosaur walking speeds and behavior.

vertebra (plural, vertebrae) One of the many individual bones that make up the backbone. The backbone includes the bones of the neck, back and tail.

vertebrate (Vertebrata) An animal with a backbone. All fish, amphibians, reptiles (including dinosaurs), birds and mammals are vertebrates.

wishbone A bone that is found in the chest area of birds and some dinosaurs. It is made when the two collarbones (called clavicles) join together. The scientific name for the wishbone is the furcula.

Index

The world's largest nonprofit scientific and educational organization, the National Geographic Society was founded in 1888 "for the increase and diffusion of geographic knowledge." Since then it has supported scientific exploration and spread information to its more than nine million members worldwide. The National Geographic Society educates and inspires millions every day through magazines, books, television programs, videos, maps and atlases, research grants, the National Geographic Bee, teacher workshops, and innovative classroom materials. The Society is supported through membership dues, charitable donations, and income from the sale of its educational products. Members receive NATIONAL GEOGRAPHIC magazine—the Society's official journal—discounts on Society products and other benefits. For more information about the National Geographic Society, its educational programs and publications, and ways to support its work, please call 1-800-NGS-LINE (647-5463), or write to the following address:

National Geographic Society
1145 17th Street N.W.
Washington, D.C. 20036-4688
U.S.A.

Visit the Society's Web site: www.nationalgeographic.com